Vicious Cycle

Books by Terri Blackstock

Predator
Double Minds
Soul Restoration
Emerald Windows

Intervention Series
1 | *Intervention*
2 | *Vicious Cycle*

A Restoration Novel Series
1 | *Last Light*
2 | *Night Light*
3 | *True Light*
4 | *Dawn's Light*

Cape Refuge Series
1 | *Cape Refuge*
2 | *Southern Storm*
3 | *River's Edge*
4 | *Breaker's Reef*

Newpointe 911
1 | *Private Justice*
2 | *Shadow of Doubt*
3 | *Word of Honor*
4 | *Trial by Fire*
5 | *Line of Duty*

Sun Coast Chronicles
1 | *Evidence of Mercy*
2 | *Justifiable Means*
3 | *Ulterior Motives*
4 | *Presumption of Guilt*

Second Chances
1 | *Never Again Good-bye*
2 | *When Dreams Cross*
3 | *Blind Trust*
4 | *Broken Wings*

With Beverly LaHaye
1 | *Seasons Under Heaven*
2 | *Showers in Season*
3 | *Times and Seasons*
4 | *Season of Blessing*

Novellas
Seaside

Other Books
Miracles
(The Listener/The Gifted)

The Heart Reader
of Franklin High

The Gifted Sophomores

Covenant Child

Sweet Delights

TERRI BLACKSTOCK

New York Times bestselling author

Vicious Cycle

An Intervention Novel

ZONDERVAN®

ZONDERVAN.com/
AUTHORTRACKER
follow your favorite authors

ZONDERVAN

Vicious Cycle
Copyright © 2011 by Terri Blackstock

This title is also available as a Zondervan ebook. Visit www.zondervan.com/ebooks.

This title is also available in a Zondervan audio edition. Visit www.zondervan.fm.

Requests for information should be addressed to:
Zondervan, *Grand Rapids, Michigan* 49530

Library of Congress Cataloging-in-Publication Data

Blackstock, Terri, 1957-
   Vicious cycle : an intervention novel / Terri Blackstock.
      p. cm.—(Intervention)
    ISBN 978-0-310-25067-8 (pbk.)
     1. Teenage boys—Fiction. 2. Newborn infants—Fiction. 3. Abandoned children—Fiction. 4. Children of drug addicts—Fiction. 5. Drug addiction—Fiction. 6. Human trafficking—Fiction. I. Title.
   PS3552.L34285V53 2011
   813'.54—dc22
                                      2010039776

The New Day Treatment Center depicted in this book is entirely fictitious, as are the characters that the author has created. They do not represent any real rehab center or any specific people, living or dead. If you or a family member is in need of a rehab center, evaluate them individually. For information about choosing the best one, see "Hope for Families of Addicts" at www.terriblackstock.com/hope-for-families-or-addicts/.

Any Internet addresses (websites, blogs, etc.) and telephone numbers printed in this book are offered as a resource. They are not intended in any way to be or imply an endorsement by Zondervan, nor does Zondervan vouch for the content of these sites and numbers for the life of this book.

Published in association with the literary agency of Alive Communications, Inc., 7680 Goddard Street, Suite 200, Colorado Springs, CO 80920. www.alivecommunications.com

Cover design: *Michelle Lenger, Jeff Gifford*
Cover photography: *George Doyle, Getty Images*
Interior design: *Michelle Espinoza, Publication Services*

Printed in the United States of America

11 12 13 14 15 /DCI/ 20 19 18 17 16 15 14 13 12 11 10 9 8 7 6 5 4 3 2 1

This book
is lovingly dedicated
to the Nazarene

Vicious Cycle

Chapter 1

I should have died.

Jordan lay on her bloody sheets, her newborn daughter in her arms, and longed for one more hit. She had never hated herself more. Her baby had come two weeks early, and she hadn't been sober enough to get to the hospital. Giving birth at home had never been part of the plan, but there was no one in her house whose mind was clear enough to care.

What kind of mother traded prenatal vitamins for crystal meth? Her age was no excuse. At fifteen, Jordan knew better than to get high while she was pregnant. Now she had this beautiful little girl with big eyes and curly brown hair, innocence radiating like comfort from her warm skin. That innocence, so rare and short-lived in her family, made the birth all the more tragic. Worse, the baby seemed weak and hadn't cried much, and sometimes her little body went stiff and trembled.

Was she dying? Had Jordan tied off the umbilical cord wrong? Her mother, who had once worked as a nurse's aide, had told her to use a shoestring. What if that was wrong? What if she'd waited too long to cut the cord? It wasn't like she could trust her mother. It was clear she didn't have Jordan's or the baby's best interests in mind.

Jordan had made up her mind to give the baby up for adoption, even though she'd felt so close to her in the last few weeks as her daughter had kicked and squirmed inside her. While she was sober, she'd come to love the baby and dream of a future for her ... one that bore no resemblance to her own. But once Jordan went back into the arms of her lover—that drug that gave her a stronger high than the love of a boy—the baby stopped kicking. For the last week of her pregnancy, Jordan believed her baby was dead. So she'd smothered her fear, guilt, and grief in more drugs.

Then last night her water broke, and cramps seized her. She had responded to her fear as she did every emotion—by taking more drugs. By the time she felt the need to push, it was too late to get to the hospital, even if there had been someone who would drive her.

She craved another hit, but she was out of ice. Her mother and brother claimed to be out too. They'd already burned through Zeke's casino win, so one of them would have to find a way to score. Maybe it was better if they didn't, though. Her baby needed her.

She wrapped the child in a dirty towel, swaddling it like she'd seen on one of those baby shows. She hadn't expected to love it so fiercely. The baby had big eyes, and now and then she would open them and look up at Jordan, as if to say, "So you're the one who's supposed to protect me?"

The door to her bedroom burst open, and Jordan's mother, eyes dancing with drug-induced wildness, swooped in with sheets in her hand. She must have been holding out on Jordan. She had a secret stash of dope somewhere that she didn't want to share.

"Up, up, up," she said with trembling energy. "Come on, baby, you've made a mess. Now let's clean it up."

Since when did her mother care about neatness? Rotten dishes festered in every room, and garbage spilled over on the floors. "Mom, I have to get the baby to the hospital. She's not acting right, and I don't know about the cord."

Her mother leaned over the baby, stared down at her with hard, steel-gray eyes. "Looks fine to me. I've called the Nelsons. They'll be here soon. They're anxious to get their baby."

The Nelsons? No, this wasn't how it was supposed to go.

Her mother released the fitted sheet from the corners of one side of the mattress and pulled it up, clearly trying to roll them both out. Jordan braced herself. "Stop! Mom, I can't."

"Get up," her mother said, clapping. "Come on. We've got to get the little thing cleaned up before its mommy and daddy come. If they come back here I don't want them to see these sheets."

"Mom—you don't get to pick her parents!" Jordan got up, clutching the baby. Blood rushed from her head, blotches blurring her vision. "I've worked it all out with the adoption agency. I'll call them and tell them—"

Her mother's face hardened even more, all her wrinkles from hard living starkly visible now. "It's a done deal, darlin'. Baby, we have to do this. It's great for our family! This is the whole reason we let you leave rehab early."

"It's not the reason you gave me, Mom. You said you

missed me, that I needed my mama while I was pregnant. But it was all a lie."

Her mother snapped the sheets. "Forty thousand dollars, baby. Do you know how much ice that'll buy?"

"Just take her to the hospital to make sure she's all right. Then we can talk about who—"

"No!" her mother bellowed, and the baby jerked and started to cry.

Jordan pulled the baby's head up to her shoulder and rubbed her back. She was so tiny, just a little ball. Her arms and legs thrashed, as if she protested her birth into the wrong family.

"Its new parents can take it to the hospital," her mother said.

"Not it—her!" How could her mother talk about her as if she were an object? "And they're not her parents. I don't know them. They're not on the list the agency gave me."

Her mother flung the soiled sheets into a corner. The blood had seeped through and stained the mattress. "Look what you did, you piece of trash! Bleeding all over the mattress."

"If you'd taken me to the hospital—"

"To do what? Let them arrest you because you were high as a kite while you were giving birth to that kid? Let them arrest me? I'm on probation. You know they can't see me like this. And you're fifteen. They might have taken you away from me, put you into foster care. Then where would you be? Or they could take the baby away and put it into foster care. Then we got nothing to show for it. I ain't gonna let that happen."

Jordan squeezed her eyes shut. If she'd only stayed in rehab, under the protective wings of New Day.

She felt dizzy, weak, but as she held the baby, her mother

threw the clean sheets at her. "Put these on the bed. But first get that stain out of the mattress."

"Mom ... I need some things." She kept her voice low. "Something to dress her in. Some diapers. Bottles."

"You can nurse her until they take her. I'm not putting one penny into this. *They're* paying *me*!" She yanked the baby out of Jordan's arms. "I'll hold it while you change the bed."

Jordan hesitated, uneasy about the fragile baby in the hands of a wild woman who didn't know her own drug-induced strength.

"Do it!" her mother screamed.

Again, the baby let out a terrified howl. Jordan took her back. "I will, Mom," she said softly. "Just let me put the baby down."

Breathing hard, her mother watched as Jordan laid the baby on the floor and tried to make her comfortable. Then Jordan got a towel and blotted at the blood stain on the mattress, watching the baby from the corner of her eye.

She couldn't get the stain out, so she grabbed the new sheets and tossed them over the mattress. Out of sight, out of mind, she hoped. As she worked, she panted, fighting dizziness. Her bones ached, and she shivered with chills, though her skin was damp with perspiration.

"Now clean the kid up. I want it to make a good impression. Wish she was a blonde. They pay more for blondes."

Jordan tried one last time. "Don't you think she'll look better to that couple if she's dressed? They're not gonna want to take her without a diaper or outfit. Get Zeke to go and get her some things."

Her mother hesitated, then walked out. A few minutes later, Jordan heard her shrieking at her brother. After a loud exchange, the front door slammed.

Jordan's hands trembled as she picked up the baby and wrapped her in the towel again. These people her mother had found to take the baby—how did they even know Jordan's mother and brother, who only hung out with losers and convicts? Forty thousand dollars was a lot of money. Maybe it meant they were desperate for a child and would be good parents.

But something about this whole scheme stank. She couldn't let it happen.

The baby's crying grew louder, then silenced as her little body arched and jerked. Was this a seizure? Panic drove Jordan to the window. She'd have to climb out with the baby and get to the car. But Zeke had taken it.

Jordan dragged a chair to the window. When Zeke came back, maybe she could make her escape. Her child's whole life hung on the frayed cord of a lot of maybes. And she knew from past experience that maybes never worked out in her favor.

Chapter 2

Looks like we've got a newbie," Lance Covington told his mother as they pulled into the parking lot at New Day Treatment Center.

Barbara glanced at the teenaged girl getting out of the car next to them. Her eyes were puffy from crying, and she looked as if her life was over. Her parents seemed even more distraught. Even from inside her car, Barbara sensed the tension rippling between the girl and her parents as they got her suitcase out of the trunk.

Barbara remembered that first day of Emily's treatment like it was last week, rather than a whole year ago. At least they'd found a place right here in their hometown, Jefferson City, so Barbara and Lance could visit every weekend. Though Emily had realized she needed help and gone to the teen treatment center voluntarily, Barbara had still battled crushing feelings of grief.

She'd taken Emily in with all the belongings they had so carefully packed to make her comfortable for a year's stay. The counselor examined every item to make certain no drugs were hidden away. Every container was opened, every pocket checked. And she paid careful attention to linings and hems, common hiding places of addicts.

The shakedown exposed a pack of cigarettes hidden in a pocket of one of Emily's sweaters. At least it wasn't drugs, but the small infraction disheartened Barbara enough to make her doubt Emily's sincerity.

"Mom, I'm giving up everything," Emily told her. "I thought a cigarette now and then would help ease me in."

Emily's explanation hadn't made Barbara feel better. What else had she sneaked in?

Doris, the intake counselor, seemed undaunted—she just tossed the cigarettes in the trash and kept paring Emily's belongings down to what would fit in a small plastic bin. When she finished weeding out the things Emily couldn't keep, Doris helped Barbara return them to her car. As she'd driven away that first day, Barbara had wept with worry over her daughter's plight. Most eighteen-year-old girls didn't have to give up a year of their lives to fight a battle raging inside them.

But now, a year later, Barbara knew it had all been worth it.

She wanted to tell those parents bringing their distraught daughter in today that it would be all right, that there was light at the end of their dark tunnel. That the year would fly by faster than they could imagine. That miracles happened here.

But telling them those things wouldn't assuage their

pain. The decision to check their child into a year-long program couldn't have been easy, and it didn't come without guilt and feelings of failure.

Barbara and Lance got out of their car and reached the main building before the fragile family did, so she opened the door for them and offered a reassuring smile. The sound of singing came from the main room, and all three newcomers looked toward it.

"It's the choir," Barbara said. "They sound beautiful, don't they?"

The girl nodded and tossed her hair back from her face, as if she wanted to look her best if any of the girls caught a glimpse of her. "I didn't expect to hear singing," she said.

The song ended as they walked into the foyer. Beyond the doors to the left, the girls in the main room erupted in laughter. Barbara looked for Emily and saw her sitting on the edge of a table, surrounded by friends. She looked so healthy, so well. So unlike her appearance when they'd brought her in a year ago.

Barbara smiled at the new girl's mother. "They laugh a lot here."

Her words, meant to reassure the grieving mother, did nothing to change her expression. To this woman, days of laughter probably seemed far into the future—maybe even a hopeless dream.

"Man, I'm gonna miss this place," Lance said.

Barbara chuckled and glanced at her gangly son, who'd grown four inches in the last year. "Where else do you have so many adoring fans?"

He laughed and regarded the new girl. "What are you in for? Wait, don't tell me—pills, right?"

"Lance!" Horrified, Barbara turned to the girl and her parents. "I'm so sorry."

The girl looked down at her feet.

"Hey, no offense, okay?" Lance said. "I didn't mean anything bad."

Barbara touched his shoulder. "Just ... don't talk."

He started to say something, and she put her hand over his mouth, eyes flashing. "Nothing!"

Lance shut up.

The receptionist wasn't at her desk, so they all stood there awkwardly for a moment, no one speaking. Finally, the girl looked back at Lance. "They let guys go here?"

"No, just girls on this campus. The boys' campus is across town. My sister's here. I visit every Saturday. This your first time in rehab?"

Again, Barbara wanted to slap him. "Lance, that's enough."

"What?" he asked. "I'm just having a conversation."

"It's none of your business."

The girl studied her feet again. This time her mother spoke. "It's not her first time."

"First time to stay for a whole year," the girl muttered with disgust. "Last time was only a month."

Lance had never been more chatty. "A month won't cut it," he said. "Takes at least a year for a brain to unfry."

Barbara covered her face and groaned.

The girl's cheekbones reddened, but she forced a smile. "It's okay."

"I'm just sayin', it's good here. Not like jail or anything. My sister hasn't hated it."

Barbara wanted to tell them that New Day had given her her daughter back when she'd almost despaired over Emily's future. But not now—this family was probably seething over Lance's lack of tact.

The receptionist came to her desk and slid the glass

back from the window. Smiling, she said, "Hi, are you the Beattys?"

"Yes," the mother said.

"Good. And you're Tammy?"

The girl nodded glumly.

"Nice to meet you. Come on back and we'll get you started."

As the girl's father opened the door to the counseling hallway, Tammy turned back to Lance. "See ya."

"Yeah, hang in there, okay? Food's good."

When the door closed, Barbara turned on her son. "What is wrong with you?"

"I was just trying to make her feel better."

"By asking what drugs she's addicted to?"

"Well, it's not like it's a big secret, Mom. She's checking into rehab."

"She's fragile, Lance, and so is her family. You shouldn't have interrogated her."

"Which one of us did she say 'see ya' to? You or me?"

"And that tells you what?" Barbara asked.

"That she liked me. That she wasn't ticked."

Barbara blew out a sigh. "Just ... if you see them again, please don't ask her questions like that. And keep your comments about fried minds to yourself. Like you're the expert, all of a sudden."

"Hey, I went to family counseling."

Barbara almost wished she hadn't dragged him there with her. The cliché was true. A little knowledge could be a dangerous thing.

The receptionist returned and nodded to Barbara and Lance. "You guys can come on back too. Esther will be right in."

Barbara thanked her and they stepped through the door.

The Beattys stood at the end of the hall, waiting to talk to Doris, the admissions counselor. Doris was tough as nails. Barbara hoped her manner didn't make the new family feel worse, especially when they began the shakedown. The girl would be frazzled by the time she was shown to the Phase 1 orientation area where she would begin detox.

Barbara said a silent prayer that the girl would hang in there and that her parents would feel relief instead of fear on their drive home.

When they were settled in the office, Esther, Emily's counselor, came in, holding a mug of coffee. "We're so excited about Emily's graduation," she said. "It's a huge accomplishment to stay the full year. I worry so much about the ones who don't. We had one walk out just this week, and she was a very tough case. Broke my heart. I have a really bad feeling about her."

"Who was it?" Lance asked.

Esther shot him a grin. "Lance, you know the confidentiality rules. I can't talk about it. But we're thrilled when the others see one like Emily get to the finish line. It reminds them that they can do it too." Setting her mug down, she opened a file, pulled out several papers. "Are you ready to have her home?"

"Depends," Lance said before Barbara could answer.

"We can't wait to have her home," Barbara said. "It'll be so good to get things back to normal."

"Barbara, we've talked about this in family counseling, but I have to go over it again, because it's so important. Emily's doing great, but you need to keep your expectations realistic. Maybe you should be looking for a new normal."

That wasn't what Barbara wanted to hear. "I hate that phrase. I still don't know what that means."

"It means that Emily's not the same person she was

before she started using drugs. And she's not the same person she was when she checked in here a year ago. You're not either. So don't expect her to settle back in as if she hasn't been away for a year. She may have problems adjusting. And temptations."

"I've been to all the counseling sessions you've offered me," Barbara said, "and I've gone to Al-Anon and my church support group, so I think I'm prepared. I know there are going to be temptations, but she's doing so well. It's been a year, and she doesn't seem to crave drugs anymore."

"Maybe not here, because drugs aren't available. But that could change when she gets out in the world where they're easy to get."

Barbara's expression fell. "I know you're right. I want this whole thing to be over."

"Don't worry, Barbara. Emily's well equipped to fight those feelings. But she might be a little moody, and she may want freedoms you're not willing to grant. That's why we have the families come in before the graduation." She folded her hands and leaned forward. "It's important that you decide now what Emily's rules are going to be. She's nineteen, so you have to give her some freedom, but she understands the need to rebuild trust. The more you outline and discuss ahead of time, the fewer problems you'll have when things come up."

"You're talking about curfews? Who her friends are? Things like that?"

"Curfews, yes, for a while. As for her friends, she knows she can't step back into the circles she was in when she was using. That's going to be a huge temptation. She may be really lonely for a while, until she makes new friends."

"So how do I make sure those people stay out of her life?"

"Don't worry about it," Lance said. "I'll make sure. If she even starts to hang out with her old group—"

"She's starting college in January," Barbara cut in. "She'll make a whole new group of friends there. And she'll be living at home for the first year or two, so we can support her and help her."

"Good. Just remember, she may still have some addictive behaviors. When my son came home from treatment, he wanted to sleep all day and stay up all night. He was late for work almost every day. Some days he just didn't go. He left messes all over the house and expected me to clean them up. He wasn't using, but he fell right back into his old habits."

"Sounds like a normal boy," Barbara said.

Lance gave her a sarcastic smile.

"Emily's had structure here," Esther said. "She's going to need it at home too. She has a schedule already—what she'll do on Mondays, Tuesdays, Wednesdays ... She really needs to have her time filled up and planned out."

The last thing Barbara wanted to be was a warden.

"So what about her car?" Lance asked. "Wouldn't you say it would build character in her to share it with me?"

Esther laughed. "I can't advise you about the use of her car, Lance. Nice try, though."

"I'm just sayin', she hasn't driven for a year, so maybe I could drive her around for a while. Then when I get my license, she and I can share the car—"

"Lance," Barbara cut in, "your permit lets you drive with a parent, grandparent, legal guardian, or instructor. Not your nineteen-year-old sister." Why were they talking about this now? Lance had gotten them off subject. Barbara looked at her watch. She had to be at work in an hour, so she needed to move this along.

She heard chattering voices through the wall. "Sounds

like choir practice is over. Lance, why don't you go talk to the girls for a while? I'll finish up here."

Lance sprang up. "Sweet. You don't need me, do you, Miss Esther?"

Esther chuckled. "No, you go ahead."

He went through the door, then leaned back in. "Hey, don't talk her into giving me any more structure, okay? I have all of it I need."

Chapter 3

Lance waited outside the community room until the girls came outside. As they did, he accepted their adoring hugs and hellos and followed Emily and her friends to the pond. His mom had been right—the girls loved him here, and that's why he never missed a visiting day. But he supposed it was time for Emily to come home. She'd grown up a lot in the last year, and he was pretty sure she could cut it on the outside without going back to drugs.

"Did you hear about Jordan?" Emily asked him in a low voice as they ambled across the grass.

"No—did she have the baby?"

"We don't know," Emily said. "She took off in the middle of the night a few days ago."

Lance stopped walking. "No way. You're kidding, right?"

"Lance, don't take it personally."

He couldn't help it. The crisp air whipped his hair into his eyes as he stared at the pond, trying to imagine why Jordan would do a thing like that. He should have known his fifteen-year-old classmate couldn't keep her commitment to stay sober.

Before she'd come here, Lance and Jordan hadn't been very good friends, since she hung out with druggies and thugs. But when he found out she was pregnant and still actively using crystal meth, he couldn't hide his disgust. One day when she came to school clearly high, her belly beginning to show through a tight T-shirt, he confronted her.

"You know, it's your business if you want to be a loser, but you should really think about what you're doing to your kid."

She squinted up at him. "What is your problem?"

"Pregnant junkies make me sick."

She reared back and slapped him. Lance caught his breath and stepped back, pressing his hand over the burning spot on his cheek. "You're out of control, Jordan, just like my sister was."

"My life is none of your business." Her tears surprised him. He'd figured she was too cold to get her feelings hurt. Feeling guilty, he leaned back against the lockers, staring at the ceiling. He shouldn't have been so harsh. She was human and she had feelings, even if she was stupid. He forced himself to look into her blotchy face. "Look, I know where you can get help."

"Nobody can help me."

"Yes, they can. If my sister can change, anybody can. She was bad off."

Jordan wiped her face on her sleeve. "I remember her."

"But she's different now. She went to treatment, and she's learning how to live sober."

"I don't have any money," she said. "My mom ... no way she'd ever spend a cent on that."

"You don't need money. Churches and Christian people support the place. It's a good place. She likes it."

"I don't know. I couldn't handle all that Christian stuff."

He saw pain in her eyes and a desperate need to break free of her chains. Maybe she really didn't want to be like this. "Just take a step, Jordan. Do it for your baby."

She touched her stomach, and for a moment, he thought she might listen.

She didn't. Not then.

But a couple of months later, as her pregnancy began to show and the desperation in her eyes grew more intense, she came to him after algebra. Leaning over his desk, she said, "Can you help me get into that place?"

He looked up at her. "What place?"

"That place where your sister is."

Lance caught his breath and got up. "Sure. They know me. I can get you in." He hoped it was true, that they wouldn't make her wait for a bed the way Emily had had to wait. If they did, she might change her mind. "We could go by there and you could talk to them. I could get my mom to take us today. She's picking me up after school."

That afternoon, he and his mother took Jordan for a tour of New Day. When they told her she could check in without paying a dime, she worked up the courage and agreed. Her mother, who needed treatment herself, had reluctantly signed the papers, probably glad to dump her on someone else.

Up until now, Lance had considered this one of his great personal accomplishments. He saw Jordan every Saturday when he came to visit Emily, and he'd watched her progress with pride.

Now she was gone, without a word of warning, without giving him a chance to talk her out of it.

He stepped to the edge of the water, picked up a rock, and threw it to the center of the pond. It dropped with a plunk, ripples spreading. He thought about Jordan's few visits from her abusive mother and brother, visits that always left her in tears. Why would she go back to that?

Emily put her hand on his back. "You okay?"

"Why did she leave?"

"I don't know," she said. "She didn't talk to any of us about it. But I don't think her mom really wanted her to get well."

"I know why she left," someone behind him said.

Lance turned to see Amanda, one of Emily's roommates. "Why?"

"She was fiending for dope, that's why."

He hoped not. She'd begun to care about the baby she was carrying, but using meth while she was pregnant could seriously hurt it. "Do you think she went home?"

"Probably," Emily said. "But it's terrible there. And she's due any day."

Lance had felt the baby kick and had been amazed by the ultrasound picture Jordan carried in her purse. What if she had gone back to drugs?

"Maybe I could try to call her," he said. "See if I could talk some sense into her."

Emily swept her blonde hair behind her ears and studied him for a minute. "It's worth a try. Tell her we miss her."

"Don't worry," he said. "If I find her, I'll talk her into coming back. I got her here the first time. She listens to me."

Chapter 4

Barbara hated working on Saturdays, but that was the day
furniture stores made most of their money. She should
be grateful just to have a job.

Last year, she'd had her own interior design business,
with an assistant and a construction crew. She'd been among
the designers considered to renovate the governor's mansion.
But a crisis with Emily had forced her to prioritize, and she'd
wound up losing the opportunity. As a result, she had to lay
off her staff and give up her studio. She'd taken this job to
keep her head above water while she did design work on the
side. Though she still got an occasional client, she hadn't yet
built back her business enough to warrant quitting this job.

She walked among the dining room tables, clipboard
in hand, looking for browsers. Working on commission
was tough, especially when the economy was bad. But her

background and experience gave her an edge. Last week she'd helped a family whose house had burned. They were rebuilding and needed to furnish every room. The commission had been a blessing from God. They'd said *she* was the blessing, since buying from her was like having their own interior decorator.

Even with that commission, things would be tight when Emily came home. Barbara would have to resume paying Emily's car insurance, buy her some clothes, pay tuition for the college classes she'd be taking in January. She hoped she could manage it all. Ever since her husband died five years ago, keeping her family financially afloat had been her responsibility. She would make it work somehow. She always had.

Her phone vibrated, and she pulled it out of her pocket and saw that she had a voicemail. She'd noticed it vibrating earlier when she'd been with a customer, but she'd ignored it. Now she listened to the message and smiled as she heard Kent Harlan's voice.

"Hey, Barb. Sorry I missed you. I was just ... thinking that maybe I could take a day or two off and come to Emily's graduation Monday. Don't know if you want me there or not." There was a long pause. "If you think it would be better for Emily if I weren't there, no problem. I want her to have a really good day." Again, he hesitated, as if some unspoken question hung between them. "I want you to have a good day too. Hope you're having a good day today."

The awkward message made her smile again. For a tough homicide cop, there was something very vulnerable about Kent.

She thought of calling him back but didn't know what to tell him. Should he come, or shouldn't he? For the last year, they'd talked on the phone a lot, and he'd found excuses to come to Jefferson City a couple of times to see her. But distance made it difficult to pursue a serious relationship. Focusing on her children was the most important thing.

Emily had been so troubled after her father's death. Barbara feared doing anything now that could revive those feelings. Depression and grief could trigger a relapse. Besides, she wanted graduation day to be about Emily, and if Kent were there, Barbara's attention would be divided. Emily's victory after committing a year to her healing was too important to diminish in any way.

Still ... Barbara would really love to see him.

"Barbara!"

She turned and saw Lily, one of her co-workers, coming toward her with a disturbed look on her face. She waited as Lily crossed two rows of recliners. "That homeless guy is back," she whispered.

Barbara looked over Lily's shoulder. The scruffy man was sitting in a Lane recliner, his feet up and his jaw hanging open. He was sound asleep.

"I'm going to call the police," Lily said. "We can't have him in here scaring the customers."

Barbara touched Lily's arm. "Just wait, please. I'll take care of it."

Lily looked back at him. "Okay, ten minutes. If he's not out of here by then, and completely off the premises, including the parking lot, I'm having him arrested."

It wouldn't be the first time. Barbara walked up the row of La-Z-Boys to the Lane section and sat down in the chair next to the man. Touching his arm, she said, "J.B., wake up."

The man stirred, and his eyes opened — bloodshot, as usual. His breath smelled rancid, and red, inflamed skin showed through his sparse, unkempt beard. His ski cap was threadbare and filthy, as if he'd found it in a garbage bin. "Hey," he said, groggy.

"J.B., I told you, you can't hang out in here."

"It's cold out," he said. "Jus' needed a place to get warm for a while."

"You have to do it somewhere else. You know that." She glanced toward the desk, aware that her co-workers watched. "I talked to your mom."

He rubbed his eyes. "Aw, no."

"She's really worried about you."

"Then why won't she let me come home?"

"Because last time you were there, things didn't go so well." There was no point in mentioning that he'd given his father a black eye and pawned his mother's jewelry.

"I won't stay here long."

"You can't stay at all. They're going to call the police. They gave me ten minutes to run you out."

Sighing, he reached for the lever to lower the footrest but couldn't find it. She helped him lower it, and he sat up straighter. "All right, I'm going."

"Come to my car with me," she said softly. "Your mom sent me some things for you. A warm coat and some gloves."

He rubbed his neglected beard. The corners of his mouth trembled, and he covered his eyes with a filthy hand.

"J.B., your mom said the offer is still open for you to go to treatment. She'll come and get you and take you herself."

"I don't need treatment," he slurred. "I don't have a problem." He pushed himself up with great effort and took a few steps, wobbling. "Haven't eaten all day," he said. "Got a few bucks?"

She took his arm and walked him toward the door. "I can't give you any money, J.B. But I have some food in the car."

As the glass doors slid open, the cold air blasted her. Sorrow crushed her heart at the thought of him being exiled into this weather. She wanted to take him home with her, but if his own parents couldn't trust him, neither could she. Six months ago, after he'd beaten up his father, his mother had joined Barbara's support group for parents of prodigal children. When she'd shown Barbara a picture, Barbara had recognized him as one of the homeless men who wandered into the furniture store now and then to escape the summer heat and the winter chill.

He had choices, she reminded herself. He didn't have to live on the streets. He could go to a shelter or a treatment center. If he worked, he could get his own place. He could even go home if he would just stop using.

But J.B. wasn't able or wasn't willing to do what it took to live a functional life. She felt him shivering as they crossed the parking lot. She pulled her keys out of her pocket and popped open the trunk.

The bag J.B.'s mother had sent sat next to the box of crackers and jar of peanut butter Barbara had bought for him the last time she went to the grocery store. "Here's something to eat," she said.

He took the box of crackers but didn't look that interested.

She handed him the bag, and he pulled out a brand new parka with a warm hood. The one he had on wasn't warm enough, and it didn't look like it fit. She wondered where he'd gotten it.

"Won't be able to keep this long," he said as he pulled it on over his other one.

"Why not?"

"Somebody'll take it." His breath steamed on the frosty air as he dug into the bag and pulled out some gloves, a scarf, and a new knit cap.

Charlotte was mothering him the best she could. But Barbara couldn't escape the irony—that her friend was dressing her son to survive, homeless, on the cold streets.

What else could she do?

Barbara had watched Charlotte, who had become one of her dearest friends, scurry around the house finding things she thought might help J.B. Charlotte was fighting her own battle with cancer. But that crisis was secondary to her worries about her only son.

Even Charlotte's "tough love" in leaving him on the streets was more for his benefit than for hers. Her hope was that the temporary homelessness would make him hit bottom. That he'd somehow come to his senses, check himself into treatment, and do what was necessary to change his life.

But there was no sign of that happening yet.

He zipped up the coat and wrapped the scarf around his neck, then dropped the crackers back into her trunk. "I'm not hungry."

"J.B., you said you hadn't eaten. Take them. Eat."

"I just need a few bucks."

"I'm not giving you money. Is there anything you want me to tell your mom?"

He thought for a moment, tears rimming his eyes. Then he turned and staggered away.

She closed the trunk and chafed her arms, watching as he made his way off the parking lot. From the back, he looked like a stooped, eighty-year-old man.

He was only twenty-three.

"J.B.," she called out.

He kept walking.

"J.B., go to the shelter. It's going to get really cold tonight."

"Hate that place," he said.

When he was off the premises, she swallowed the lump in her throat and headed back inside. Lily waited at the glass doors as Barbara went in. "Did you tell him not to come back?"

"He knows. He's just cold."

"We can't have homeless people hanging around here."

"I know."

"You shouldn't feed him. It makes him come back."

"He's not a stray dog, Lily. He's my friend's only son." She hurried into the bathroom, grabbed a tissue off the sink, and dabbed at her eyes.

She would have to call Charlotte later and tell her J.B. had gotten the coat. But today was a chemo day. Charlotte had it on Saturdays, since she worked during the week. Maybe she should wait until tomorrow.

Barbara studied her reflection in the mirror. Kent said she looked like Michelle Pfeiffer, but the movie star didn't have deep lines around her mouth or grief lines between her brows. Family problems had aged her, as it had her friends.

Had she done the right thing for Charlotte's son? Maybe she should have let Lily have him arrested. At least he'd be warm tonight, and relatively safe.

It was so hard to know what to do.

Her phone vibrated again, and she looked down at the readout. Lance. She clicked it on. "Hey, sweetie. What's up?"

"Nothin'," he said. "I was thinking about Jordan. Mom, do you know her mother's name? I want to get their number from Information."

She pictured Jordan's mother, who looked like she'd been using drugs for decades. Though she was probably much younger than Barbara, she looked three times older. "It's Maureen. So you're going to call Jordan?"

"Probably. She needs to go back to treatment. Using drugs while she's pregnant has got to be really, really bad for her kid."

"It wouldn't hurt to call her. I'm sure she'd appreciate that you care."

He sighed. "It's just that if she's using, she probably won't talk to me. She won't want me to know."

"All you can do is try. Just understand that you can't make her do anything. Her mother can, since Jordan's a minor, but knowing her, it's not likely that she will."

"Maybe I should talk to her mother too."

"Just remember, the choice is Jordan's. If she doesn't want your help, you can't force her to accept it, and you'll have to leave it alone."

"But, Mom, the baby ..."

"I know, honey. That baby needs a hero." Silence hung heavy over the line. "Listen, I have to get back to work."

"Yeah, okay."

When Barbara hung up, she prayed a silent prayer for J.B. and Jordan—and for the innocent baby about to enter a chaotic world. Dabbing her eyes again, she left the bathroom and walked to the front door just as a family approached from the parking lot. There were two teens with them. That was a good sign. When a family came with adolescent children, it usually meant they were planning to make a purchase.

Either that, or they wasted a lot of her time.

She met them as they entered the store. "Hi, may I help you?"

The mother looked disinterested. "We just want to look around."

"Great, feel free." Barbara handed them her card. "I'm Barbara. Just so you know, I'm not just a salesperson; I'm an interior decorator. No extra charge."

It didn't seem to impress them, but she followed at a distance so she could help the moment they had a question. She needed another big sale, and she wasn't going to let this family get away.

Chapter 5

Lance told himself he wasn't doing anything wrong taking his sister's car, because he almost had his driver's license. In three months, the whole driving thing would be a non-issue. Having to wait until sixteen was ridiculously random, anyway, especially when a baby's life was at stake.

The shallow reassurance didn't soothe his conscience. If his mother found out about this, he'd be grounded until he was thirty. He'd just have to get the car back before she got home. But calling Jordan wouldn't cut it. He couldn't convince her of anything over the phone, especially if she was high. But if he stood with her face-to-face, maybe he could sway her.

He dropped into the driver's seat, jabbed the key in the ignition, and started it up. Emily's Accord wasn't the car he would have chosen. He was more of a Corvette kind of guy, or maybe a convertible Mini Cooper. But the only wheels in his future were those on his skateboard.

He adjusted the mirror and checked himself out. He looked good behind the wheel. Comfortable, like he drove all the time. His mother let him practice a lot, and he was a natural, if he did say so himself.

As he backed out of the driveway, Lance called Information on his cell phone, asked for an address for Maureen Rhodes. After a moment, the computer texted him the address — 1630 Simpson Road. He knew right where it was.

He drove the few miles to Simpson Road, constantly checking his rearview mirror for flashing blue lights.

The street was filled with old, mildewed houses with rusted cars on cement blocks in the yards, garbage molding in torn trash bags on the street.

He drove past them to a stretch of woods, the trees providing a stark contrast to the dilapidated neighborhood. After half a mile or so of woods, a lone house came into view. The house number was painted in fading, dirty white on the rusted black mailbox. 1630. This was it.

The yard was unkempt and overgrown. The paint on the house was peeling, and in places the eaves hung unevenly, apparently rotten. New Day was a palace compared to this.

He left his car parked on the street and walked across the yard that was mostly dirt and tall clumps of weeds. The screen door was torn and crooked on its hinges, and the front door was open. He knocked on the frame.

"Come in," somebody yelled.

Feeling awkward, Lance opened the screen and stepped inside. At once, he was hit with a rancid mixture of scents. Rotten food, body odor, cigarette smoke ... He coughed, wondering if he should go back outside, but he didn't want to be rude.

Beyond the front room, in the kitchen doorway, he saw Jordan's mother with a cigarette hanging out of her mouth. Maureen was skin and bones, no more than ninety pounds of knobby joints and angular skeleton. Some of her teeth were rotten, and her chin had that look of toothless age. Her hair was greasy and hung in her face; dark circles sank under her eyes. When she saw him, she took the cigarette out of her mouth and stared at him. "What do you want?"

"Um ... is Jordan here?"

She squinted as she blew out smoke, then pushed past him and looked out the screen door. "I was expecting somebody else." She turned back and studied him. "Oh, you're that girl Emily's brother, right?"

"Yes, ma'am," he said. "We're worried about Jordan because she left treatment. Is she here?"

"She ain't feelin' good. Come back another time." She opened the screen door, dismissing him.

But Lance hesitated. "Please, Ms. Rhodes. I just want to talk to her for one minute."

"I told you, she's sick."

"Sick how? Is the baby okay?"

She put the cigarette back in her mouth, narrowed her eyes. "Son, that's none of your business," she said. "Now I'm expecting company, so I need you to leave."

The house didn't look in any condition for company. He glanced through the small living area to the kitchen. There were dirty plates and glasses all over the counter, and garbage spilled out of a trash can. The carpet was caked in mud and dirt, and cigarette butts lay wherever they'd been dropped.

Lance heard another car arriving outside, and Maureen opened the screen door. "There they are. Finally. Now, go on. I can't have you here."

Lance started toward the door but then heard someone

in the hallway. He turned around. Jordan came into the living room, wearing leggings and a big, baggy T-shirt. Her face looked pale and had a gray cast, and her long brown hair was tangled. "Lance, what are you doing here?"

She'd been crying. Her face was swollen and puffy, and her hands trembled. Her stomach still looked bloated, but nothing like it had the last time he'd seen her. "Jordan, you had the baby?"

"Yeah, this morning," she muttered.

Maureen let the screen door fall shut and gave her daughter a stern look. "Go back to your room and get the baby. They're here."

Maureen went outside, letting the screen door bounce shut behind her. Jordan stepped to the window and peered out.

"Are you all right?" Lance asked quietly.

Jordan stared at the man and woman getting out of the car. "Those people. I don't want them taking my baby."

Lance followed her gaze. "Who are they?"

"My mother and my brother have some kind of deal worked out. I don't want it." She wobbled, as if she might pass out, and caught herself on a chair.

Lance grabbed her arm and steadied her. "Are you okay? Shouldn't you be in the hospital?"

"My mom wouldn't take me. I had her here at home."

"At home? Why?" She didn't answer. "Jordan, where's the baby?"

"My room." She straightened as another car pulled into the yard—the blue Dodge he'd seen at New Day when her family visited. Zeke got out of the car and went to the visitors, greeting them like they were old friends. "Finally, he's back," she said bitterly. "Mom sent him to get diapers and bottles, but he probably stopped off to get high."

"Is the baby okay?"

Her voice flattened. "I don't know."

He twisted his face as he tried to make sense of this. "Has a doctor seen her?"

"No." She turned to a table near the door, moved papers and clutter. "Where is the other set of car keys?"

The couple with Maureen and Zeke closed their car doors and headed to the porch. Jordan backed away from the window. "Lance, I need your help."

"Okay. You want me to take you to the hospital?"

As the visitors reached the porch steps, Jordan turned and ran back up the hall.

"Jordan!" Lance called after her.

The bedroom door closed, and he heard the lock click as her mother ushered the couple in. The screen door squeaked as they stepped into the house.

The man and woman were well dressed. They glared at Lance. "Who's this?" the man asked.

"Some friend of Jordan's," Maureen said. "Kid, I told you to leave."

Zeke pushed in past the others and stared Lance down. "You hear her, dude? She told you to go."

Lance didn't move. "Ms. Rhodes, Jordan doesn't look good. She should be in the hospital and so should the baby. If you won't take her, I will."

"I'll take care of Jordan," Maureen said. "Don't you worry about it." She stormed through the house and yelled, "Jordan, bring the baby! We're waiting."

Lance just stood there, astonished at what was happening. "Ms. Rhodes, are you giving the baby to them?"

She swung back around, her eyes glowering. "How many times do I have to tell you to get out of my house?"

"Jordan's upset about this," he said to the couple. "I

don't think she's ready to give the baby up." Maybe they would listen. No adoptive parents wanted to deal with an indecisive birth mother, did they?

But the man's eyes flashed. "Get him out of here, Maureen, or we're calling the whole thing off."

"No!" Panic crossed Maureen's face. "He's leaving!" She took Lance's arm and pushed him toward the door.

Lance jerked free. Something wasn't right here. Jordan was being railroaded. He moved back toward the hall. "Jordan! Jordan!"

She didn't answer. Apparently, she didn't want him here any more than her mother did. But hadn't she said she needed his help? What was that about, if she was going to lock herself in her room?

"I'll get the kid myself!" Maureen yelled. She pushed Lance out of the way and tried Jordan's doorknob. Locked. She banged on the door, shaking the house.

There was still no answer.

Lance heard Zeke's heavy footsteps rattling up the hallway. The rage on his face startled him.

"You! Out now, or I'm gonna smash your face in!" Zeke grabbed Lance by the shirt and dragged him back into the living room.

Lance tried to pull away. "Maybe I should just call the police!" He jerked free, pulled his cell phone out, and started to punch in 911. Zeke grabbed the phone and threw it against the wall. When it hit the floor, he crushed it with his foot. Then he picked up the pieces and threw them out the door.

"Hey!" Lance yelled. "That was my phone!"

As Lance charged him, Zeke grabbed him by the throat. Jordan's brother was skinny from drug use too, but he was several inches taller than Lance. Zeke's wild eyes suggested he could snap Lance's neck without a thought. "You leave now, you little cockroach, and if you say one word to the police, I'll find you and rip your head off. Got that?"

Lance knocked Zeke's hand away. "She's your sister," he choked out. "The baby's your niece!"

Zeke took him by the collar, ran him to the door, and threw him out. Lance tripped going down the front steps and landed on his hands and knees in the crabgrass. Getting quickly to his feet, he looked for his phone. He found the pieces in the dirt, the glass front smashed. He tried to turn it on, but it wouldn't power up.

Sweat dripped into his eyes, despite the chilly wind. He looked around, dazed. He couldn't go back in. Zeke might kill him.

He rushed back to Emily's car, slammed the door, and locked it in case any of the lunatics inside came after him. Then he pulled onto the street. He'd hurry home and call 911. Maybe it wouldn't be too late for the police to help Jordan.

But as he turned the corner onto the next street, a baby's cry ripped out. He slammed on the brakes and looked into the backseat. A newborn baby lay on a pillow on the back floorboard, eyes screwed shut, face red, crying as if it understood perfectly the mess it had been born into.

Chapter 6

Lance got out of the car and threw open the back door, lifted the baby off the floorboard. The tiny child was wrapped in a towel, squirming and grunting as he held her. He looked out the back window. No one was following him. He half expected to see Jordan running up the street to get her baby. Clearly, she had taken it out of the house through her bedroom window and put it in his car. No wonder she hadn't answered Lance when he'd called out to her.

Where was Jordan now? What did she expect him to do?

He put the pillow on the front seat and laid the baby down. Carefully, he worked the seatbelt around the pillow, knowing this wasn't safe. He sat there a moment, trying to decide what to do. His phone was smashed, so he couldn't call his mother or the police.

He had no choice but to take the baby home. There was

no way he could return her to that chaos. She could be killed or given away to strangers. Jordan had said she needed his help. Well, he was going to help her.

The baby kept crying, so he put his finger in her mouth, wondering when he'd washed his hands last and wishing he had something to feed her. Jordan hadn't left him a thing—no bottle, no pacifier. He drove home carefully, slowing around curves and turns, stepping on the brakes gently so the baby would stay put.

When he got back to his house, he didn't park Emily's car down the driveway where it had sat for a year. Instead, he pulled up to the garage, opened it with the remote on the visor, and drove inside, closing the door behind him. If any of the neighbors saw this it would be too hard to explain.

Carefully, he slid his arms under the baby's, lifted the little thing off the pillow. She was so light, so fragile, so tiny. He held her out in front of him, studying her. Jordan had diapered her with a hand towel and safety pins, but the baby had nothing else on. She started to cry, so again he pressed her to his shoulder, careful to hold her head as he took her into the house and back to his room.

She wasn't even a day old, but she was a living, breathing baby, the same one he'd felt kicking when Jordan had let him touch her stomach at New Day. This baby was a miracle. The fact that she'd survived her mother's first few months of pregnancy, when Jordan was still using meth, proved that God was looking out for her. To be born at home, in such neglect, to a meth-addicted mom who was practically a kid herself . . .

Jordan's thinking was muddled, yet she'd thought clearly enough to save her baby from that couple who'd come to take it.

He jostled and patted the baby, trying to make her stop crying, as he racked his brain for what to do. If he called his mother, she would certainly call in the police, and they'd take the baby away from him before Jordan had the chance to come and get her back.

The baby finally stopped crying. He had done something right.

"See?" he whispered in a soft voice. "I'm not gonna hurt you. I'm your friend."

Carefully, he laid the baby on his bed and covered her with part of his bedspread. Raking his hands through his hair, he took a few steps back, trying to decide what to do. If the police got involved, who knew what would happen to her? Maybe something good. Maybe they would get Jordan out of that house and arrest everyone else.

Or they might give the baby right back to her family, which meant she could be adopted by that strange couple, or set on a lifelong track of foster care, going from home to home. He couldn't let that happen to her, could he?

He needed advice. Someone who could tell him what to do, without going ballistic.

He picked up his landline phone and dialed the number for New Day. The weekend counselor picked up the phone.

"Hello, it's a New Day."

"Hey," he said. "This is Emily's brother, Lance."

"Hi, Lance." He recognized the gruff, phlegmatic voice of Sue, one of the counselors.

"Listen, I need to talk to Emily. It's real important."

"Sorry, Lance. She's already had her quota of phone calls for the day."

"But it's an emergency. Seriously, I need to talk to her."

"I'm sorry. You'll have to wait until tomorrow. Rules are rules."

"This is about Jordan Rhodes," he said.

Sue hesitated. "What about her?"

"I saw her today. I went by her house. She's not doing good. She needs to come back to treatment. But that's not the thing. She's had the baby."

"Is it okay?"

He looked at the child lying on his bed. "Yeah. No. I mean, it was born at home, and I don't really know. Jordan's not thinking right, and her mom is crazy."

"We don't take babies, Lance, but if you get her to call us we can help her find a rehab where she can keep her. Or is she still going to give it up for adoption?"

"I don't know. You don't understand." He cut his sentence off, knowing better than to tell her what had happened. "I'm just thinking the baby ... it's in trouble." He had to keep this secret, just long enough for Jordan to come get the baby. But did she even know where he lived? How would she find him?

The baby started to cry, and the counselor heard it. "Lance, are you with Jordan right now?"

"No," he said.

"Let me talk to her. Maybe I can convince her to come in."

"She's not here."

"I hear the baby. I know you're with her. Just put her on the phone."

He hung up and sat on the bed. What should he do? The baby was probably hungry. How was he supposed to feed her?

He took her into the kitchen, opened the refrigerator, and grabbed a carton of 2% milk. Maybe this would work. But what would he feed her with? It wasn't like she could drink out of a cup.

He pulled open a drawer, found a Ziploc bag. Maybe he could make some kind of nipple from it. Taking her back to his room, he laid her on the bed again. Then he poured some milk into the bag, zipped it up, and pricked a hole in the corner with a safety pin. He put it into the baby's mouth. She tried to suckle.

Her mouth filled up too quickly, so he pulled it out and gave her a chance to swallow. She was cute, with that brown, curly hair. He didn't even know her name. Jordan had told him nothing about her.

Sadness ached through his chest. What would happen when this kid grew up and learned that her mother had been too high to deliver her in a hospital? That she'd put her in somebody's car to get her away from her crazy grandmother? She'd need a dozen shrinks.

He gave her the bag back, let her suckle a little more. This time she sputtered and choked. Setting the bag down, he picked her up, and her little head rolled back. Quickly he caught it, put her to his shoulder, and jostled her again. He felt milk running down his shirt. This was never going to work.

He needed a bottle, but how was he supposed to get it? Throw her back in the car and take her to the nearest drugstore? He couldn't keep riding around with a baby lying on his seat. Getting pulled over for not having a license would be bad enough. How would he explain having a baby that wasn't in a car seat?

He tried to think. Jacob! He had his own car, so he could make a run to the store. Lance grabbed the house phone and punched in his friend's number.

"Whassup, man?" Jacob's voice was grainy, as if he'd been asleep.

"You wouldn't believe me if I told you," Lance said. "Hey, I need a huge favor. Can you run to the drugstore for me and get a few things?"

"The drugstore? Call your mom. I just woke up."

"It's three o'clock!"

"It's Saturday, dude."

"Come on, it's an emergency."

"I don't even have any money, man."

Lance went back to his room. "You have the birthday money your grandparents gave you. Use that, and I'll pay you back when you get here." Lance opened his dresser drawer and dug around, hoping he could find some cash somewhere. "Please, Jacob."

"Okay, okay, what do you need? If it's anything embarrassing, I'm not doing it."

He wished he could just call ahead and have it ready, so Jacob wouldn't have to know anything. But that wasn't possible. "I'll tell you, but no questions, okay? I'll explain everything when you get here."

"It's not illegal, is it?"

"No. It's ... I need a baby bottle and some baby milk. What do they call that stuff babies drink?"

"Are you kidding me?"

"No. Just listen. I also need some diapers."

"No way I'm going in a drugstore to buy diapers and bottles. What's going on, man? You babysitting?"

There wasn't time to explain. "Yeah, I'm babysitting for a friend. I'll tell you everything if you'll just bring it. Please hurry."

"Are you at home?"

"Yeah. Seriously, man, it's a big emergency. Hurry up, okay?"

When he hung up, he tried to give the baby another drink of milk. This time it spilled on her face, and he quickly wiped it off. No, he'd have to wait for the supplies.

He smelled something in the diaper and peeked in one leg. "Oh, no. This really isn't funny, dude."

Forty-five minutes later, Jacob came with the bag of

things he'd asked for. When Lance met him at the door holding the baby in his arms, Jacob gaped at her. "Man, that's a tiny one. Whose baby is that?"

"Jordan Rhodes," he said.

"The doper? What are you doing with her kid?"

"Don't call her a doper. She was trying to get sober. She just wanted me to watch her for a little while."

Jacob grunted. "Why would you say yes?"

"I didn't exactly have a choice." He led Jacob back to his room and put the baby down on his bed. "First I've got to change her diaper. You ever done this before?"

Jacob threw his hands up and shook his head. "Hey, don't look at me."

Lance opened the diaper and winced at what he saw. "Aw, man. That is seriously sick."

"You need some of those diaper wipes. I didn't get any of those."

"Go get some toilet paper out of the bathroom. Wait, get a washcloth. Wet it first."

Jacob hesitated. "Lance, this is insane. Why don't you call your mom to come help you?"

"Just do it, man."

Jacob left and came back with the washcloth. Lance removed the makeshift diaper and cleaned the baby the best he could. "How do people do this?"

Jacob backed toward the door. "I have to go."

"No, man! You gotta help me. Open the diapers."

Jacob sighed and tore into the plastic bag. He pulled out a diaper, examined it, then handed it to Lance.

"Can't be that hard," Lance said, opening it and laying it under the baby. It was huge. He peeled off the tabs, folded up the front, and tried to stick it together. "It's too big. It'll fall off. What size did you get?"

"Hey, I didn't know there were sizes!" Jacob looked at the bag. "Six to nine months. How old is this one?"

"Like ... six to nine *hours*."

Again, Jacob grunted. "What kind of mother leaves a day-old baby with some kid who doesn't know anything?"

Lance sighed and looked around for something to make it work. He had some masking tape on his desk. He grabbed it and tried to tighten the diaper. It didn't look good, but it was better than nothing. Maybe it wouldn't fall off.

The baby began to cry again, and he picked her up. "Okay, time to feed her. I hope you did better with the bottles."

"Give me a break, okay? I did the best I could."

Lance pulled a box of bottles out of the bag. They were packed with sanitary nipples and a can of formula. He led Jacob into the kitchen as he bounced the baby. "Open the can and pour it in there for me."

Jacob did as he was told, tightened the nipple onto the bottle, then thrust it at him. Lance sat down and positioned the screaming child on his legs. He gave her the bottle. The child latched on, suckling like she was starving. "Sweet!" he said softly. "She's quiet."

Jacob sat down on the ottoman in front of him. "Okay, dude, tell me about this chick who drops a baby on you. Do you two have something going that you haven't told me about?"

"No! I just know her from school, and I would see her at New Day when I visited Emily. She bailed on treatment and had the baby, and when I went over to her house to talk her into going back, her family was chaos. People yelling, going whacko. And then I get in my car to leave, and a block away I realize she stuck the baby in my car."

"Just like that?"

"She was trying to protect it from all that insanity in her house. It was seriously bad."

"So call the police, man. Call your mom."

"No, because it'll look really bad for Jordan. I don't want her getting in trouble. I'm expecting her to show up any time and get her back."

Jacob watched Lance feed the baby for a few minutes. "Aren't you supposed to burp it or something?"

"How?"

"You hold her up and pat her back."

"Do I do it now, or after she's done?"

"Man, I don't know. How long have you had her?"

"I don't know. An hour and a half, maybe."

"And Jordan hasn't come yet?"

"No."

"And she hasn't called?"

"No."

"So what if she's getting high somewhere and letting you do all the work? What if she has no intentions of coming?"

Lance looked down at the suddenly contented child. "I'll worry about it then," he said. "For now, I think we're good."

"What about when your mom gets home? She's not gonna let you keep it."

"Jordan will come before that," Lance said.

Chapter 7

The moment Barbara pulled into the driveway, she noticed that Emily's car had been moved. She rolled into the garage next to the Accord, her chin set, and got ready to lambaste Lance. He was chomping at the bit to drive, but surely he wasn't dumb enough to think he could drive Emily's car, park it in a different spot, and not pay for it big-time.

She wasn't in the mood for this. She'd had a long afternoon. Though she'd managed to sell two beds to the family who'd come in, she'd also had to work out refunds for another family who didn't like the custom furniture they'd just gotten. It had taken hours to work all that out.

Exhausted, she locked her car and went into the house. Things were quiet. No television or music blaring, as it usually was. Lance wasn't laid out on the couch playing a video game with a friend.

She walked up the hall. His door was closed. "Lance?" she called.

He opened the door a few inches and slipped out quickly. Keeping his voice low, he said, "Hi, Mom."

She set her hands on her hips. "Did you drive Emily's car?"

He faltered for a moment, as though he hadn't expected that. How could he think she wouldn't notice where the car was parked?

"I . . . I moved it so Jacob could pull in. I'm sorry I didn't put it back."

"Oh, really? Why? There was plenty of room for his car in the driveway."

Was his face pale?

"He's not a very good driver, Mom. You should notice his fender next time. I did Emily a favor."

She grunted. "Thanks for letting me know. I won't let you ride with him anymore."

He opened his mouth to protest, then let out a sigh. "Whatever." He put his hand back on the doorknob.

That wasn't like him. His story was clearly untrue, and now he was walking away without a protest. "What were you doing?"

"Just sitting in my room."

"Everything okay?"

"Yeah."

She frowned. "Is someone in there, Lance? You're talking awfully quiet."

He shook his head quickly . . . too quickly. "No, I was just taking a nap."

A nap? There had been days when she'd come home and found him asleep on the couch, with a bag of nachos on his stomach and the TV blaring. But never did he go into his room in the middle of the afternoon, turn off all electronics, and go to sleep.

But they'd had to get up early for visitation with Emily, so maybe he was tired.

The phone rang. Barbara hesitated, watching her son.

"You gonna get that?" he asked.

"I'm not finished with you," she said, heading back to the kitchen. The caller ID said it was Charlotte. She picked it up. "Hello?"

"Barbara, I know I caught you just getting home."

Charlotte's voice sounded weary, raspy. It must have been a tough day of chemo. "No, it's fine. How are you?"

"Okay today. They gave me something for nausea."

"Did you have to go alone?"

"Yeah, but it was all right. I took a really great audio book and listened to it the whole time. But I was wondering if you happened to see J.B. today."

Barbara wished she had better news. "I did. I gave him the stuff you sent. He put it right on."

"How did he seem?"

"A little agitated. Tired. I tried to give him some food but he wouldn't take it."

"Did he ask for money?"

"Yes."

"Don't give it to him. Don't ever give it to him." Her voice cracked.

"I didn't."

"He'll use it for drugs, you know."

"I know."

"If I could just get him some help."

Barbara knew how hard it was when the person you loved didn't want that help. Charlotte had tried having J.B. legally committed, but he'd created so much chaos in the treatment center that they'd let him go. His years of drug abuse had rendered him mentally ill—with bipolar and personality disorders. Or had those mental illnesses led to his self-medicating with illegal drugs?

No one knew for sure which came first, and it almost didn't matter. The fact was, he was like this now. He needed help, but he wasn't going to get it until he was willing.

"We'll keep praying for him," Barbara said. "He knows you love him."

"Does he?" Charlotte's voice faded out. "Well, anyway, I hope your day went well. Is Emily excited about graduating?"

"Ecstatic. But right now I'm worried about Lance."

"What's going on with Lance?"

"I don't know. He's just acting weird. Napping in his room, which, in itself, is pretty suspicious." She didn't see the usual mess he left for her to clean up, except for some milk spilt on the counter and a Walgreens bag.

Maybe he'd ridden with Jacob to the drugstore.

She went to the trash can to toss the bag, stepped on the pedal that made the top come open. Sitting on top of the trash was an open can of Similac. Frowning, she picked it up. "What is baby formula doing in my trash can?" she said into the phone.

"Baby formula?" Charlotte asked.

"Yes. An empty can of Similac."

"I'm drawing a complete blank."

Barbara sighed. "I'd better go. I need to talk to him."

She hung up and went to the hallway again, knocked on Lance's door.

After a moment, he opened it, cracking it only wide enough to slip out. Then he closed it behind him again. "What?" he asked.

"What's going on with you? Is there something in there you don't want me to see?"

"No, ma'am."

That was a dead giveaway. He never called her ma'am. "Then why do you keep closing the door like that?"

"My room's a mess. I don't want you to get mad. I'll clean it up."

That didn't fly. Lance's room was always a mess, and he never cared, no matter how many times she told him to clean it. She brandished the can. "Lance, what is this?"

He took the can, a blank look on his face. "I don't know. It isn't mine."

His ears started to redden, the way they always did when he lied. "Then whose is it?"

"I don't know, Mom."

He still kept his voice low, and he looked nervous and kept his hand on the doorknob.

"Did you have someone over today?"

"Just Jacob."

She stared at him. Why was he lying? She didn't buy that he didn't know about the formula, but before she could question him anymore, he went back in and closed his door. She heard the lock click.

Suddenly she heard an unfamiliar sound.

A baby crying.

Frowning, she put her ear against the door. Yes, it was a baby!

She tried to open the door, then knocked loudly. "Lance, what is that I hear? Do you have a baby in there?"

There was no answer for a moment. The baby's cry grew louder. "Lance! Open this door!"

Finally, the door came open, and she saw her son standing with a tiny, screaming baby in his arms.

"Mom, I know you're gonna freak out, but I need you to chill. Something's wrong with her, and I don't know what to do!"

Chapter 8

Where did you get that baby?" Barbara shouted.

"Mom, I'll tell you everything. Please! Just help me."

Barbara pushed aside her shock and took the baby, which seemed to be convulsing. She laid her on the bed, examining her carefully.

"I didn't do anything wrong, Mom. I went to Jordan's to see if she was okay, and there was this big fight. Her family's all crazy."

"This is Jordan's baby?"

"Yes. They were trying to make her give the baby to these people, and she didn't want to. And while I was arguing with them, she must have snuck out and put the baby in my car. I didn't see it till I drove off."

"What were you doing driving?" she shouted.

He started to answer, but she said, "Never mind, we'll

talk about it later. You're right, something's wrong with this baby. We have to take her to the hospital."

"Should we call an ambulance?"

"It'll be faster to just take her. Come on, get my purse." As she picked the baby up, Barbara saw the masking tape around the diaper. Was that his or Jordan's handiwork? She wrapped the baby in the towel and headed for the garage.

"Maybe she's just hungry," Lance said. "I have a bottle in my room. I tried to give her some but she started jerking!"

"It's a seizure, Lance. She should have been in the hospital from the beginning. She's a meth baby."

They got outside, and Lance opened the driver's door. "You hold her, and I'll drive."

Barbara didn't want to let the baby go. "Okay. Be careful."

She got into the passenger seat and pressed the button to open the garage door. Lance started the car and backed slowly out of the garage. "Mom, she wasn't doing that when I found her. She was okay, mostly. I took good care of her."

"Why didn't you call me, Lance? Why would you keep a brand new baby all afternoon?"

"I knew you'd call the police, and I didn't want Jordan to get in trouble. I don't know why she hasn't come to get her yet." He glanced at the baby. "Is she okay?"

"She stopped shaking. When was she born?"

"Today. She was born at home."

Barbara sighed. "There's no telling what's in this baby's system."

As they got to the end of the driveway, the baby began seizing again. Barbara put her in her lap. "She's doing it again. Maybe we should call the ambulance after all, so the paramedics can take over."

"Okay, give me your phone!"

He stopped in the driveway and dialed 911.

Almost immediately, there was a siren, and a police car with blue lights flashing pulled in behind him, blocking him in.

"Hello, 911."

Lance looked in the rearview mirror. "Uh ... never mind, the police are here ... somehow. But we need an ambulance—"

"Sir, what is your emergency?"

Barbara looked out the back window as two cops got out of the squad car. Another cruiser pulled up behind the first one. Where had they come from? Barbara got out and called to them. "Help! We need an ambulance for a baby. She's having a seizure."

One of the cops jogged up and took the baby out of Barbara's arms. The other one yanked Lance out of the car and threw him against the back door. Barbara sucked in a breath. "What are you—"

"Are you Lance Covington?"

Lance looked as confused as Barbara. "How did you know that from me dialing 911?"

Barbara followed the cop who had the baby. "Yes, he's Lance Covington. What's going on?"

The officer snapped cuffs on Lance's wrist.

"Hey, I have a driver's permit!" he cried. "My mom was in the front seat!"

"You're under arrest for kidnapping an infant—"

"What?" Barbara spun around. "No! He didn't kidnap her! Are you crazy? We were calling an ambulance! He was trying to help her!"

But no one was listening as they read Lance his Miranda rights.

Chapter 9

Jordan stared at her face in the mirror. Her eyes were swollen and bruised, and she thought her nose might be broken. Her head was sore and bloody where her mother had ripped her hair out.

She felt like she was going to faint.

She hated herself for letting the dragon of addiction catch up with her again, stalking and hounding her, breathing fire into her sleep. She'd been warned by rock stars in songs they wrote about addiction that the dragon's talons cut deep, and breaking free of him was nearly impossible, but the songs made it sound mysterious and glamorous. That beast scorched the thoughts of every addict she knew.

At New Day, one of the Bible verses they'd drilled into her brain was the one about guarding her thoughts—taking them captive. But how did you do that when you were the prisoner, when your master had never really let you go?

The craving for meth had become overwhelming. She'd ignored the obvious consequences — that at fifteen her teeth were rotting from her past abuse, that her skin had scarred after years of being covered with meth sores, that her brain was in a constant fog ...

A sane person wouldn't have gone back to that dragon, but she'd never claimed to be sane. She'd sold her sanity years ago when she started down her mother's path.

She sank down to her bed, unable to look at herself anymore. If her baby was safe, the beating would be worth it.

Her mother had gone ballistic when she realized the baby was gone. After she'd beaten Jordan, Jordan heard yelling in the living room, the man threatening her mother, and her mother begging for time to find the baby.

At first, Jordan had felt a feeble sense of satisfaction that she'd actually done one thing right for her child. But then her mother demanded that Jordan tell where the baby was, and since the beating hadn't worked, she pulled out another weapon. A syringe full of meth that she would give her ... if she would tell her where the baby was, then lie to the police.

Jordan had finally caved. When the police came, she told them Lance had kidnapped the baby right out of her arms.

She'd gotten her shot of meth as soon as the police left, but the high had been short and had done little to numb the pain and worry. What if they arrested Lance? What would they do with the baby? Maybe, with the police involved, she could get the baby into the hands of Loving Arms, the original adoption agency, and they could find her a home where sober people would love her and care for her. Maybe the baby would actually have a chance. Maybe the family cycle of drugs and violence would end with this baby.

But if her mother's plan worked, the baby would be returned and given to those people who had come for it. She couldn't let that happen.

Why had she left New Day? She should go back, but now there was so much pain. She needed a few more fixes to get through it. Meth was the only comfort she'd ever really known.

The dragon wasn't just her tormenter. It was her savior. Her lover. It courted her with memories of glorious highs, and blocked out memories of shame and regret. It flashed hope and healing in her mind. Sometimes it took away the pain, and that was worth any price.

But even as she acknowledged that thought, enemy questions missiled through her. Did it block out memories of an abandoned baby? A friend accused of a horrible crime?

It wasn't right. Lance had only come because he cared about her. This was how she repaid him?

And the baby—her sweet, nameless baby, with those big trusting eyes that looked right into Jordan, as if she knew her and didn't even care that she was a worthless slave who couldn't control herself.

That looked like grace—the grace they'd talked about in rehab, the grace she'd learned about in Bible studies there.

Grace. That was a perfect name for her. Little Grace, who'd done nothing to deserve the family she'd been born into.

Jordan's mother banged on the door. "They caught your little boyfriend!" she yelled. "And they're taking the baby to the hospital."

Jordan went to the door and threw it open. "Was she okay?"

"They said she was convulsing and underweight."

"I told you she needed to be in the hospital!"

But there was no point in yelling at her mother. It was Jordan's fault the baby was in that condition. She'd been so high when she was in labor that she'd barely realized it when her water broke.

As she thought of the baby, her breasts began to hurt, and milk leaked through her shirt. The reminder of her failed motherhood made her long for another hit of meth.

But she had to clear her head and tell the people at the hospital what adoption agency she was using and that the baby needed a decent mother and father, not the ones her mother had chosen. The baby's sickness would buy her some time.

"What about Lance?"

"He's going to jail," her mother said, laughing. "Picture that little dirt wad in a cell. Bet his prissy mother never expected that."

Jordan slammed the door and locked it. She turned her back as her mother banged on the door and screamed about respect.

She needed another fix, just to give her strength. But she wasn't going to get it here. Her mother was holding out on her, using the drugs to control her.

As Maureen ranted, Jordan opened her window and crawled out again. When her feet hit the dirt, she steadied herself against the side of the house, dizzy. Would she be able to make it several blocks to the motel where she could score? She hurried across the yard to the street. The wind was cool, whipping through her hair. She could do this. Just a few blocks. She walked slowly, her mind fixed on her destination, the place where her friends were as messed up as she was. Someone there would see how bad she was hurting and share.

One more hit ... that was all. Then she could live with herself again.

Chapter 10

The Atlanta crime scene was full of evidence, but even without it, Detective Kent Harlan could quickly close this case. A woman dead from stab wounds, her husband sitting in the kitchen, still clutching the knife that killed her. He'd even confessed, claiming she deserved it because she'd made his life miserable for twenty-seven years.

The CSI techs would gather all the evidence and log it, and Kent would complete the paperwork that would put this case to bed. But it was going to be cut and dried.

His phone rang, and he pulled it out, checked the caller ID. He grinned when he saw Barbara's name. He stepped out of the apartment and put the phone to his ear. "I wondered when you were gonna call me back."

He expected to hear a smile in her tone, but instead he heard panic. "Kent, Lance was just arrested."

"What? What for?"

"Kidnapping!"

For a second he couldn't process it. Lance arrested for kidnapping? It didn't compute. Finally, he asked, "Barbara, what happened?"

As she explained everything that had led up to the arrest, he trotted down the stairs to the ground floor and crossed the parking lot to his car.

"Kent, what can I do? They've taken him to jail. They're booking him now. They say that Jordan accused him of taking the baby!"

"She said that? She signed an affidavit?"

"Yes! She knows that isn't true. She put the baby in his car. Lance is innocent. What are they going to do to him?"

Kent racked his brain for an answer. There wasn't much she could do, not until the arraignment, but maybe he could do something. "Barbara, I'm coming to Jefferson City."

"Kent, that's thoughtful, but—I need help now ... tonight."

"I have a friend with a plane. Maybe he can fly me there tonight. He was going to do it tomorrow anyway if you'd let me come to Emily's graduation."

"But what can you do?"

"I'll know when I get there. But I don't want you to go through this alone."

She was quiet for a moment, but he knew she was crying, and it made him feel helpless. "In my wildest dreams, I never thought Lance would be in jail. He's a good kid. He meant to help her ..."

"Barbara, just hold on. I'm on my way, okay? Get Lance an attorney immediately, and demand to be present during the interview."

"I can do that?"

"It's up to them. But at the very least, you can watch. Don't let him talk until the attorney gets there. He's a minor and you're his mother, so you have the right to demand that."

"But won't that make him look guilty? I want him to be able to tell them what happened."

"He can tell them with the attorney there. Barbara, there's no hurry. The baby's in the hospital. Tell him to take his time and wait for the lawyer."

"It's Saturday night. What if I can't get one here tonight? He'll have to stay in jail, won't he?"

He didn't want to say it, but he had to. "Probably. But let's not cross that bridge until we come to it. Do you know somebody you can call?"

"Yes, there's an attorney at church who's a good friend."

"Call him, then."

He glanced at the apartment's entrance; the investigators were bringing out bags of logged evidence. "I'll call you when I have an arrival time. What airport can we fly into?"

She hesitated a moment. "Jefferson City Memorial, I guess. Or Garrison, a smaller private airport."

"All right, we'll probably use that one."

"What do I do in the meantime? Should I stay at the police station? Should I go talk to Jordan? They haven't told me anything about bail."

"They have to wait for a judge to decide. The attorney can get some answers for you." He wished he lived closer. Atlanta was way too far from Jefferson City. "Just stay at the station until you're sure they won't let you bond him out, then go home until I call. Don't go to Jordan's. Do you hear me? Wait until I can go with you."

He hoped his coming would make things easier for her. She'd carried too many burdens alone. Maybe they didn't have a full-fledged relationship yet—not the kind he wanted—but they were friends. He had to be there for her, and for Lance. She was right. Lance was a good kid. Not the kind who deserved a night in jail.

He started his car and pulled out of the parking space. Andy, his partner, tapped on his window. "Where you goin', man?"

"I have a family emergency," he said. "I have to take some personal days."

Andy frowned. "Your brother okay?"

"I didn't say it was my family. I'll call the chief on the way to the airport. You can handle this case. It's a no-brainer."

Andy chuckled. "Thanks for the vote of confidence. When will you be back?"

"When the emergency is over."

He glanced in his mirror as he drove off. Andy stood with his hands on his hips, watching him drive away. Kent hit a speed-dial button on his phone.

His buddy Blake answered quickly. "Hey, Kent! What's up?"

"Blake, I need a favor. Can you fly me to Missouri tonight?"

Blake, who was in the men's group at the church Kent had been attending for the last year, owned a Cessna 182. He'd just gotten his instrument rating, and he loved any excuse to fly.

"Yeah, I guess I could. Can't wait till tomorrow?"

"No. Barbara's having a crisis."

"Another one? Her daughter hasn't relapsed, has she?"

"No, not that. But she needs my help."

He heard the smile in Blake's voice. "Did she call you and ask you to come?"

"Sort of."

"That's good, right? Means you're important to her."

"I'm the only cop she knows. Still ..."

"You got it, man. I can be there in about an hour. Can you meet me then?"

"Perfect. How long will the flight take?"

"A few hours. We may have to make a stop for fuel."

"Whatever we have to do. I'll pay for it all. Hotel and everything."

"No worries, we're good. I love night flying. See you then."

Kent hung up and headed home, quickly packed a bag. Barbara's tone reminded him of the way she'd been a year ago, panicked and grieving over Emily's plight. Trying to do what was best for her daughter, she'd hired an interventionist to convince Emily to go to treatment. Then she'd put Emily on a plane to Atlanta with the woman, who'd promised to get her to rehab safely.

When the interventionist was found dead in the parking lot of the Atlanta airport, with no sign of Emily, Kent had investigated the case. He'd met the grieving mother at the lowest point in her life, but her strength and the power of her faith and love had moved him more than any woman ever had. He hadn't expected to fall for a woman who lived 650 miles away and had two teens, one with so many problems. And it wasn't fair now that she had to endure another crisis, this time with Lance. If it was at all in Kent's power, he would help her again.

He got to the airport before Blake, so he sat in his car and prayed. Praying—something he'd never done before he met Barbara—had now become a habit. He hoped God was still listening.

Chapter 11

Jail wasn't part of Lance's plan for his life. He'd been appalled when his sister got arrested for DUIs, and had vowed never to do anything that would lead to his own arrest.

And here he was. The old saying was true: No good deed goes unpunished.

Okay, sure—he deserved a ticket for driving without a license. Maybe even a fine or a suspension of his permit. But not jail. He should have known not to get tangled up with a girl who was on drugs. Addicts were like octopuses, wrapping you up, manipulating and draining you, dragging you down. He'd told Emily that so many times when she was hanging with those losers. Why hadn't he taken his own advice?

Shame twisted his stomach as he walked through the police station, his hands still cuffed behind his back. His mother, who had followed them to the precinct, warned him not to tell them anything until she got an attorney here. He hoped the lawyer would get here soon, because he honestly didn't know if he could keep his mouth shut if they pressured him to talk.

The cop sat him down in a metal chair in a cold, small interview room and released his handcuffs. He looked around for a camera and found one mounted in the top corner of the room, just like on those cop shows. They'd record what he said, and people would analyze his story. It was downright creepy.

A man he hadn't seen before came in and held out his hand. "Lance, I'm Detective Dathan. I'm going to be taking your statement."

He shook. "Nice to meet you." It seemed like a lame thing to say, even a little silly, but maybe if he pulled out all his manners, they'd realize he wasn't some ordinary thug.

The man slid his chair out behind his desk. It scraped on the concrete floor. Every noise in here seemed amplified, as if it were designed to intimidate.

Detective Dathan was a perfect customer for the Big and Tall Shop. At around six-four, his meaty, imposing arms covered most of the table. "So ... why don't you tell me what happened?"

"I ... I've already explained it to the officer that arrested me."

"I know, but let's just go through it again."

Lance felt his pulse throbbing in his throat. "I'm sorry, sir, but my mom wanted me to wait until she gets me a lawyer."

The door flew open, and Lance jumped. His mother stood in the doorway with a uniformed cop behind her. "Bob, this is the mother," the cop said. "She wants to be present for the questioning."

Lance met his mother's eyes, hoping they didn't throw her out.

The detective groaned and rubbed his face. "Lady, that's not the best idea."

"He's a minor," she said. "I'm his mother."

He sighed and got up. "All right. Joe, go get her another chair."

Lance sat stiffly, relieved to have someone on his team. His mom could make them see the truth. She always fixed everything, even when it seemed impossible. When the chair was brought in, she sat down next to him. The detective took his seat again, looking peeved.

"So ... we were saying ..."

"That I need to wait for a lawyer," Lance said, glancing at his mother for approval.

"I've called our attorney, Gus Thompson," Barbara said. "He should be here soon."

The detective slapped his knees, then got up. "Okay."

"I mean, I don't have anything to hide," Lance said. "It's not that. I had the baby, but Jordan did give her to me."

His mother touched his hand, squeezed it to shut him up.

The man slowly sat back down. "Just handed her over, huh? Then forgot and called the police?"

His mom squeezed tighter.

"No sir."

"Well, she says you took the baby forcefully."

"No way! She didn't say that."

The man's eyes widened. "I have the complaint right here."

Sweat dripped down Lance's temple. "If she said that, she lied."

"The police report says she had bruises on her face and body."

Barbara sucked in a breath. "Does she claim Lance did that?"

"No. It was an observation the officer made."

Lance's ears burned. "Her mother did that!" he cried. "She's crazy and violent. She's a meth addict too."

"So you felt it was the right thing to do to remove the baby from that environment?"

"No! I didn't remove it!"

Barbara slammed her hand on the table. "That's enough! I know enough about the law to know that you can't keep questioning him once he requests an attorney."

Detective Dathan didn't like that. Rubbing the stubble under his chin, he said, "When they re-engage us, lady, we're allowed to continue. And that's what he did."

Lance looked at his mother. "What does that mean?"

Barbara pointed at him. "It means, don't say another word until the lawyer gets here, Lance!"

The detective got up and jerked Lance to his feet. "Then let's go."

Lance stared up into his face. "Go where?"

"To booking, and then to the holding cell."

"No! You're gonna lock me up? Mom!"

Barbara tried to block the door. "Please, just let him sit here until the attorney comes. It won't be long."

"No, lady. We don't let our perps hang out with their mommies. Either we're questioning him, or he goes in the cell."

Lance could see that there was nothing his mom could do to change this, so he straightened his shoulders and lifted his chin. "It's okay, Mom. I can go."

She started to cry, that same frustrated, helpless weeping he'd seen so many times when Emily was making them crazy. He would have given anything to make her feel better.

Barbara followed the detective and Lance out of the room, and she looked across the desks to the door. Where was Gus? He'd promised to hurry.

On the other side of the room, she saw Judge Hathaway walking through. Though Barbara didn't know much about the law, she had learned some things from Emily's arrests and from the arrests of the children of the moms in her support group. Judge Hathaway had been the one who'd heard Emily's first case of DUI. He was probably the one who would decide whether they would set bail for Lance tonight. She crossed the room and caught him in the hallway. "Judge, can I talk to you for a minute?"

The judge turned. He had a golf tan, and the crinkles at the corners of his eyes suggested he spent a lot of time smiling ... or squinting. She hoped he was a reasonable man.

"Sure. What's up?"

"I'm Barbara Covington. My daughter Emily came through your court a couple of years ago."

"I remember Emily Covington," he said. "She's the girl who disappeared last year."

"Yes," she said. "She's doing great now. But this isn't about her. It's my son. He was arrested for kidnapping today. But he didn't do it. The teenaged mother is a friend of his, and she gave him the baby to protect it from her abusive family, and he was keeping it until—"

"Ma'am, this is inappropriate. This is what court is for."

Desperate, she grabbed his arm. "Please—it's Saturday. Can't you set bail tonight, and then I guarantee I'll have him in court Monday morning? He's fifteen. He's not a flight risk, and he's never been in any legal trouble, ever. He's a good kid. This whole thing is absurd!"

The judge didn't seem moved. "Kidnapping is a serious charge, ma'am. I don't know if that's prudent here. I'll have to take this under advisement."

She knew what that meant. Lance was going to wind up spending at least a couple of nights in jail. "He only went there to try to talk his friend into going back to treatment. The girl is a mess, and so is her family."

"Look, I understand your concern. But I have people to answer to."

The judge wouldn't want people saying he'd let a kidnapper back out on the streets the very day they caught him with a baby. Besides, he probably had distraught parents arguing for their children every day. "This is all going to be cleared up," Barbara said. "Jordan will tell the truth if they can get her away from her mother. I know she will. The public isn't going to go crazy over this, because it's all just a mistake. I know this is an election year—"

The judge jerked his arm away, clearly insulted. "I'm not thinking of politics, Ms. Covington. I'm thinking of the rule of law."

His tone was dismissive, cutting her off. As he walked away, she wondered if she'd made it worse.

Lance was going to spend the night in jail.

Chapter 12

It was the first time Kent had flown with Blake, and as they lifted off the small runway and into the night sky, turbulence bounced them. Kent clutched the door handle.

"Just hang on till we get through these clouds. Should be clear a few miles out."

The moonlight was bright when not obscured by clouds. He hoped they wouldn't become engulfed in them, disorienting Blake. Wasn't that what happened to John Kennedy Jr.? "You ever flown at night, Kent?" Blake asked him, his voice sounding tinny through the headset.

"Not like this," he said.

"Nervous?"

"A little."

"Don't sweat it. Look at all the lights. It's gorgeous. And it's a lot easier to see the airport with it all lit up."

Last month Kent had worked a homicide case at a small private airport in Atlanta, and the lights hadn't been kept on at night. "What if the lights aren't on?"

"I can turn them on myself using the radio microphone key. I checked in advance in the Airport Facilities Directory, and if I press the key four times for that airport, the lights will come on. Piece of cake. We'll be fine."

Adjusting his headset, Kent looked out the window. He couldn't see the usual landmarks, like rivers. But he could see the lights along the highways. "You sure you know how to get there?"

"Got the GPS," Blake said into his mike. "It'll take us right there. Probably take about five and a half hours."

Kent raised an eyebrow. "Why? Flying commercially, it's only about an hour and a half."

"Yeah—flying a big jet at 30,000 feet. But in this thing, flying at about 4,500 feet at 120 miles an hour, it takes a while. It's 533 miles by air, and we'll have to stop once to refuel. We'll probably be there about eleven thirty. So what did Barbara say when she found out the cavalry is coming?"

Kent had told Blake all about his feelings for Barbara. It was because of her influence that he'd found a church and gotten involved in the men's group where he'd met Blake. Now the guy was his racquetball partner and one of his closest friends. "She sounded relieved that I was coming to help her. I don't have any clout with the police department there. But there are some things I can offer. At least she won't be alone."

"I think this is a God thing."

Kent looked at him. "How do you figure that?"

"It's the perfect opportunity to take things to a deeper level with her. An answered prayer."

Kent hoped that was true, that God was intervening and

fueling this relationship. Despite his visits to Jefferson City, he hadn't been able to move things along on his own. "I know you won't believe this, but I'm not doing this to seize the opportunity. I'm seriously concerned about Lance."

"He'll be okay."

"I'm not so sure. A kidnapping charge? That's pretty serious."

"Well, when we get there I'll text all the guys and get them to pray."

At nine o'clock, they landed in Jackson, Tennessee, to refuel, and Kent got out of the plane to stretch and use the bathroom. Before he got back in, he called Barbara.

"Kent?" Her voice was anxious. "Are you here already?"

"No, only halfway. I'm hoping to be there by eleven thirty or so. Can you pick us up?"

"Of course. Kent, they're keeping Lance tonight. I talked to the judge but I don't think he'll let him out. We're going to have to wait until Monday unless I can get Jordan to drop the charges."

"He'll be okay, Barbara."

"No, he won't! He's just a kid, and he'll be in there with dopers and criminals." He winced at the pain in her voice. "What was he thinking? Taking the car, finding a baby, and keeping it? He didn't even call me. He should have taken it straight to the police."

"Where are you now?"

"I'm at the police station, but I'm thinking of going to Jordan's. I've got to talk some sense into that girl."

"Barbara, no! Wait until I get there."

"I can't! It'll be too late then to show up at her house. But if I can find her there now and let her know that Lance, who's supposed to be her friend, is in jail because of her— maybe she'll tell the truth."

"Is there anybody you can take with you?"

"No, I don't have time to find anybody."

"Then get the police to go with you."

"I've already asked. They said they already have her statement. It's Saturday night, Kent. Nobody wants to go to a lot of trouble."

"Then get your attorney to go with you. Is he still at the station?"

She sighed. "Yes, he's just about to go into the interview with Lance."

"Then after he's done there, take him with you, Barbara. Promise me."

He heard muffled voices, then she came back to the phone. "Okay, Gus said he'd go with me."

"Great." He checked the plane—the refueling truck was driving away, and Blake was climbing back in. "Just be careful. We're about to take off again. I'll try to text you from the air when we're about thirty minutes out. We're landing at Garrison Airport."

"I'll be waiting."

He hung up, feeling that tug on his heart that he always felt when he spoke to her. As they took off again, he prayed that God would go with her and Gus, surrounding her with protection. Jordan had to tell the truth about Lance. Otherwise, this would be a colossal mess, and he didn't know how they would get Lance out of it. He'd been found with the baby, after all. On paper, that didn't look good.

Chapter 13

Lance was relieved when they brought him out of the holding cell and took him back to the interview room. Gus Thompson, an attorney who'd once coached Lance in the church basketball league, stood waiting for him with his hands in his pockets.

"Lance, how's it going, buddy?" Gus shook his hand like they were greeting each other at Sunday school.

"Terrible," Lance said, aware of the heat on his cheeks. "They think I kidnapped a baby!"

Gus shushed him until the guard had left them alone. "Okay, sit down and tell me everything. From the very beginning. Starting with how you know Jordan Rhodes."

Lance spilled it all out, and when he finished, Gus folded his hands on the table. "Okay, Lance, all this seems like it should be relatively easy to prove. I'll be here during the interrogation, but be careful how you tell the story. Don't say anything that might lead them to think that you felt the baby would be better off if it was removed from the home."

"I may already have."

"What did you say?"

"I told them about the chaos there, and the detective started putting words in my mouth, like I was saying that I wanted to take the baby away from all that. But that never even crossed my mind. I knew I couldn't take that baby. I didn't even see it before I found it in my car."

"All right, don't panic. Just answer them slowly, and think before you speak. Remember that anything you say can be misinterpreted. I'll stop you if I think you're not being clear or if they're taking it down the wrong track."

"Okay, but do you think they'll believe me?"

"It doesn't really matter at this point, as long as the girl claims you kidnapped the baby."

Lance grunted. "Then somebody should go talk to her. I know her mother made her say that. If they could get her alone, she'd tell the truth."

"I'll try to get the police to do that. But they're not obligated. If they won't go, your mom and I will."

"But am I going to have to stay in jail?"

"Probably, in the detention center. Just until Monday, or until Jordan clears things up."

"Two nights in jail with a bunch of criminals? I can't do that!"

Gus patted Lance's cold hands. "It may not come to that, Lance. Don't panic yet."

"But I shouldn't have to go to jail for something I didn't do!"

"I know, Lance, and it isn't over yet. Just know I'm going to do my best to get you released tonight."

But as the detective came back in, Lance realized the truth. His life was in the hands of a meth addict.

Chapter 14

They weren't going to release Lance. Barbara had already concluded that they didn't care about her tears or her pleading, and they didn't care whether Lance was innocent. It all boiled down to the unreliable statement of a known methamphetamine addict who hadn't even been sane enough to get to the hospital to have her baby.

Two nights in juvenile detention would seem like an eternity to Lance. And it could even be longer. If Jordan didn't back down from her statement, he could go to prison.

But Barbara couldn't let her mind go there. Jordan had to back down. Barbara would convince her.

When she watched them load Lance, handcuffed, into the van to transport him to juvenile detention, she stood on the dark sidewalk in a daze.

Gus touched her shoulder. "Barbara, he'll be okay."

She ignored his reassurance. "Gus, can we go to Jordan's now?"

Gus hesitated. "Are you sure that's a good idea? You and Lance have both said it's a violent and wild place where everybody uses drugs. How far do you expect to get with people like that?"

"If Jordan changes her story, Lance can get out tonight."

He sighed. "All right, but I have to tie up some loose ends inside. Go home, and I'll call you when I'm finished."

She headed home and went into the dark, empty house. She went back to Lance's room, saw the bag of diapers on his bed, the masking tape, the bottle.

The truth was, he'd tried to take care of the child. He should have come to her, yes. He should have called the police the moment he found the baby. But he'd been trying to do what was right for the child and for Jordan. After watching his sister suffer, he felt compassion for those in her shoes, and he'd thought he could help Jordan.

God, what are You doing?

She sat down on Lance's bed, rubbing her face. Lance shouldn't have borrowed the car and driven without a license. He shouldn't have gone to the house of an active drug user. He shouldn't have argued with her mother.

And when he'd found the baby ...

But *shouldn'ts* wouldn't get them anywhere now. The girl who'd gotten Lance into this mess was the only one who could get him out.

Even in her selfishness, even in her fogged thinking, maybe Jordan would care enough about Lance to change her story.

Barbara didn't even know where Jordan lived, and her phone book wasn't where she'd last left it. She racked her brain for the girl's last name, but if she'd ever known it, she'd forgotten. Her mother was Maureen. But Maureen what?

Emily would know. Barbara grabbed the phone, dialed New Day.

"New Day. This is Tia." Tia was the night counselor whom Barbara barely knew.

"Tia, this is Emily Covington's mother, Barbara. I need to speak to my daughter."

"I'm sorry, but she's used up her phone calls for the day. Besides, the girls aren't allowed to take calls after eight."

"Tia, this is a family emergency. If you don't let me talk to her, I'm going to have to come there."

She hesitated. "All right, if it's an emergency. I'll go get her."

Barbara breathed a sigh of relief and closed her eyes as she waited. After several moments, Emily came to the phone.

"Mom? What's wrong?"

"Lance has been arrested."

"What?"

When Barbara was finished explaining, Emily said, "That dork drove my car?"

Barbara wanted to scream. "Emily, is that really the worst thing you heard me say?"

"No, I'm just saying, if he hadn't done that, none of this would have happened."

"I need Jordan's last name and her address or phone number."

"I don't know her address, but her last name is Rhodes." She spelled it. "Mom, did they really put him in Juvie?"

"Yes. Pray for him. Get everyone there to pray."

"We will. Mom, Jordan's in deep trouble with her addictions, but she does have a heart. I really think if you talk to her she'll change her story. Her mother is horrible, and she probably made her say that."

"But why? Why would Maureen do that? It's not as if she cares about the baby—she didn't even get Jordan to the hospital when she was in labor. Even after the baby was born addicted to meth, she didn't get her to a doctor to see if she was all right."

"It's probably a control thing. She's the reason Jordan's addicted in the first place. But if Jordan does give the baby up for adoption, the counselors said she can come back here. She'd have to start over from the beginning, but she needs that."

"I'll tell her, if I can find her," Barbara said.

She hung up and changed clothes. Her feet were killing her in these heels, and she'd been wearing this dress all day. She put on a pair of jeans and tennis shoes and waited.

When Gus finally called, she told him she'd pick him up at the police station. Pulling out of the driveway, she prayed that God would help them find Jordan at home. The girl was their only hope.

Chapter 15

The porch light was on when Barbara and Gus pulled up to the Rhodes house, and bugs flew around it. The yard was neglected, the grass a foot tall where it grew at all, and the house looked like it needed a coat of paint and some repairs.

Her heart sank as she thought of Lance coming here alone today. What was he thinking?

"Barbara, if they give us trouble, we leave. No fighting. We're not dealing with rational people here."

She agreed.

The porch looked rotten and unsteady. Stepping up onto it, she knocked on the door. Gus stood on the rickety steps behind her.

The door squeaked open, and Maureen peered through the screen door with red, bloodshot eyes. "What do you want?"

Barbara had met her a time or two on visitation days at the treatment center. They'd never exchanged more than a passing greeting, so she wasn't sure the woman would recognize her. "Maureen, hi, I'm Emily and Lance's mother."

Maureen narrowed her eyes. "I know who you are."

"I need to talk to Jordan."

"She ain't here. She went out."

Barbara doubted that—the girl had just given birth. "Maureen, we really need to talk to her. My son is in jail tonight."

"Where he should be." Maureen looked past her to Gus. "Who are you?"

"Gus Thompson." He stepped forward and reached his hand out to shake. But Maureen didn't open the screen door to take it. "I'm Lance's attorney."

Barbara hoped the authority in his voice would get some results. But Maureen just laughed. "He's gonna need one."

"Maureen," Barbara said, "you know Lance didn't do anything like what Jordan claims. She put that baby in his car. This is all just a huge misunderstanding, and we can clear it up very easily."

"I told you, she ain't here."

Barbara concentrated on softening her voice. "Where is she?"

"I don't know, probably with some of her no-account friends."

"She just had a baby. She shouldn't be hanging out with her friends. She should be in a hospital."

"Don't tell me what my daughter should be doing. Worry about your own reprobate kids."

Barbara drew in a long breath. "I do, Maureen. That's why one of them has been in treatment for a year. And I worry about my son. Why would she say that he kidnapped the baby? You were here. You know that isn't true."

"You're right. I was here. He came in here ranting about how she needed to go back to treatment, and when she wouldn't go, he beat her up and grabbed the baby and took off."

Barbara almost went through the screen door. "Why are you lying? He's fifteen! Lance has never done anything to you. No one in our family has ever done anything to you. Lance was trying to help Jordan, because he cares about her."

"Do I need to call the police again?"

Barbara took a step back and tried a different approach. "Let me appeal to you as a mother. I know you love your daughter. I love my children, and I'd do anything for them. Please—the baby's safe now, and everything's okay. Just . . . please get Jordan to drop the charges."

"If you want to help your son, teach him to stay out of other people's business. Now get off my property or I'll have you arrested for trespassing and harassment."

Gus handed Maureen a business card. "Ms. Rhodes, when your daughter comes home, would you have her call me?"

Maureen took the card and tossed it on a table just inside the door.

Gus took Barbara's elbow. "Come on, Barbara. Let's go."

Barbara would just have to get to Jordan some other way. If she was somewhere in the house, maybe she'd heard her. But she couldn't count on that. Barbara stalked back to her car. If she really had gone out, maybe Emily's friends would know where Jordan hung out. Maybe someone at New Day could tell her. She knew Gus wouldn't consent to beating the bushes for the girl. She'd have to wait for Kent.

She prayed they could still find Jordan before Lance had to spend the night in jail.

Chapter 16

The holding room at the juvenile detention center was a bright Pepto-Bismol color, though this was the side for boys only. Lance wondered if that was meant to humiliate the tough guys who landed here.

It was a busy night. He stood at the door of his holding cell, watching through the dirty glass as they booked another eight losers. Their cursing shook the place, the cuffs on their wrists probably the only things keeping them from attacking the cops who handled them. Some of them had bloody bruises, and one had a swollen black eye. They'd clearly been fighting. He wondered if they'd all been on the losing side.

He sure hoped they wouldn't put them in the same holding cell with him. But there had only been three doors like this one when they processed him. If there were only these holding cells, some of them would undoubtedly end up in here with him.

He backed across the room and sank onto a bench. It was built into the wall—probably so no one could pick it up and throw it. There was nothing in here you could use in a fit of violence. Except fists ... teeth ... feet ...

He raked his hands through his hair. He'd never survive this night.

How do I get out of here?

He wondered if the baby was all right. If she was fed and diapered, if he'd done all the right things with her. He sure hoped he hadn't made anything worse for her.

Jordan's mother had probably gone nuclear when she realized the baby was gone. She'd probably threatened Jordan to try to get her back. Jordan would have had to tell the police some story to cool her mother off.

But didn't she understand what her lies would do to him? Did she even care?

No, of course she didn't. She was selfish, like all active drug users. She only cared about herself and getting that next high. Whatever she had to do, whoever she had to sell out, however she had to lie, she would. He'd learned all about it at New Day—their need to lie and steal to get drugs to numb the pain. But the lying and stealing led to more problems and more pain, so they needed more drugs to feel better. And that meant more lies and stealing. More problems. More cravings for drugs. It was a vicious cycle that took miracles to break.

The door clanged and scraped open. Lance stood up as the guard ushered three guys in. The one with the bloody lip was first, followed by a kid who looked no more than twelve and the kid with the black eye.

Suddenly he felt like a little mouse in a cage with rabid rats.

"Any trouble from you," the huge guard told the new-comers, "and I'll put you in lockdown, you got it?"

The smallest kid had the biggest mouth, and he told the guard what he could do with his lockdown.

When the door clanged shut, all three turned toward Lance. He tried to stand tall, but the kid with the black eye was taller. He wished he hadn't showered today, that he looked a little dirtier, a little less clean-cut. He hoped his cheeks weren't burning red. He hated that about himself, that his every emotion burned in full color splotches on his face.

"How long you been in here?" the little one, who happened to look the most dangerous, asked.

Lance shrugged. "About an hour."

"So are we spending the night here in this cell?" the kid asked.

The big guy shook his head. "No, man. This is just a holding cell. They'll take us upstairs to the pod."

"What's the pod?" the kid asked.

"A cell with a bunch of rooms in it around a circle."

"So we'll all be together? Reno will smash my face in."

"Not if I'm there," Black Eye said.

Lance wanted to laugh, since it looked like Reno had already smashed all of their faces in. But he didn't dare.

"Will they keep us separate from them since they arrested them first?"

"Doubt it," the kid with the fat lip said. He turned to Lance. "What are you in here for?"

Lance swallowed. "For something I didn't do."

The three laughed. "No, really. What did you do?"

Lance drew in a breath of courage. "I don't want to talk about it, okay?"

"You got a attitude?" Bloody Lip asked him.

"No."

The kid took menacing steps toward him. "Whatsa matter? You too good to talk to us?"

"Apparently not," Lance said, "since we're all in jail."

The little guy came closer and slapped his fist into his palm, right in front of Lance's face. Lance refused to flinch. He was sure he could take this kid if he had to, but not all three of them, and the other two were sure to join in.

And if he got in a fight, he'd probably have to stay longer. It wasn't worth it. He wondered if that girl checking into New Day this morning had felt this way when he asked her what she was in for.

"Okay, if it means that much to you …" He thought of telling them he was in for ripping the face off the last dude who smarted off to him, but he decided to play it straight. "I'm in for kidnapping."

"Kidnapping who? A girl?" Bloody Lip asked.

"No, not a girl. A baby."

They stared at him. "Your own kid?"

Lance knew they'd never understand. "No. A friend's. I didn't take it. It's a long story."

"You give her money for it?"

Lance stared at the kid. "No, I didn't give her money."

"But she was gonna get some, right?"

Lance shook his head, confused. "What are you talking about?"

"She on dope? This girl who had the baby?"

Lance shrugged. "Yeah, meth. Why?"

"Dude in the hood is always looking for pregnant tweakers. Waves drug money in their face. Wads of cash."

Lance frowned. "For what? What does he want with the babies?"

"He only wants the baby girls. Sells them to some dudes in South America."

"It's easy money, man." The little guy was clearly hopped up on something, and he tore out a laugh. "Dude, wish I could get pregnant. I could use some cash." He couldn't sit still and paced across the floor, fidgeting and agitated. The other two sat down, but their knees jiggled.

They reminded him of Jordan. He wondered if they were on meth too. "Who is this dude? The one who sells the babies?"

"Man, I ain't tellin' you that. He'd slice me up."

Lance thought that over. Surely that wasn't the situation with Jordan. The people waiting for the baby were clean-cut. And Maureen and Zeke had arranged this themselves. He thought back to what the man had said. He'd threatened to call off the whole thing, and Maureen went crazy, begging him not to. Was it possible that money was involved? Was that why Maureen was so dead set on giving the baby to them?

The boys started arguing about the fight that had gotten them there. "I told you not to get into it with them," the little twerp said. "How can we get out of a possession charge?"

"Hey, you're the one who called the cops, you moron," Black Eye said. "There was stuff all over the place, right out where they'd see it. They saw us cookin'! We're not goin' down for possession, but for manufacturin'. That's real bad, man!"

"Hey, I was tryin' to keep him from killin' you."

"I'd rather be dead! Now the cops are gonna score with our stuff, man, and all that money is wasted."

"Reno would have put a bullet through your brain. He had a gun."

"You could've at least hid our stuff before you called 911, fool."

Lance winced, certain of what would come next. Instead of jumping on the name-caller, the boy kicked the stone wall, as if he could walk up it. "You call your old man?" he asked the other guy.

"Naw, man. I called Mag."

"Mag? She can't bail you out."

"Ain't nobody bailin' me out. My old man sure don't have no cash."

"I called my mom. She told me to sit here, that I deserve it. She wouldn't come."

Lance thought back to the night Emily had been arrested for a DUI. His mother, who'd been at the end of her rope, had refused to get her out too. Emily had to spend the night in jail.

He hoped she didn't get the same idea with him. "If it just wasn't the weekend," he said. "I have to wait until Monday to get bail set."

"Man, us too. Two nights in jail, at least. I hate this place!"

"Been here before?" Lance asked.

"Five times," Black Eye said.

Lance wondered what could make someone do enough to get put in here five times. Once was all it would take him. He was a fast learner.

The little guy backed up and got a running start, then kicked the wall higher, as though he could walk up it like Harry Potter. Then he fell onto the concrete floor, hurting his shoulder.

Black Eye erupted. "Stop it, you idiot! I've had enough of you."

The kid got back up, fire in his eyes. This was going to be bad. Lance glanced at the door, wishing for an escape.

The best he could do was stay out of the way.

Chapter 17

It wasn't easy to convince the counselor at New Day to let Barbara see Emily so late. Though Emily would be completely free in just a couple of days, the rigid rules that kept these girls clean and sober still applied to her.

When they finally let her into the rec room to talk to Emily, her friends came with her. Barbara tried not to look frantic.

"Mom, did something else happen to Lance?"

"No, but I need your help. Jordan isn't home, and her mother wouldn't tell me where she is. I need for you guys to tell me where she hangs out."

Emily looked back at one of the girls—a brunette who'd blossomed from a scrawny, unhealthy addict into a beautiful young woman in the last few months. "Karen, you hung out with her. Do you know where she could be?"

"I know a few places," the girl said reluctantly. She glanced at Emily. "I'll bet she's at Belker's."

Barbara saw the knowing look on Emily's face. "Yeah, I bet you're right."

"Belker's?"

The girls all looked at each other, silent. Emily finally met her eyes. "He's ... someone we all knew."

"A dealer?" Barbara asked.

No one answered, and she knew why. Though they were living in sobriety, they still didn't want to face the repercussions of ratting out dealers. Breaking the code of silence, even among those who'd escaped the addictive lifestyle, was deadly.

Barbara tried again. "Girls, you all know Lance. He's a good kid. He shouldn't be in jail. If you have any idea where I can find Jordan, please — "

"I think I know."

The voice was nearly inaudible. Barbara turned to see who'd spoken. It was Lindy, a tiny redhead.

"We used to hang out a lot at ..." Her voice trailed off as someone came in, and Barbara turned to the door. It was the new girl she'd seen checking in this morning — the girl named Tammy.

Lindy got quiet.

"What, Lindy?" Barbara pressed. "You were saying?"

"I don't know. I forgot."

"You didn't forget. You were about to tell me — "

"Just that she'll come around. I know she will. She really likes Lance."

That clearly wasn't what Lindy had started to say. Barbara realized that Lindy didn't yet trust Tammy — and was reluctant to say anything sensitive in front of her.

Barbara looked at Emily, who sent her a look that told

her to stay calm. Maybe she could get the information when she was alone later with Lindy.

Defeated, she went back to her car, praying that God would give her some direction. How could she find Jordan?

It hit her then. The police would have taken the sick baby to the hospital. If Jordan cared about her baby at all, she'd probably show up there.

It was a safe place to confront the girl, and going there was a way to kill time until Kent arrived. Barbara turned her car around and headed to the hospital.

Chapter 18

Barbara found the nursery on the third floor of the hospital. She went to the window and checked out the newborns. Most of the bassinets were empty. The mothers probably had the infants in their rooms.

Farther back from the window were several incubators holding small babies attached to monitors. A young mother and father stood near one, stroking their child and talking softly.

Nurses moved from bassinet to bassinet, seeing to the needs of these tiny charges. Barbara found the door and stepped tentatively inside.

A nurse came toward her. "Can I help you?"

"Yes, I'm a friend of the Rhodes family. I just wanted to see how the baby is."

"She's doing better. She's right over there, in an incubator."

Barbara looked where she pointed and saw the baby sleeping on her back in a glass crib, attached to monitors. Her little belly rose and fell with each breath. "Her family isn't here?"

"No, nobody's been here for her since she came in by ambulance."

Sorrow rushed over Barbara. Once again, this baby's needs were being neglected by her family. Had Lance cared more about her than her own flesh and blood? Tears filled her eyes. "Could I ... rock her or something?"

"Sure, we can always use volunteers to do that."

The nurse scooped the baby up and put her in Barbara's arms.

"Do you know her name?" the nurse asked.

Barbara shook her head. "I don't think they've named her yet. If they did, they didn't tell my son."

"Your son?"

"He's a friend of the mother."

The nurse pulled a rocking chair over. "You can rock her right here. Just don't let the leads pull off, and watch the IV on her foot. It was the best place to find a vein on her. She's having some drug withdrawal."

Barbara nodded. "Her mother's a crystal meth addict."

"That's what the tox screen showed, among other things."

Barbara knew that Xanax was probably in the mix, since meth addicts used anxiety drugs to cushion their crashes. Withdrawing from that drug would have neurological implications for the baby. She hoped she could overcome it.

The nurse nodded. "We've got her on some medication to help with the seizures. It makes her really sleepy."

Barbara sat down, enjoying the feel of the child in her arms. It brought back so many memories. When Emily and Lance were babies, when John had been alive and they'd on a whole new phase of life called Parenthood, everything had seemed perfect. She'd never in her wildest dreams imagined herself a widow with one child in drug treatment and the other in jail.

Failure throbbed through her head.

"Is she going to be all right?" she managed to ask.

"Probably. She may have some developmental delays, but lately we've seen some good studies that say these babies can rebound and do very well, depending on their care."

That was what worried Barbara. If Jordan kept this baby and continued to use crystal meth, what kind of life would she have? It was a violent home, rife with beatings and hostility—not a safe place for an innocent infant.

She rocked the baby, counting her tiny fingers and toes, trying to imagine Lance taking care of her. She didn't think he'd ever held a baby in his life. Of all people, why would Jordan choose to give the baby to him?

Maybe because she knew Barbara would be there to help. Or maybe she just hadn't had time to think. She'd probably been trying to save her baby any way she could.

As she rocked the child, she kept looking toward the window and the door, hoping Jordan would show up. But she never came.

Barbara's phone beeped, and she saw the text she'd been expecting from Kent: *We're thirty minutes out. See you then.*

She responded, *I'll be there waiting.*

She checked her watch. It would take fifteen minutes to get to the airport. That gave her fifteen more minutes with the baby ... fifteen minutes to wait for Jordan.

She stroked the baby's curls, wondering if the trauma of her first day out of the womb would scar her for life. Barbara prayed that God would intervene and help this child. He was the only one who could.

Chapter 19

Fatigue took hold of Kent as they made their final approach. Blake self-announced, since there wasn't a tower and no one working the radio at the small airport this late. As the plane touched down, Kent scanned the area for Barbara's headlights.

"There she is, buddy," Blake said into his mike.

Kent spotted her car in the parking lot beside the small building. His heartbeat sped up as adrenaline kicked in. How long had it been since he'd seen her? Four or five months, at least. He hoped he didn't look too rough, too old. It had been a long time since he'd showered and shaved this morning.

He pulled some breath mints out of his pocket, popped one in his mouth.

"Can't wait to meet her," Blake said.

"Do me a favor. Don't let on that I've told you anything about her."

"No problem. I won't embarrass you."

Blake pulled the plane onto the tarmac and cut off the engine. Kent welcomed the silence after the plane's noise. "Go ahead and say hello," he said. "I'll tie her down and meet you at the car."

"I don't know how to repay you for this, Blake. You're the man."

"Yeah, well, if I ever get murdered, you can find my killer."

"It's a deal."

Kent waited until the prop stopped turning, then got out and headed around the small building to Barbara's car. She opened her door.

"Kent!"

Even in the dim light, she looked more beautiful than he remembered, though her eyes were red and she'd cried off any make-up she may have had on earlier. She threw her arms around his neck, and he lifted her a few inches off the ground and squeezed her.

"It's so good to see you," she said into his ear. "Thank you for coming."

He held her a little too long, savoring the feel of her small frame in his arms, the tightness of her embrace, the feel of her neck against his lips. He set her down and pulled back. "What else could I do? I can't let Lance go down for something he didn't do." He took her hand and led her back to the car. "Have you found Jordan?"

"No. She's not at home or at the hospital." She told him what she'd done in the hours since they'd last spoken. Kent breathed relief that she hadn't gone off half-cocked to hunt down Jordan alone. She was an independent woman, and he would have bet that she'd disregard his warnings in order to help her son. It wouldn't have been the first time.

But she had listened and taken the attorney with her to the Rhodes house, and here she sat ... safe and whole. Maybe now he could really help her.

When Blake got to the car, he introduced himself with an amused grin on his face. "Blake McCallister. Nice to meet you, Barbara."

"Nice to meet you," she said. "Thanks for bringing him."

"I always love making cross-country night flights. It's pure fun."

They all piled in the car, Blake in the backseat. Kent couldn't take his eyes off Barbara. "We can take Blake to a hotel, get our rooms, and then you and I can go and talk, if that's all right."

"Sounds good." Barbara glanced at Blake in her rear-view mirror. "Do you work with Kent, Blake?"

Blake shook his head. "No, we're in a men's group together at church."

Church. The word brought a faint smile to Barbara's lips. Kent knew that surprised her. He'd told her he was going to church, but he hadn't elaborated, afraid she would think he was only trying to impress her.

"You're in a men's group?" she asked Kent. "What do you guys do?"

"We study the Bible," Kent said. "Insult each other. Watch games together."

"And we learn how to be manly men," Blake said with a laugh as he slapped Kent's shoulder.

His laughter was contagious. "Oh, I doubt either of you need help with that."

"Tell it to my wife," Blake said.

Kent chuckled and rested his arm on the back of her seat. "Don't listen to him. His wife adores him." He squeezed her shoulder. "You okay?"

"Better now," she said, and her soft smile sent warmth through him. "I hope you can help. Lance has already been in jail for hours. I have to get him out. I can't rest knowing he's there."

"I'll do my best to resolve this tonight," he said.

He hoped he wouldn't let her down.

Chapter 20

Lance shrank into a back corner of the concrete cell, try-ing to stay out of the way, as fists began flying. His cell-mates had turned on each other, even though they'd come in here as friends. They fought as if trying to kill each other, rage and blood behind every blow.

By the time the guards slid the door open and broke up the fight, Lance was drenched with sweat. He was nearly limp with relief when the guards marched all four of them out of their holding cell, Lance included, then led them upstairs to change into their prison clothes.

"I see any more trouble from you stupid juvies, and I'll take care of you myself," the guard warned the bruised, bloody boys.

Stupid Juvies. He couldn't believe he was considered a

juvenile delinquent. What if his school friends heard about this? How would he ever face any of them again?

Up on the next level, he was handed a mattress, blanket, jumpsuit, and flip-flops. The guard looked bigger and scarier than Mr. Bilhorn in history class, and he wasn't bound by laws about teachers touching students. Lance had the feeling that this guard got his kicks slapping kids around when they smarted off to him.

After being treated in a way that would have been called abuse in any other setting, Lance stepped into his orange jumpsuit. It didn't fit. The pants were too long. He looked like an idiot with the legs rolled up around his ankles, but he supposed that was the point.

The boys were divided into three groups headed for three destinations, depending on their ages. Only one of the guys was his age—the one with the bloody lip. They were handed off to another guard, then herded onto the elevator and taken up to the fourth floor.

Stepping out of the elevator, Lance saw the glass-enclosed pod he'd heard about in holding, and the guards' room high above, where they observed the kids. The glass doors to the pod opened and the guard ushered them inside. Some of the guys clustered on the other side of the room got to their feet and leered at the newcomers with murderous eyes, and Lance felt the threat radiating over the room. Why were they looking at him like they already hated him?

He stood taller, chest out, refusing to show weakness, or they'd be on him in a moment, like hungry animals after fresh blood.

"I'll kill those guys." The words were muttered behind him, and he glanced back. Bloody Lip was leering at the guys across the room, and Lance realized that this guy was the target of the hatred they felt. He decided to move away from the kid as soon as he could.

The guard led them to an empty cell with two beds and a desk. "Put your stuff down and wait for me. I'll be back."

Lance set his mattress down on one of the metal beds and glanced back at Bloody Lip, who lingered in the doorway, looking out as if expecting to be jumped. "Probably nothing'll happen here," Lance said. "The guards are watching. Those guys won't want to get in more trouble than they're already in."

"You don't know those dudes." The kid turned around, tossed his foam pad onto the other bed. "I hate it here. I can't believe I came back."

"If we're roommates we ought to know each other's names. I'm Lance."

The kid stared at him. "What kind of name is that? Lance."

"Guess my mother had a white knight complex when she named me. Lancelot? You know, the prince?"

The guy breathed a derisive laugh. "How 'bout I just call you Prince?"

Lance didn't think that would go over well here. "I'd rather you didn't. I don't like nicknames. What do you want me to call you?"

"My name's Turk."

"Turk?" The guy looked Hispanic. "You don't look like a Turk."

"I do believe in nicknames, okay? Been called that since I was two."

Lance glanced at the plastic ID card clipped to Turk's jumpsuit. The kid's name was really Juarez.

Turk sat down stiffly, his shoulders boxed and tense.

"So do you think anybody'll come bail you out tonight?" Lance asked.

"I don't have nobody to come."

Lance shrugged. "I have my mom, but I don't know what she can do this late at night." His mouth was dry. He wished he had something to drink, but he doubted they had vending machines in a place like this. He didn't have any money anyway. "They think I stole a baby. Who would do that?"

"Don't matter what the charges are. If you don't have nobody to bond you out, you just sit here until you rot or till some dude gets around to your paperwork and realizes they've held you too long."

Lance knew his mother would never let that happen. "What about your mom?"

Turk got up and went to the door, peered out again. "You talk a lot, you know that?"

Lance swallowed. "Sorry."

Silence passed between them for a few moments, then finally, Turk turned back. "Not that it's any of your business, but I never depended on my mother, even before she killed herself."

Lance sucked in a breath. "Suicide?"

"No, she OD'd on heroin."

"Wow. I'm really sorry."

"Don't be. I didn't shed one tear. All she gave me my whole life was grief." He said it as though he was livid at Lance for asking, as though the memory had dragged up more violence.

Lance was sorry he'd asked. Why couldn't he just keep his mouth shut? He looked at the floor, feeling a little more sympathy toward the kid.

Turk's chin jutted out. "I been on my own since I was fourteen, and I do just fine."

Lance's eyes narrowed. The kid was apparently Lance's age, since they'd ended up in the same group. Fifteen, maybe sixteen. Why wasn't Turk in foster care? Maybe the government just didn't know about him.

Had he really been fending for himself since his mother died? He imagined being the child of a heroin addict. Turk had probably been raising himself for a lot longer than a couple of years.

"You got a dad?" Lance asked quietly, knowing he shouldn't.

Turk blew out a laugh. "Yeah. Sure. I got a sweet old man who'll drop everything and come bail me out and then go out back and toss a baseball around with me. That's probably the kind of Daddy you have, right, Prince?"

Lance's throat got tight. "My dad died."

For the first time, Turk met his eyes. Did he think that gave them some point in common? As if he couldn't bear the look on Lance's face, he turned away. "Yeah, well, I never knew mine."

"Grandparents? Aunts or uncles?"

"My granddad's in jail for life. I only seen him a couple of times when we went to visit."

Lance tried to imagine a grandfather in jail. It was too weird. "What did he do? Kill somebody?"

"Yep."

Lance tried not to look shocked.

"All my relatives are dead or in jail or drunk somewhere." An undercurrent of anger rippled on his voice.

Lance sat quietly, studying Turk. He had no right to judge his cellmate, he realized. Turk hadn't had the same start Lance had, with a mom and dad who loved him and saw to his every need and protected him from trauma and pain.

"Somebody at school will miss you. Won't it get around

that you got in a fight and they picked you up? Maybe a teacher or somebody—"

"Dude, I ain't been to school since sixth grade. You writin' a book or somethin'? You with *20/20*? Actin' like you're interviewin' me."

Lance grew quiet and thought about all the judgments he'd made before about dropouts. He'd considered them losers. But if you were born into a family with dopers as parents ... if your only male role model was a convict in for murder ... if nobody woke you up and made you go to school each day ... how would you be likely to turn out? Lance went to school because he was expected to. Every morning when his alarm went off and his mother came and said, "Lance, get up," he was expected to get dressed and go to school. But if that wasn't expected, if instead the only thing anyone expected was for you to drop out of school and get high and roll in and out of jail ...

It was, of course, the kind of life Jordan had. But knowing that wasn't enough for Lance to forgive her for this.

"Your lip looks bad. Doesn't it need stitches or a Band-Aid or something?"

Turk touched it, then examined his fingers. "I don't need anything. Wouldn't matter if I did."

The guard came back in, gave them the few supplies they were allowed to have, and told them to get out on the floor. "You're not allowed in your room until I say, got that? But when I say go back to your rack, you don't breathe, think, talk, or do nothing but go to your rack. And if I hear anything from either of you, I'll throw you in lockdown and you can lay there and see how you like that."

Lance swallowed and said, "Yes sir."

"All right, out here where I can see you."

Lance cleared his throat. "Uh ... sir?"

The guard speared him with a look. "What?"

"Is it possible that someone could come for me tonight? I mean, to bail me out or whatever?"

"No, it's not. If there was a possibility of you being bailed out, they'da left you in the holding cell at the county."

Lance's heart sank. "What if the charges are dropped? If the girl who accused me finally tells the truth? Could they let me out then?"

"If pigs start flying, we'll let you know. How's that?"

His cellmate sat down on his bunk, looking between his knees to his feet. The guard grabbed him up by his collar. "Didn't you hear me? I said get up and get out there right now."

For the first time, Lance saw fear on Turk's face. "Those dudes ... they're gonna jump me."

"Not if you keep your head down."

"We didn't finish the fight. The police busted it up."

"You finish it here," the guard said, "and I'll be the one who wins."

"Somebody's gonna wind up dead, man. Might be me. Can I just stay in here?"

The guard had no sympathy. "Nope. Out there. Now. Lights out is in an hour. You can come back to your cell then."

As they stepped out of their cell, Lance cast a leery glance at the gang members across the room. They watched with dangerous grins as Turk came out. Lance didn't want to get caught in the fray, so he headed to a corner. He wasn't here to make friends or enemies. He was just here to wait. His mother would figure something out.

All he had to do was try to be invisible. Maybe if he stayed off everyone's radar, he would come out of this with a few good stories and no broken bones. But as the gang members pushed off from their wall and meandered across the room, Turk gravitated toward Lance.

Lance slid down to the floor, sitting on his haunches. "Man, if they're coming for you, don't stand by me, okay? I don't want to fight."

"I can stand wherever I want."

Real mature, Lance thought. But he saw through Turk's bravado. The kid didn't want to face his enemies alone. Turk was breaking out in a sweat as the leering guys now in the middle of the room called out, taunting him. His face twisted in rage as he stared them down.

"Look, I've never been here before," Lance muttered, "but I'm just thinking that they might not jump you if you quit staring at them like you're gonna pull a Steven Seagal on them."

"That's what I'll do if they come near me," Turk said.

"Just chill, okay?"

"I can't. They'll think I'm weak."

"And what good will it do for them to think you're dangerous?"

"It'll keep me alive."

Lance shook his head. When a guard walked in front of the glass doors, staring pointedly, the dudes coming toward them turned away. Lance breathed a sigh of relief.

Turk slid down the wall and sat next to him on the cold concrete floor. "What time did he say he puts us in our cells?"

"The time doesn't matter, since we don't know what time it is now."

Turk tore his eyes away from the gang across the room and gave him a cryptic stare. "Kidnapping, huh?"

Lance closed his eyes. "I didn't do it."

"I'm starting to believe you."

"Good, at least somebody does." Lance sighed. "Man, my buddies at school aren't gonna believe this."

"Where you from?"

"From here."

"I never seen you before."

"I probably don't hang out where you do. I'm in tenth grade at Jefferson High."

"Man, school is for losers."

"Losers? You mean people who want to grow up and get jobs they like? Nice, safe places to live?"

"Too many rules. I hated getting up, listening to a bunch of stupid teachers trying to control me."

"It's easy. You show up, listen, hang out with your friends. How hard is that?"

Turk's attention veered back to the gang members across the room. "My boys ain't in school neither."

"Yeah, well, maybe if you went to school you wouldn't have time for gang fights."

The bar was set pretty low for Turk and his buddies. No high school diploma, no chance of college, no prospects of decent jobs or a future. It was almost like these guys were *trying* to make things harder on themselves.

He looked around the room at these boys who were now marked as criminals, wondering which of them were fighting through life virtually alone, like Jordan, who was born into turmoil. No wonder the prisons were full and dope dealers had a booming business.

Chapter 21

Kent didn't know how he was going to help Barbara, since he didn't know anyone at the Jefferson City Police Department. But the case with Emily last year had garnered him national attention, even though he hadn't sought it. After she was found, he was interviewed on most of the major cable and network news programs. Her hometown PD had undoubtedly watched those programs too, and he hoped they'd remember him well enough to be cordial.

As he and Barbara walked into the police department, he said, "Let me do the talking. It would be best if you just sit off to the side. Let me see what I can find out, one cop to another."

The station was lit with fluorescent bulbs that gave the illusion of daylight to those who worked the graveyard shift. Several cops worked at their desks, either booking arrests or filing reports. A sergeant who looked like he hadn't yet adjusted to the night shift sat at a front desk talking to a flustered man whose car had been stolen.

Kent waited until the theft victim was referred to another officer who would take his complaint. Then he leaned on the chest-high desk. "How you doin'? I'm Detective Kent Harlan, Atlanta PD."

The man frowned as if trying to place the name. "Sergeant Harper. Nice to meet you. What brings you here? We got a case in common?"

"No, nothing like that. I handled the case of a Jefferson City resident a year ago. You might remember—Emily Covington's disappearance?"

The man's bushy eyebrows shot up. "Yeah, and that murdered woman. I knew I recognized you!" He grinned and called across the room. "Hey, Crawley, get a load of this! We got a celebrity here!"

Kent hadn't expected that. He shot a look back at Barbara, and she smiled and ducked her head. A couple of men came to introduce themselves, and when he had the chance, he said, "Turns out Emily Covington's brother, Lance, was arrested today. I got to know the family real well while we were working on the case, and Lance is a good kid. Would you mind if I took a look at the police report? I want to see what Jordan Rhodes alleged."

Less than a minute later, he was at Scott Crawley's desk, and they were pulling up the info on Lance's case. He read over the report. There really wasn't anything there that Barbara's attorney hadn't already told her. "The arresting officer, Todd Miles. I'd like to talk to him if he's still on shift."

"He got off at eleven, but he never goes straight home. I might be able to catch him."

As Kent waited for Crawley to reach Miles, he ambled

back up to Sergeant Harper. "Hey, Sergeant, do you know anybody at Juvie?"

"Yeah, I got a couple of buddies there."

"Listen, do me a favor. This kid, Lance Covington, he's in school, he's making good grades, never been in trouble. Not a druggie, doesn't fight—a dream kid, you know?" Sure, Kent was stretching it a little, but compared to some of the kids this sergeant probably saw every day, Lance was a white knight.

"Yeah?"

"So if you have any pull, see if you can get them to put Lance in lockdown tonight. Just to keep him safe, you know? I think he's being set up for this. Be a real shame if anything bad happened to him under those circumstances."

The sergeant leaned closer, looking mischievous. "What's with you and the kid's mom? She's sitting over there pretending like she's not here, watching you work us."

Kent grinned, and Harper laughed.

"It's okay, man, I understand. She's not bad. And I can see how it came together—I mean, you were the hero who found her daughter."

"Actually, she found her daughter before I did. But she's been through a lot. Single mom, trying to do the right thing. Finally gets her daughter clean, about to graduate from a year in rehab, and now this."

The sergeant stole another look at Barbara. "Yeah, I could see earlier she was pretty upset. She saw the judge and shot through here like a heat-seeking missile."

"She's trying to protect her boy. Can you do me that favor? It would mean a lot."

"I'll give it a shot. If they have a couple of lockdown cells empty, they might do it."

"I'd appreciate it."

As the sergeant picked up the phone, Kent saw Crawley waving him over. "I've got Miles on the phone. He says he'll talk to you."

Kent took the phone. "Hey, Miles. Kent Harlan here."

"Yeah, nice to talk to you. I saw you interviewed a couple of times after the Covington case."

He hoped that would work in his favor. "Did you know Lance is related to Emily?"

"No, not until now. His mom looked familiar, but I didn't realize it was her. Now, if I'd seen Emily, I would have realized it. Her picture was all over the news for weeks."

"So who filed the complaint? Jordan Rhodes or her mother?"

"Her mother called first. I responded to the call and found Jordan beaten up ... bloody lip, black eye, looking pretty feeble. They told me she'd had the baby this morning."

"What was her emotional state?"

"Seemed upset. Like any mother whose baby was kidnapped."

"So what did she say happened?"

"You read the report. I was pretty thorough."

Obviously, this guy wasn't a talker. "But did she sound credible? Or did she sound like her mother was coaching her?"

There was a pause. "Her mother was there, trying to help her get the story out."

"Any coercion?"

"I didn't think so. Just an agitated mother helping her teenage daughter talk to police."

"Did they seem high? Disoriented?"

"Maybe, but I didn't see anything out in the open. I figure things aren't quite on the up and up if she gave birth at home. It's not like they're health fanatics who planned a home birth. But the story made sense. I figure the kid saw the condition of the house and decided to get the baby out of there. Could even be the father."

"He's not the father," Kent said. He knew he couldn't be sure of that, but from Barbara's account, Jordan had just been an addict Lance knew from school, someone he'd helped get into treatment. He'd never given his mom any sign that he'd had an intimate relationship with her.

"I know he says she put the baby in his car," Miles said, "but who knows which story is true? The fact is, we found him with the baby."

"You found him in the process of taking the baby to the hospital. Didn't that tell you anything?"

"Hey, he could have been skipping town for all I know."

"He called 911 before you showed up. You can confirm that."

"We'll do that tomorrow." There was an irritated pause. "Any other questions?"

"Did you call an ambulance for the girl?"

There was a pause. "I wanted to, but the mother swore she'd take her to the hospital."

"So let me get this straight. They never said Lance had beaten her?"

"Well ... that's why I didn't put that in the report. The mother implied it ... but Jordan said no, he wasn't the one. She said he wouldn't do that."

That was a good sign. That meant the girl had a conscience, that there was a line she wouldn't cross. Truth was, Lance would be in less trouble if he had beaten her instead of taking her baby. But a fifteen-year-old girl probably wouldn't realize the implications of a kidnapping charge.

If he could only find Jordan and talk to her alone, he felt sure he could get her to change her story. He thanked the cop, and as he hung up, Harper motioned him over. "Good news. They did have some empty lockdown cells. They're putting him in one. He won't like it, but he'll be separated from the population."

Relief washed over him. "Thanks, man," Kent said. "Maybe now his mom will be able to sleep."

Kent managed to convince Barbara that there was nothing more he could do tonight, so they headed back out to her car. As Barbara drove home, Kent explained everything he'd learned. When he told her about Lance being separated from the other juvenile offenders, she burst into tears. "Really? He'll be safe?"

"He was probably safe before, but this should give you a little peace of mind."

"It does." She wiped her eyes. "Thank you, Kent. I wouldn't have even thought of that."

"He won't like it. He'll think they're singling him out for punishment. He won't know they're doing him a favor."

Barbara leaned her head back. "I know. But still ... it's the best thing. Sometimes things happen to us that seem cruel." Her voice rasped, and she cleared her throat. "But it's just that we don't know the whole story. Sometimes there's stuff going on that we can't see ... God protecting us ... testing us ... molding us ..." She glanced over at him. "That's what I tell myself, anyway."

"I think it's true. Lance will see that when it's all over."

She smiled fully for the first time since he'd gotten here. She was beautiful when she smiled. "You really have gotten to know God, haven't you?"

"Did you think I made the whole thing up?"

"You just haven't talked about it a lot. I mean, you told me you were going to church, but that was all."

"I didn't want you to think I was using religion to impress you."

"It does impress me."

He knew she wouldn't have considered dating anyone who wasn't a Christian, so he'd started going to church. Her faith in the midst of trials, her certainty in the depths of desperation, had made him doubt his doubts about God. But once he started attending, he found things he hadn't expected. A sense of belonging, of hope, and of truth that resonated deep in his soul. Even if their relationship didn't go anywhere, he would always owe her for that.

"So . . . I guess you can leave me at the hotel. Tomorrow, I'd like to get started early if that's all right. It's Sunday, so the chief probably won't be in, but I want to try to find him. I need him to give me access to the department's resources while I'm here. Do you mind picking me up and taking me to the department?"

"Why don't you take Emily's car?"

"Are you sure?"

"Yes. It's just sitting there. That way you'll have more freedom."

"But—what will you be doing?"

When she looked away, he touched her shoulder. "Barbara, look at me."

Headlights of passing cars lit her face and the tears in her eyes. "What?"

"I don't want you going to look for Jordan. We'll look together, okay? I want you to wait for me. Lance will be all right, so you don't have to rush into anything unwise."

"But maybe I can catch her—if not at home, then at the hospital."

"All right—while I'm at the police station, go look at the hospital. But don't go to her house or anywhere else to look for her, okay? I know you. Last year, you went to some very dangerous places looking for Emily. Please don't do that this time. I'm here to help with that. Promise me."

She smiled. "I promise. I appreciate your caring."

He kept his hand on her shoulder as she turned into her driveway, and she clicked the garage door opener. The light came on and she pulled in.

She didn't pull out of his reach. "Thank you for coming, Kent. It's just like old times, huh?"

He chuckled. Old times meant murder, lost innocence, terror. "Yeah, but what can I say? I'm thankful for any crisis that gives me an excuse to see you."

She laughed then. "You don't need an excuse."

He met her eyes in the car. "Well, it's good to see you again."

"I'm really glad you came," she said softly. "When this happened, you were the first person I thought of to call."

His chest burned with that knowledge. "I'm glad. I like being needed."

"People need you all the time."

"Yeah, if there's a murder or something, I'm the guy to call. But for anything less than murder ..."

"Kidnapping, for instance?"

He grinned. "Yeah, take kidnapping. Nobody ever calls me for that."

She laughed harder then, and the sound played like a song in his head. He didn't want to get out of the car. He wanted to just sit here like this, for hours, listening to the lyrical sound of her laughter.

Barbara took his hand that rested on her shoulder and laced her fingers through his. She hadn't imagined that any-one on earth could make her feel better in these circum-stances, but Kent had. "I don't believe nobody needs you.

You have lots of friends. One guy dropped everything to fly you to Missouri."

"He loves any excuse to log hours."

"He seems to think a lot of you."

"Yeah, but he doesn't give me warm fuzzies like you do."

Again, she grinned. His hand felt good over hers, his rough thumb stroking her skin. She wished he were staying here tonight, sleeping in Lance's room. But if he did, the neighbors would think something was going on, and she didn't want that to get back to her kids. It was always better to avoid the appearance of impropriety.

Besides, he did have a hotel room.

"So tomorrow, when we find Jordan and she confesses, how quickly do you think we can get Lance out?"

"That's a lot of ifs. But I feel good about the possibility that she'll tell the truth," he said. "The arresting officer told me that she was having trouble with the accusation. Her mother tried to make her say Lance hit her, but Jordan said he would never do anything like that."

"Really? She said that?"

"Yes. That tells me she's conflicted. She doesn't want him in trouble. If we can catch her away from her mother, I think we'll get somewhere. And if she does change her story, we can get him out pretty quickly."

Barbara hoped that was true. She shivered in the cool air and chafed her arms.

"Come here."

She leaned into him over the console, and he slid his arm around her. His warmth blanketed her.

"Do you think you'll be able to sleep?" he asked her in a soft rumble.

"Actually, I do now, thanks to you. I thought I'd be up all night, but you've made the burden a little lighter."

"That's my job. Putting women to sleep."

Maybe it was the endorphins from all the tears or just the relief of knowing Lance was safe. But she found herself laughing again. She laid her head on his shoulder.

When he kissed her, her heart turned to warm wax, sliding into her chest, making her ache. She touched his face, felt the sandpaper stubble. His lips were slightly chapped, but she liked the feel of them. He had his own unique taste, one that lingered.

He pulled back, and she let her hand slide down his chin. Their eyes met and held, and she couldn't think of a thing to say.

Finally, he whispered, "That was nice. I've missed you a lot."

She smiled, feeling like a teenager. Then she thought of Lance in jail, and her smile faded. What kind of mother was she? She drew in a deep breath and pulled back, but she didn't want him to think she was turning cold. "I've missed you too," she whispered. "I just ... feel kind of guilty. Making out in the car when Lance is ..." Her voice trailed off.

"Lance knows we kiss."

"I know, but ... tonight?"

She saw his disappointment, but he didn't argue. "Tomorrow, then." He opened his door, and she took the cue and got out on her side.

She went around the car and stood close to him as she dug through her purse, trying to find the extra key to Emily's car. She found the key, pulled it out. "The car should be clean."

"It'll be fine. I'll call you in the morning, okay?"

"All right. Sleep well."

He stood there for a moment longer, then touched the

back of her head, pulled her toward him, and pressed a kiss on her forehead. "Good night, Barbara."

Barbara couldn't account for the feelings coursing through her as she went in. She watched through the window in the door as he got into Emily's car. When he'd driven away, she closed the garage door and went into the den.

She lowered herself onto the couch, wondering how it could be that, in the midst of such a trial, she could still have such fierce feelings for Kent. She'd tried for the past year to keep her feelings for him from getting too intense, since their distance apart made it impossible for them to be together often. But that distance hadn't cooled things at all.

Here she was, thinking of him, when her son was in lockdown in the Juvenile Detention Center. How could she ever have a relationship when her kids were so troubled and so many miles lay between them? She had to be careful and not let her heart take her down the wrong path. Too much was at stake. Even if she got Lance out of jail tomorrow, Emily would be home Monday. Then there would be a whole new truckload of worries.

It was a time for sacrifice, not indulgence.

If only she could make her heart follow her head.

Chapter 22

Lance couldn't keep a low profile for long, not with Turk sticking so close to him. When the guard outside the glass turned away, Turk's enemies crossed the room toward them.

Turk rose to his feet, his chin set like he was preparing for mayhem. Lance felt a little sick.

One of Turk's tormenters took the lead. "We got unfinished business, Turk. You real bad now, ain't you? Let's see how you hold up in here with my boys."

"I'll hold up just fine, Cash, and don't count on them guards keepin' me from rearrangin' your teeth."

Lance sprang up. "Everybody calm down, okay? We're all stuck here, so just chill. Why get yourselves in worse trouble?"

Hate-filled eyes turned on him. "Who are you?" Cash stood a couple inches taller than Lance, but he weighed twice as much and looked like he was pumped up with steroids.

"I'm nobody," Lance said, refusing to back away. "I'm not in this."

"Then stay out of it," Cash sneered. He grabbed Lance's throat with a tattooed hand, his face inches from him. Lance told himself not to react, just to freeze like he would in the presence of a snake.

Then Turk lunged, attacking Cash's face like a monkey ripping into a banana. Cash fell back, then rallied and swung. Lance moved away as the other boys whooped and yelled, surrounding the two fighters like hungry animals.

Suddenly the glass pod door slid open, and three guards rushed in, brandishing billy clubs. Lance backed against the wall to let them pass, glad he wasn't part of the fray. They grabbed the fighters by their collars and wrestled them out the door. One guard shouted for everyone to back off. "I'm throwin' them in lockdown, and any of you who make trouble can go there too."

Lance watched through the glass as Turk and Cash were manhandled until they were out of sight. But before they closed the glass doors, one of the guards came back in.

"Covington! Lance Covington!"

Lance raised his hand. "That's me."

"Come with me," the guard ordered.

Lance got to his feet, his heart pounding. Maybe his mother had figured a way to get him out. He followed the guard and the glass doors closed behind him. He hoped he never saw the place again.

"This way," the guard said. Ahead of them in the hallway, Turk and his sworn enemy were being thrown into lockdown cells.

"Am I getting out?" Lance asked.

The guard grunted. "You're going to lockdown."

Lance sucked in a breath. "Me? Why? I didn't fight. I didn't do anything."

The guard ignored him and kept walking.

"Can you tell me why? What did I do?"

"I'm just doing what I was told."

Tears of rage filled Lance's eyes, but he fought them back as they came to a door that looked like it was made of iron. It had a tiny window in it and a slot that he supposed was for food trays. The door opened, and he looked inside. There was a metal bench welded to the floor so it couldn't be moved, and a metal toilet without a lid. That was it. Nothing else.

"Go on in."

Lance held back. "I left my mattress and blanket in my cell."

"I'll bring you another mattress. You can't have a blanket."

"Why not?"

The guard wasn't interested in answering questions. "Come on. It's almost my break."

Lance felt the blood rushing to his cheeks again. As frightened as he was of being in there with kids who'd just as soon attack him as look at him, he hated being singled out for punishment.

"Is there a TV? Anything to do?"

"No. Nothing you can hurt yourself with."

He sighed. "How long do I have to stay in here?"

"Until they tell me to take you out."

"But ... if I don't know why I'm getting punished, how can I do better?"

"Just shut up and get in there." The guard shoved him into the room.

Lance stumbled in and looked around. The room wasn't

any bigger than eight feet by five. "There's no bed. Where do I sleep?"

"Put the mattress there," the guard said, pointing to the bench. "That's your bed."

Another guard appeared with the rolled-up foam pad they'd given him as a mattress. Lance dropped the pad on the bench and turned back to the door. "Is there anything to eat? I missed dinner, and I'm starved."

"You'll have to wait for breakfast."

"Is there anything to read?" He knew he was pressing his luck, but he didn't want the guard to leave. What if they forgot about him in here? "No!" The door slammed, its clank echoing.

Lance stared at the door, already feeling claustrophobic in the small, sterile room. He unrolled the pad on the bench and sat down, wondering how he'd sleep on this. The room was freezing. Emily had complained about that when she'd spent the night in jail. She said they kept it cold to keep people calm. That people fought when it was warmer.

That didn't work here.

This was so unfair. He didn't even belong here in the first place—and now they were throwing him into lockdown? The boredom was going to kill him.

He sat on the bench and pulled his feet up, wishing for socks. The orange flip-flops were too small for his feet, and his toes were like ice.

He lay down, stretching out on the pad that wasn't more than a couple of inches thick.

He wished he could turn time back to earlier today, when he'd gone to Jordan's. He never should have driven Emily's car without a license. If he hadn't, none of this would have happened. But driving without a license shouldn't result in lockdown.

He prayed that God would forgive him and get him out of here.

Soon he was bargaining with God, promising to do better, to read his Bible more, to stop the occasional cussing. He'd stop giving his mother a hard time. He'd be nicer to Emily.

He heard Turk in the cell next to him, screaming profanity and threatening Cash across the hall, as if he could pull a Superman and bust through the door. Lance wanted to tell him to shut up, that he was only hurting himself. But he kept quiet, his arm over his mouth, muffling the sounds of his own despair.

Chapter 23

Barbara woke at four the next morning, groggy from a labored night of shallow dreams. As she made a pot of coffee, she wondered what Lance's night had been like. Had he suffered in lockdown? Had he felt betrayed?

She prayed that Jordan was safe, that she was coherent, that she would come to her senses and tell the truth. What condition must the girl be in after having a baby at home and being beaten by her mother? Barbara hoped Jordan was alive.

As she drank her coffee, she read Scripture, searching for wisdom that could guide her through these rough waters. It was Sunday, but she didn't feel free to go to church. Her son needed her. If she could get him out today, then maybe tonight they could all worship together.

At eight, she drove to the hospital, again hoping that

she'd catch Jordan checking on her child. But there was still no one there for the nameless little Rhodes baby.

The nurse allowed her to rock the tiny bundle, and Barbara fought back tears as she did. The child looked a little stronger today, and they had her in a little pink T-shirt. Some kind nurse had fluffed her wispy curls, and they circled her little head like a brown halo.

God, please give this little girl a good life. She's going to need an extra measure of help from You.

She ran her knuckle along the baby's cheek, and their eyes met. In that moment, as innocence and trust blinked up at her, Barbara felt a fierce sense of protection. But the baby wasn't hers to protect.

She couldn't even protect her own children.

Through her tears, she saw movement outside the display window, where relatives and visitors could peer in at their little miracles. Maureen Rhodes stood in the hallway, talking to a nurse. Barbara caught her breath. Could Jordan be with her?

Maureen would scream or hiss like a character from *Invasion of the Body Snatchers* if she saw Barbara with the baby. She looked around for a way of escape. If she went out the door she'd come in, Maureen would see her. But there was another door that exited into the adjacent hall. She quickly returned the child to the bassinet and made sure nothing had pulled loose. The nurse came toward her. "Are you leaving so soon?"

"Yes, I have to go." Barbara glanced at the window again. "Her grandmother's coming, and ... we don't get along."

The nurse turned and looked through the window as Barbara slipped out.

In the hall, Barbara leaned against the wall. Her forehead

was sticky with perspiration, though a chill hung in the air. She felt like she'd just committed a crime. If Maureen saw her here, she'd probably call the police.

Barbara waited for several minutes, then walked quietly to the corner and peered around. Maureen was gone. Forcing herself to breathe, Barbara moved toward the nursery window. Maureen had gone inside, but the door was still open behind her.

Jordan was nowhere in sight. The nurse led Maureen to the baby. Maureen showed no emotion. She didn't melt when she saw the baby, and she didn't try to pick her up. Her shrill voice carried over the room full of fragile babies, as she coldly questioned the nurse about the baby's condition.

No wonder Jordan put her baby in Lance's car. What kind of person was Maureen?

Lord, please don't let them release the baby until this is sorted out.

She had to find Jordan—not just for Lance's sake, but for the baby's as well.

She decided to leave by the stairwell, just in case. As she headed down to the lobby, her cell phone rang. She dove into her purse for it. The caller ID said "New Day."

She clicked it on. "Hello?"

"Mom?"

"Emily, did you find out anything?"

"Yes, I did," she said, her voice low. "Nobody wanted to talk in front of Tammy last night, because she's new and she may not stay. None of us would ever rat out a dealer in front of people we didn't trust. Anything could happen."

"Then you think Jordan's with a dealer?"

"Probably," she said. "She hangs out a lot with a dealer named Belker. He works from several different locations. He has a mobile meth lab, so he can move fast. But the Serene

Motel is one of his favorite places, and it's closest to where Jordan lives."

Barbara stopped on a landing. "Emily, do you know this guy?"

She was quiet for a moment. "Yeah, he sells other drugs too, not just meth. I used to buy from him sometimes."

"And you don't know his full name?"

"Just Belker."

"Do you have a phone number or anything?"

"Not anymore. But, Mom, I could be wrong. I just know that she was close to Belker, and she hung out with him a lot. He even put her to work doing things to pay for her drugs."

"Put her to work? Doing what?"

"Mom," Emily said, as if Barbara should know what she meant. "She doesn't even know who the baby's father is. He put her to work ... selling what she has."

Barbara's heart sank. Jordan had just had a baby, and she'd been beaten and abused. Would this Belker person abuse her so quickly after that?

Evil weighed down on her, heavy and smothering. What was she going to do?

"Mom, if you figure out where she is, don't go all Super Woman. I know how you are."

"I won't. Kent is here. He's helping me."

"Oh." The word fell flat. "How did *he* know about all this?"

"I called him. I didn't ask him to come, but I'm glad he did."

"That's good, I guess."

Barbara didn't have time to analyze that reaction. "Emily, don't waste any of your phone calls today. If you hear anything else, please call me back."

"I will. Lance better get out today. All the girls want to tell him good-bye. And I want him at my graduation tomorrow."

"So do I," Barbara said. "So do I."

As soon as she hung up, she called Kent and told him what Emily had said.

"All right," he said. "I'm on my way to meet the chief of police. I'll ask him if he knows about this guy Belker."

"If they know him, wouldn't they have arrested him?"

"Probably have. But they get out. Just wait for me, Barbara. Don't go anywhere without me, okay?"

"Why does everyone keep saying that?"

"Because you will."

"I promised you I wouldn't. Just hurry, okay?"

"Okay. I'll call you the minute I'm out of this meeting."

Chapter 24

Barbara didn't want to go home and just wait, so she went to a nearby Burger King and ate a breakfast croissant in her car. This reminded her so much of that time a year ago, when she'd been in Atlanta, eating alone while waiting to hear word on Emily's whereabouts. She had never wanted to be in this situation again.

When she finished eating, she drove around aimlessly, waiting for Kent's call. She drove down the street where she worked, pulled into the parking lot, and into the space where she parked every day. The store was closed on Sundays, so the lot was empty. She checked her watch. Only a few minutes had passed. Maybe she should just go home and wait.

Then she saw someone at the Dumpster on the side of the parking lot, pulling out a large cardboard box that had once held a recliner. Reflexively, she checked her door lock.

Then she saw the man's coat.

It was J.B., in the coat she'd given him yesterday. She started the car, drove toward the Dumpster, and rolled her window down. "J.B.?"

He dropped the box as if he'd been caught stealing.

"J.B., it's okay. You can have that box if you need it."

Recognition cleared his eyes. He stepped toward her car. "Did my mother send me anything?"

"No, I haven't seen her since I gave you the jacket." She wanted to tell him that Charlotte was going through chemo, that her cancer was eating her alive. But that might make him feel so guilty he would self-medicate again. Or worse, it might make him go home and force Charlotte to deal with him. No, she couldn't tell him that.

Then it occurred to her that he might know Jordan. "J.B., can I talk to you for a minute?"

He came closer, and the breeze whipped his scent in. He smelled unbathed and drenched in smoke, and his breath was rotten, as if something inside him was dying and decaying.

"I need your help."

"Mine?" He stared blankly. "You need my help?"

"I'm looking for a girl. Her name's Jordan Rhodes. She's really sick right now and she's been beaten. Do you know her?"

He shrugged. "I know a girl named Jordan. She's a kid. Like fourteen or something. She was pregnant, but now she's not."

Barbara's heart jolted. If he knew she was no longer pregnant, then he'd seen her in the last twenty-four hours. "She's fifteen, and she had the baby yesterday. I need to find her. Where is she?"

He stared at her for a long moment, his eyes glossy. "I need cash," he said.

"J.B., I can't give you money. But I've helped you in other ways, and you know it. I need you to help me now. Please, tell me where I can find her."

"Just ten bucks," he demanded.

She stared into his red eyes, and her gaze swept over his leathery face and jaundiced skin. What if she gave him the money that bought the hit that killed him? No, she couldn't do that. She'd never be able to look Charlotte in the eye again if she did.

"No money, J.B."

"A hotel room then. It's gonna get cold tonight."

A hotel room. Yes, she could do that. "All right," she said. "Get in. Show me where she is, and I'll get you a room."

He abandoned the cardboard box that would have been his home tonight and got into the car.

She pulled out of the parking lot. "Is she at the Serene Motel?"

"Yeah," he said.

"Do you know what room?"

"The one on the corner. First floor. I'll show you."

"How long has she been there?"

"Saw her last night," he said.

Barbara got quiet, knowing she promised Kent and Emily that she wouldn't go there alone. She would just let J.B. point the room out to her, and then she would take him somewhere else.

She was quiet as she drove. "J.B., I know it's cold out, and tomorrow, you won't have a room. But you can always call New Day's men's program. They'll take you in and help you get your life straightened out."

"My life is straight. I'm doing what I want."

"You want to sleep outside in cardboard boxes? If you got clean, you could get a job, a place to live—"

"Job doing what?"

"Lots of things."

"Nobody's telling me what to do. I'm my own boss."

His logic made no sense, but she couldn't make him see it. His mother had tried many times. "Just remember, New Day is a safe place to sleep every night for a year. Good food. And a chance at a future."

As she reached the Serene Motel, she didn't turn into the parking lot. Instead, she pulled into a McDonald's across the street and parked in a space facing the motel. "J.B., point out her room for me."

"That corner one ... see, that one at the back there? Left of the stairs. She was there last night. All I know."

She stared at the room's door. It looked quiet, not like a drug dealer's place of business. She supposed everything was different at night.

She went to the drive-through, got J.B. some food, then drove him to the Day's Inn up the street. She went into the office with him and paid for a night's stay with her credit card. She gave him the key card, then watched him go into his room, carrying his little bag of breakfast. She hoped he remembered to eat it.

At least he'd get some sleep and be warm for a little while.

As she drove away, she thought of Emily's phone call and her familiarity with the dealers who would still be accessible to her after her graduation. It would be so easy for her to get drugs again. In one moment of weakness, she could relapse. When she got out of rehab tomorrow, how would she stand?

Barbara had so hoped that things would be stress-free when Emily came home. That she could pick up where she left off in the family, before the drugs. That she'd get a job until school started in January, make new friends, rebuild her life.

But now she would come home to this crisis that was overshadowing everything. It wasn't fair. It would be hard for Emily to make it under the best of circumstances. How would she make it now?

She went back to McDonald's, sat in the parking lot with her car facing the Serene Motel, and waited to hear from Kent. Then they would go in and find Jordan.

Chapter 25

It didn't take long for Kent to get a message to the chief of police through the sergeant he'd met at the department last night. Though it was Sunday, the chief called him and offered to meet at a Starbucks.

Kent found the chief sitting in a corner, wearing a suit and tie and checking his BlackBerry. "Chief Levin?" Kent said.

The man stood, smiling like an old friend. "Kent! Great to see you in person. I followed the Emily Covington case real closely last year. Good work. It's a pleasure to meet you."

"You too. Thanks."

The chief straightened his tie. "Sorry about the suit, but I'm an usher at church. Heading there after we talk." He motioned for Kent to take a seat. "You want coffee?"

"No, thanks. I don't want to keep you any longer than

I have to." He told the chief about Lance's relationship to Emily and about his own connection to the family. "He's a great kid. I believe his story that this girl who accused him of kidnapping was being pressured by her mother. Check Maureen Rhodes's rap sheet. She's got a pretty long criminal record."

"I did before I came. You're right."

"So what I'm wondering is if I can use some of your resources while I'm here. I'd like to use your databases and have access to the detective working the case."

"Yeah, that would be Bob Dathan. I'll tell him to share what he has with you. He's young, just passed the detective exam three months ago, so he could learn from your experience."

Kent had hoped for cooperation, but he hadn't expected this much. "I appreciate that, Chief. Do you happen to know about a drug dealer in this area who goes by the name of Belker?"

"Yes, we've locked him up before. But he hires expensive lawyers and gets out in no time. He's constantly on the move, so we have trouble tracking him. You know how it is."

He did know. To catch the guy near the top of the food chain, they needed a lot of hard evidence. The addicts always knew how to sniff him out, but a guy like that would be careful.

"Why do you ask?"

"We just heard that he's Jordan Rhodes's supplier."

"Right. I was going to try to talk to her, get her side of the story. But her mother claims she's not home. Kid just gave birth yesterday. I figure if she really went out, it was to get drugs. If I knew where this guy was headquartered, maybe I'd find her there."

"I don't know. Last I knew he was operating from a motel on the north side of town, but that place shut down. But feel free to talk to any of my detectives. One of them may have more updated data on him."

"Okay, I will if you don't mind."

The chief leaned in, elbows on the table. "Listen, do you spend a lot of time in Jeff?"

"Not as much as I'd like."

Levin grinned. "So ... Barbara Covington. Are you seeing her?"

There was no point in hiding it. "Trying to. But long distance things are difficult ... and she has a lot going on."

"I ask because ..." He stroked his lip with a finger and seemed to consider what he wanted to say. "Because the city council has approved the budget for me to hire another detective. It's a supervisor's position, over the whole Criminal Investigation Section. Not homicide, like you're used to, but you have more murders in Atlanta than we have here. You'd be over seven detectives and a civilian evidence technician. You're a perfect candidate for the job."

Kent blinked. "You're kidding."

"No, I'm not. I've been looking for the right person, and I'm not impressed with any of the applicants so far. But if there's any possibility you might be interested ..."

He thought of saying yes, right here on the spot. But it was complicated. His relationship with Barbara was still young. Taking a job here might put too much pressure on her.

Besides, he liked working in homicide. Did he really want to start investigating burglaries and drug deals?

"Well, I appreciate that, Chief. I'll think about it."

"Meanwhile, I'll have Detective Dathan give you a call, since he's the one working this case. Make yourself at home,

Detective. Check us out thoroughly. Get to know the other guys. And if you want to talk seriously about the position, give me another call."

As Kent was leaving Starbucks, Barbara called. "I may have found her," she said. "I'm across the street from the Serene Motel, and I've been told she's in one of the rooms."

He got behind the wheel of Emily's car. "You've been told? Who told you? Barbara, what have you been up to?"

She sighed. "I talked to the son of a friend of mine. He gave me the information. He's not extremely reliable, but I think he's telling the truth. He knew she'd had the baby, so he had to have seen her yesterday or last night. Don't worry, I'm not doing anything until you get here. I'm keeping my promise."

"All right," he said. "Stay right there. I'll be right over."

She gave him directions. "Why is it that every addict in town knows that drugs are dealt from this motel, but the police don't?"

"They move a lot, Barbara. When they find them, they have to catch them at it, and they need probable cause for search and arrest warrants. And as soon as they arrest one group, another one pops up in the same area. And when they do catch them, they want to make sure they have enough evidence to make a conviction stick."

"But there are dealers all over Emerson Street. Just drive down there and you'll see. Middle-school kids are finding these people, and the cops can't? If the drugs weren't so easy to get—"

"Barbara, it's the same everywhere. There are drugs in every town."

"I know," she said. "I'm not mad at you. I'm mad at the police in general. That they would lock up my son, who's done nothing, when there are drug dealers operating meth labs and crack houses, and nobody cares. It's a war. These things are taking our children out in horrifying numbers and nobody cares."

"No, you're wrong. There are people who care. And I just had a good talk with your police chief. He seems competent and sharp. He's offered me access to his resources."

"Good. Then can you get the police to come with us to find Jordan?"

"Not yet. Jordan hasn't technically done anything wrong. If you've found her, hopefully we can get her to answer the door. Anything beyond that ... well, we'll cross that bridge then."

Barbara was skeptical as she waited for Kent to get there. If Jordan looked out the window and saw them at her door, what incentive would she have for letting them in? She prayed that Jordan wouldn't hide, that she'd let them in and be willing to talk.

Finally, Kent showed up and pulled in beside Barbara. He got into her car, and she pointed out the room J.B. had identified.

"All right, we'll go over there and see if she'll let us in. But if we run into anybody else, you let me do the talking, okay?"

"Fine with me. I don't have any experience with meth users."

"It's a dirty drug. It does some serious damage to the brain, and sometimes it makes users hallucinate. They see things that aren't there. Back home, I arrested a guy once who saw snakes slithering around his house. He got out a gun and shot at them. When he came to his senses, his children were dead."

She caught her breath. "He thought they were snakes?"

"That's right. It seems like something right out of Satan's playbook. How else can you explain people ingesting something that has battery acid and rat poison as ingredients?"

Her face twisted. "That's in crystal meth?"

"It's deadly. They can get pretty violent when they're on meth. When they're high, they have the strength of four men. So what I'm telling you is that if anything starts to happen, you back off and do what I say. Got that?"

"Okay. You don't have to tell me twice."

They crossed the street and went to the room at the back corner of the building. Barbara knocked softly.

There was no answer. The drapes were pulled closed, and there was no way to tell if anyone was even inside. What if J.B. had led her wrong? What if he'd simply been manipulating her?

Kent knocked harder, with more authority, but still no one answered.

Barbara wanted to cry. "What do we do now?" she asked him. "Can we go to the office and ask if she's here?"

He shook his head. "She probably didn't check in. We could knock on other doors, see if anybody will talk to us, but it's doubtful they would."

Barbara wasn't about to give up now. As he spoke, she tried the knob. It was unlocked. "Kent ..."

"Barbara, you can't walk in without a warrant, even if it's not locked."

"I'm not a cop," she said, and before he could stop her, she pushed the door open.

Light from the outside poured into the darkness, illuminating the girl on the bed. It was Jordan, lying there alone, and her bed was stained with blood. Barbara ran to her side and shook her. "Jordan! Wake up, Jordan!"

The girl was limp. Barbara turned her over. Her face was gray with purple bruises, and dark circles stained her swollen eyes. She looked dead.

"Call an ambulance," she cried. "Kent, is she ...?"

After he'd punched in 911, he touched Jordan's neck. "She's alive," he said. "Pulse is weak, though."

As Kent spoke to the dispatcher, Barbara lifted Jordan's head and tried to wake her, but she didn't stir. The girl had given birth to a baby at home, endured a beating by her mother, then run here where she was bleeding to death, probably from the aftereffects of childbirth. Or maybe she'd been beaten or abused again after she got here. She may have even overdosed.

Barbara kept trying to rouse Jordan as they waited for the ambulance. In moments, she heard sirens. Kent went out to wave them down. As the ambulance pulled in, glassy-eyed waifs stumbled out of their motel rooms to see the latest casualty.

The EMTs got Jordan on a drip, then loaded her into the vehicle. "I'll ride with her to the hospital," Barbara told them. "Kent, you follow and meet us there."

Barbara got in and sat next to Jordan, holding her cold hand. As they flew to the hospital, she prayed that Jordan would come back around and take the second chance to start her life over. If this wasn't hitting bottom, she didn't know what was. The next level was certainly death.

Chapter 26

The sound of voices penetrated Jordan's consciousness, and she struggled to open her eyes. Bright light made her wince, and blurred faces moved in and out of her vision. Where was she? This wasn't the motel room where she'd taken a handful of downers to end her pain. It was a hospital. She jerked as she realized an IV was dripping blood into her veins.

"Jordan, can you hear me?"

She tried to focus on the blonde woman who was way too close. She smelled of vanilla. Then, as Jordan's vision gradually cleared, she recognized Barbara.

"Jordan, we found you at the motel. You'd lost a lot of blood, and you overdosed. We almost didn't get you here on time."

The woman waited, staring, as if she expected Jordan

to thank her. But Jordan felt no gratitude. Only the seeds of a fragile rage.

"Why?" Jordan whispered through dry, cracked lips.

"Why what?"

"Why'd you bring me here?"

"To save your life, honey. How do you feel?"

The question ramped her rage up a notch. How did she think she felt? She tried to sit up. "Who asked you to do that? It was none of your business."

Barbara didn't seem to know how to respond to that. "Jordan, I know you didn't want to die."

She couldn't sit up. She was too weak. Instead, she turned on her side, away from Barbara. She felt her stomach, the loose, empty skin. It hadn't been a bad dream. It was real. "You don't know anything about me."

"I know things are complicated. That you're in pain. But death isn't the answer, Jordan."

Why was this lady interested in her? What did she want?

Then she remembered Lance. Of course. Barbara didn't really care about her. She was here for her son.

Anger spread through her veins, making her want to rip the IV out. But there was also guilt. Jordan had lied about him and gotten him into trouble. He didn't deserve that.

"Jordan, you have a baby to think of now. You can't clock out and leave things unsettled, or the wrong people will adopt her."

Jordan squeezed her eyes shut. "Where is my baby?"

"Here, in the neonatal unit. She's getting better."

Good. Those people hadn't taken her yet. "What about Lance? Where is he?"

"He's in jail."

Jordan rolled to her back, her wrist over her eyes. This was all wrong. "I didn't want him to go to jail."

"Then why did you tell the police he kidnapped your baby?" Her voice was gentle, not harsh like Jordan would have expected. "Do you know how many years he could get for a crime like that? All he was doing was trying to help you."

"He shouldn't have come to my house. I don't know why he has to stick his nose in everything."

"Jordan, he didn't take your baby. I want you to talk to the police. I want you to tell them the truth."

"Then I'll get in trouble for lying."

"You can explain the pressure you were under with your mother. "

"Then my mom will go to jail. Then what will I do? They'll throw me in some foster home."

"Jordan, is she the one who beat you?"

Jordan wouldn't answer.

"If she is, then you need to tell the police. You could go back to New Day."

"But then I have to follow all those rules and give up everything that makes me feel better."

"Drugs don't make you feel better, Jordan. Look at you!"

The door swung open. "What are you doing here?" Her mother stood in the doorway, looking like she hadn't bathed in days. The smell of her friends' meth lab floated around her, infecting everything in the room. Jordan wanted to scream.

Who called her? Why couldn't her mother just go back to not caring?

Barbara stood up and faced her. "Maureen, I found your daughter half dead. I called an ambulance."

"Get outa my way." Maureen pushed Barbara aside, then bent down and bobbed her head over Jordan. "How you feelin', baby?"

Jordan wanted to spit in her face, but her mother would hit her again, and her bruises were still tender. "I'm fine."

"You don't look fine." Her mother shot Barbara an accusing look. "See what he did to her?"

"Mom, don't. Lance didn't do this to me."

She felt her mother's anger rippling like a current on the air. Her sharp eyes cut through her, warning her to shut up.

"I was just talking to Jordan," Barbara said, "about the lie she told the police about my son."

"She didn't lie," Maureen insisted. "And if you don't leave this room right now, I'll file charges against you too. We'll get the whole family locked up."

"For what? For saving her life?"

"For harassment. I'll get a restraining order so you can't come within fifty feet of her."

"Come on, Maureen." Barbara's voice was getting loud. "You don't think that's going to stop me."

"Is that a threat?"

Barbara bent over Jordan. "Jordan, it's not too late to change your story. Please set the record straight so I can get Lance out. Don't punish the people who try to help you."

Jordan lay frozen, staring at the track marks on her arm and the needle dripping fluids into her.

Maureen grabbed Barbara's arm and jerked her to the door, yelling at the top of her lungs for a nurse. Jordan wanted to spare Barbara this, but bucking her mother's authority would only result in broken bones and more blood. It wasn't worth it. As Barbara left the room, Jordan lay there in the mess she'd created and knew she couldn't clean it up now.

Chapter 27

Barbara found Kent waiting for her in the waiting room near the neonatal unit, where he'd gone to make some phone calls. Shaken, she came in and dropped down next to him. "What's wrong?" he asked. "Did she wake up?"

Her hands were trembling. "Yes, and I almost had her. But then Maureen came in and threw me out."

"Oh, so she finally showed up, huh? At least Jordan's safe here. If Maureen tries to bash her face in, she'll get busted."

"Kent, she was so close to changing her story. I don't know what to do."

He took her hand. "I could try talking to her."

"No, it's no use while her mother's there. She's thoroughly intimidated. We'll have to wait." Barbara glanced wearily around at the others in the waiting room. A young couple who sat across the room looked like they hadn't slept in days. She wondered if they had a baby struggling for its life. Her heart ached for them.

"So what do you want to do?" Kent asked.

She sighed and shook her head. "I don't know. I need a spy, someone who works here who can keep an eye out and tell me when Maureen leaves."

"She will leave. She isn't the type of mother who would hang around 24/7. You know anybody who works here?"

She thought a moment, then it came to her. Karen Thompson, Gus's wife, worked as a floor nurse for Obstetrics and Gynecology. She must be on this floor. She got her phone out, scrolled through her numbers, and called the receptionist at her church.

The receptionist, an elderly woman who'd brought her daily casseroles when John died, answered. "Calvary ... I mean, hello?"

"Loretta, it's Barbara Covington. I hope it's okay that I called you on your cell phone. I knew you wouldn't be working on Sunday."

"Hey, sweetie. You can call me anytime. What can I do for you?"

"I need a phone number. Do you have Karen Thompson's cell number?"

"Know it by heart," Loretta said. "I've been carrying food to them ever since Karen had her gallbladder out. Her cell phone is 555-3248."

Barbara felt terrible that she'd forgotten about the surgery. "Do you know if she's back at work, Loretta?"

"I think she is, darlin'."

As Barbara hung up, she felt a dismal sense of inadequacy for not meeting others' needs the way Loretta did. How many people in her church were suffering, and she'd either forgotten or failed to notice? She'd seen Karen's name on a prayer list somewhere and had slid right over it. She hadn't even mentioned it to Gus last night.

She almost decided not to call her, but she couldn't think of anyone else. She could at least ask. She dialed the number, paced as it rang.

"Hello?" The voice was quiet, a little rushed.

"Karen, this is Barbara Covington. Am I catching you at a bad time?"

"No, but I'm at work. I have a minute, though. How are you?"

Barbara went to the door, looked up the hall. "I'm at the hospital on your floor, I think," she said. "Listen, are you at the nurses' desk? I need to come talk to you for a minute."

"Sure. Is something wrong? Gus told me about Lance."

"I'll tell you about it in a minute if you have some time to talk."

"Sure. Come to the nurses' station on the third floor."

Barbara clicked off the phone and got her purse. "Kent, do you mind waiting? She's right down the hall."

"Take your time."

There was something nice about having someone waiting for her. She headed down a parallel hallway to avoid Maureen. At the nurses' desk, she saw her friend. "There you are."

Karen looked tired. "Good to see you, Barb. What's up?"

Barbara hugged her. "First, how are you?"

"I'm fine. It was pretty much Band-Aid surgery. Just a little tired. So who are you visiting?"

Barbara launched into the story about Jordan. When she finally finished, she said, "I know this is a lot to ask, but since you're here, would you mind keeping an eye out for when Maureen leaves so I can come and talk to Jordan?"

"Sure," Karen said, glancing toward Jordan's room. "I'm on a twelve-hour shift. She's not my patient, but I walk by that room a lot. It's no problem."

"Oh, thank you. I'll keep my phone with me and come at a moment's notice."

"Barbara, what about the baby?"

"She's in the nursery. Baby Girl Rhodes—they haven't named her. She had some seizures, probably from drug withdrawal. But she looks good. I saw her this morning."

Karen's eyes rounded. "Is Jordan planning to give her up for adoption?"

"Probably. She was registered with an adoption agency when she was at New Day. Loving Arms Adoption Agency, I think. But her mother has picked another adoptive couple, so it's up in the air."

Karen deflated. "Oh. Well, I was just thinking … You know Madeline and Ben Thompson, my brother-in-law and his wife?"

Barbara knew the couple from church. "Sure. What about them?"

"They've been trying to adopt for over three years. She's had four miscarriages. If the girl is thinking about giving the baby up, I know they'd love to talk to her about it. They had the home study a year ago and were approved. But they have to wait until a baby is available, which could take years—unless a mother chooses them."

Barbara knew what Madeline and Ben had been through with all the miscarriages. They'd managed to turn their tragedy into a testimony. "We can introduce them when her mom leaves, if Jordan's in the right frame of mind. I can't think of a better couple to be parents."

Karen glanced back at the desk. "You know what? I think I'll swap with someone so I can get her as a patient.

Might not hurt for me to get to know her. Then I'll have more credibility when I introduce Madeline and Ben to her. And I'll know the minute her mother leaves."

Barbara took her hand. "I can't promise anything, Karen. We're kind of sworn enemies to that family right now, and Jordan doesn't have a record of making good decisions. Besides that, are you sure Madeline will want a baby that already has health problems?"

"Yes," Karen said. "She can handle it. They've told the adoption agency that they would take a special-needs baby. Somebody has to. God didn't put that baby here to be ignored and neglected."

Barbara wasn't sure it was wise to get Ben and Madeline tangled up with the Rhodes family. But there was no way to take it back now. Maybe it would miraculously work out.

And at least now she had an ally on the hospital staff.

Chapter 28

That night the moonlight was bright, illuminating the trees beyond the gate to New Day. Emily watched the trees' shadows dance and sway in the breeze, promising danger beyond those gates.

Tomorrow, she'd walk out of here for the last time and start her life over. She didn't want to admit it, hadn't even admitted it to her counselor, but she was scared.

A year had given her neurotransmitters time to heal. She'd learned all about it — how the opioid receptors in her brain had been damaged by all the drug use. It took a year — sometimes two — for the brain to heal and the cravings to fade away. And they had faded. For the past few months, she hadn't spent much time dwelling on getting high. The dragon that had mastered her for so long wasn't her master anymore.

Yet this weekend had been tough. Just the knowledge that she'd soon be free had worked on her psyche, and she felt the dragon's call again. Cravings had reared back up inside her, leaving her confused and worried.

"You okay?"

She turned and saw her friend Tia, her black hair blowing in the wind. Tia was older ... in her late forties, and she had a tremor that looked like Parkinson's, but was actually the result of years of drug use. Unable to get a job anywhere else, she'd convinced New Day to hire her after she'd graduated from the women's program and had managed to stay clean for two years.

"Yeah, I'm fine," Emily said.

"Thought you'd be in there having fun with the girls. After tomorrow, you won't see them."

"I just needed some time to think."

Tia sat down next to her on the picnic table. "Girl, I know what you're going through. I been there."

Emily grabbed her hair and twisted it to keep it from blowing in her face. "I want to be strong. I have so many plans."

"Long as you keep moving forward, you'll be all right. But sometimes it's not so easy. Two steps forward, one step back."

"No. Backtracking isn't an option. I have this one shot. I'm not going to blow it."

Tia gave a dry laugh. "Don't get cocky now. You get out there and get all high and mighty, thinking you don't need anybody keeping you sane—"

"My mother will keep me sane. My brother will keep me grounded."

"They're not always gonna be there. It comes down to you, my friend."

"And you don't think I can do it?"

"I know you can do it. You have a better chance than the rest of us who go home to a house full of dopers."

"Then what? You think I'm cocky, but I'm trying to be confident."

"I'm saying that if you get cocky, you'll think you can do anything, go anywhere, be with anybody, drink anything, smoke anything ..."

Emily swallowed. "So you're saying not to be so confident that I don't know my own limitations, right?"

"Knowing you're weak—that's what makes you strong. Remember when Paul asked for God to take away that thorn in his flesh?"

"I remember."

"And what did God say?"

Emily stared into the air. "My grace is sufficient for you, for my power is made perfect in weakness."

"Right," Tia said. "Paul said, 'When I am weak, then I am strong.'"

"So I should try to be weak?"

"No. You should be strong by recognizing that you're already weak."

Emily let her hair go, and it flapped crazily in the wind. She got up and hugged herself, warming her arms. "I'm worried about loneliness."

"Yep," Tia said. "Loneliness is big."

"For a year I've been surrounded by girls all the time. Before that, there was always some guy. But when I get out, there's nobody I can call. I can't hang out with any of the people I knew before. My best friend Paige is still shooting up. I have to stay away from her."

"Got that right."

"It's weeks before school starts in January. So I just sit

around and wait? Watch TV? Play on the computer? Don't go anywhere?"

Tia slapped her legs and got up, put her arm around Emily. "You'll figure it all out. But nobody said it'd be easy. It's easier to go back to the dope house and get high. Short-term easy. But then you wind up like me."

Emily felt the tremor in Tia's hand, the weakness in her stance. She walked like a woman much older than she was, and she looked like someone's grandmother. "I want to go to college," Emily said. "I want to have a career, and meet a nice guy who doesn't have all the baggage I have. I want to have a family."

"You can, girl. Wish I'd got a clue when I was your age. It's all up to you."

Emily deflated and sat back down on the table, looking up at Tia. "What if I mess up?"

"Then you catch yourself, you get back up, and you turn back right. You don't use failure as an excuse to keep failing."

Fear tightened Emily's lungs. "What if I'm no different than Jordan?"

Tia bent down and put her face in front of Emily's. "Emily, you're ready. You can do this. You have all the tools. And you have God going with you this time. You cling to Him, He'll help you through it. Your life don't have to be a series of relapses. Some people get better on the first try."

"It's not really my first."

"Then the third. Some people get better on the third or the fifth or the twelfth try. The rest of us ... we have harder heads. We don't learn until everything's taken from us."

Tia knew what she was talking about. Her two children wouldn't speak to her; her family had moved without leaving a forwarding address. She'd once supported her habit by selling herself, but even that wasn't an option anymore. No one wanted someone who looked as old and damaged as she.

But losing her options was the best thing that had ever happened to her, because it brought her to rehab, where she got the support she hadn't had anywhere else. Two years of sobriety after a lifetime of intoxication was a miracle. If Tia could do it, Emily could. No excuses.

The door to her cottage opened, and light spilled out. "There she is!"

She heard laughter as the girls came out, coming to coax her into a night of giggles and celebration.

Tomorrow she would leave this era of her life behind. She hoped she was up to the challenge.

Chapter 29

As Barbara and Kent drove home from the hospital, Barbara's spirits sank even lower. She'd been sure she would get Lance out today, but Jordan hadn't come through. The thought of his spending one more night in jail made her nauseous.

She stared out the window as Kent drove. "Emily's getting out tomorrow. I was going to decorate the house to welcome her home. I was going to shop for her favorite meal. I had all kinds of plans."

"We can still do that. I can help you decorate for her. And then I'll go to the grocery store. They have all-night stores here, don't they?"

She gave a grim laugh. "You'd do that?"

"Of course. I'm here to help you."

The words gave her hope that she could do this, after all. Back at her house, she found the streamers and banners she'd bought last week at a party supply store. She'd bought one that said "Welcome Home," planning to paint Emily's name on it to make it more personal.

There wasn't time to do that now, and her heart wasn't in it. Besides, she hoped to welcome Lance home too. She showed Kent where the ladder was, and he helped her hang the banner. "How does it look?" he asked. "Is it straight?"

She stood back to look, but tears sprang to her eyes. "I don't know … it's all wrong."

"Really? It looked straight to me."

"No, I mean … my decorating for a celebration when Lance is in jail. What if the judge doesn't let him out tomorrow?"

Kent hammered the nail through the banner to secure it, then came down the ladder. "Barbara, stop beating yourself up. You're the best mom I know. You're trying to do what's right for both kids, but you're in a terrible spot. The kids know that. They're not going to blame you for it."

"I just wish it weren't like this. Why is it that nothing ever turns out the way I think it will?"

"How did you envision Emily's graduation day?"

She dabbed at her eyes. "I wanted to be happy. I wanted to just overflow with joy, like the father in the Prodigal Son story in the Bible. Kill the fatted calf, put a robe on Emily and a ring on her finger. I wanted her homecoming to be meaningful."

"What do killing the fatted calf and the robe look like today?"

She sighed. "I don't know. Making her favorite meal. Having a dinner with lots of laughter. Making her feel a little spoiled and pampered. Maybe taking her shopping for some new things that I can't afford."

"All those things can still happen. If we get Lance out tomorrow, you can still do that tomorrow night."

She rubbed her neck. It was getting stiff, and she ached clear down into the muscles of her lower back.

"Come here," Kent whispered. He pulled her down to the couch and began to massage the muscles of her shoulders and neck. She closed her eyes as he rubbed comfort into her, remembering when John used to do this for her. It was so long ago she'd almost forgotten. Long before his cancer and her role as caretaker.

She loved being taken care of. "That feels like heaven."

His eyes were soft as he met hers. "To me too."

As he kneaded her muscles, she took his hands, stopping him. "I like having you here," she said. "I know you need to go home tomorrow. You have a job to get back to. But this has been nice, in spite of everything."

He brought her hand to his lips. "I'm not leaving tomorrow," he said. "I'm going to stay until Lance is out for sure, and if you'll let me, I'd still like to go to the graduation."

"But you're missing work. I feel so selfish."

"Stop. Having you call is the nicest thing that's happened to me in weeks. Usually when I visit, I have the sense that I'm pressuring you. Like, because I'm here, you have to hang out with me."

"What? I love it when you visit."

"It's not always that easy to tell."

She looked at him, stricken. Had he really believed she wasn't interested in him? All this time, she'd tried so hard not to read too much into things or expect anything from him. The kids complicated her life, and she didn't want to assume he would want to share the craziness with her. But for him not to see the adoration in her eyes ... "Kent, you make my life so much better."

Their eyes locked, and her heart betrayed her. It led her down a path that her head knew not to go down. But as he moved closer, as his lips grazed hers, her head wasn't in control.

She lost herself in the possibilities implied in his kiss. Maybe there was a chance for them. Maybe God had set it up. Maybe distance was not an insurmountable problem.

Suddenly the doorbell rang. They jumped apart, and she stared at him for a moment. "I don't know who that could be."

He sat up straighter. "Well, let's see."

She went to the door, turned on the porch light, and looked out the window. It was Charlotte, with Linda, from her support group. She opened the door. "Hey!" she said too brightly. "I didn't expect to see you."

"We wanted to help you with food for the next couple of days," Charlotte said. As the two stepped inside, Barbara looked at her sick friend. She looked pale, and she wore a ski cap that covered her thinning hair. Her hands trembled as she held her casserole dish, so Barbara took it from her hands.

Kent got up and came to meet them.

"Kent, these are my dear friends, Charlotte and Linda, from my support group."

Kent greeted them, and Barbara didn't miss the surprised grins on both of their faces. She updated them on all that was going on, and before she knew it, they had taken over the decorating and had the house looking like a party zone. They even made a banner for Lance's room, welcoming him back home as well.

Their very presence made the night seem less heavy, and she enjoyed seeing how Kent interacted with them. They liked him, and neither could wipe the smile off their faces. She knew she'd never hear the end of it.

By the time Kent left for the hotel, her spirits had lifted. She could do this, she thought. God had sent her comfort and support. She wasn't alone.

Chapter 30

Monday morning came with a blaring alarm, jolting Barbara from a nightmare. Sleep had been challenging, and when it finally came, it had been riddled with dreams of Lance and Emily in Jordan's condition, bruised and swollen, lying limp on a motel bed.

But they weren't in that condition. They were healthy and whole.

Apparently, Maureen hadn't left the hospital before Karen's shift was over, and Lance had been forced to spend another night in jail. She hoped he was still in lockdown. His arraignment was sometime this morning, so she shook away her fatigue and got ready. She had to be there at nine and wait through all the cases until they got to Lance. Emily's graduation was at one, so they might be cutting it close. She refused to consider the possibility that the judge wouldn't let Lance out today.

Kent met her at the courthouse and sat beside her as all the felony and misdemeanor cases were heard. She fidgeted through cases of DUIs and domestic violence, shoplifting, and drug possession. Judge Hathaway seemed terse and irritable as he set bond on each case quickly, uninterested in explanations or excuses.

When those in street clothes had all been heard, they brought in the inmates, still in their prison clothes. When Lance came in, dressed in an orange jumpsuit, Barbara burst into tears. He looked at her with round, pleading eyes. "Mom," he mouthed.

She gave him a reassuring nod. If John, her husband, had a glimpse from heaven, he would be ashamed that she had let their lives get so out of control. The sight of her son in prison garb almost sent her over the edge.

Kent took her hand, and she fought her way back from the land of regrets and remembered that this was not Lance's fault. His life had not spiraled out of control. This was just a glitch—and they would solve it soon.

When the judge called Lance's name, Barbara sprang up and went to the small wall separating the gallery from the bench. She hoped he remembered what she'd told him the night Lance was arrested.

"You're his mother, right?" the judge asked her.

"Yes sir," she said.

He waved her in. "Come on up."

She stepped through the small door and hugged Lance as he went to stand before the judge. He looked so young, so vulnerable. But he had no cuts or bruises. The lockdown had kept him safe.

Gus joined them at the front.

"Lance," the judge said, "I've looked at your case, and it appears that you've been charged with kidnapping of an infant. Is that right?"

"Yes sir, but I didn't do it."

"This is not the time to plead your case," he said. "I'm just here to set your court date."

"Your honor," Gus cut in, "we're asking that you let him out on bond. He's a minor. He doesn't have transportation. It's not likely that he's going to flee."

The judge read the file through reading glasses perched on his nose. "All right, then, I'm setting your bond at fifty thousand dollars. Lance, if you get someone to post bond and you don't show up in court, they'll lose that money. Do you understand?"

"Yes sir."

He looked at Barbara. "His court date is set for December 21. At that time he'll have a preliminary hearing, where he can enter a plea."

Barbara nodded. "But, sir, I don't have fifty thousand dollars."

Gus put his arm around her shoulders. "You'll only have to pay the bondsman ten percent," he whispered.

"Oh, okay."

Lance fell into his mother's arms and she held him as they both wept. Finally, as he was taken to process his release, they told her she could pick him up at the jail.

When she and Kent were back in the car, Barbara finally relaxed. "Now we have time to get Lance cleaned up and go to the graduation. I'll have my family together tonight after all."

Kent smiled. "And at least we have some breathing room while we wait for Jordan to tell the truth."

"She has to do it soon," she said. "I want this whole thing to go away before Lance has to be back in court."

Chapter 31

Barbara found a bail bondsman in the yellow pages who agreed to meet her at the jail. When she arrived, Barbara was stunned to see that she was a little old lady who looked like she'd just come from a church luncheon. Kent followed Barbara into a stairwell outside the jail office and listened as the woman went over the conditions of the bond. "I need $5,000 now from you," she said.

Barbara dug in her purse. "I can put it on a credit card, right?"

"No, hon. I'm afraid I need cash."

"Oh." Her heart sank. She didn't have five thousand cash.

Kent touched her hand. "Don't worry about it. I've got this."

Barbara frowned at him. "Kent, no! I can't take it from you. I can try to get a bank loan."

"You can pay me back," he insisted. "Besides, as soon as Jordan tells the truth, we'll get our money back."

Barbara turned to the bondswoman. "Is that true? If the charges are dropped, you'll refund the money?"

"Most of it. All but my fee."

How had she gotten into this? Borrowing money from Kent was way over the line. But if she wanted to get Lance out today she had no choice.

She sat with the bondswoman, going over the paper-work while Kent ran out to a bank and came back with the cash. While they waited for Lance to be released, others began to show up to get their loved ones out.

Some of them stared at her, probably because she didn't look like a mom whose child was in jail, but she had learned over the last couple of years that it could happen to any parent.

Finally, the door to the jail area opened and Lance shot out. "Mom!"

She sprang up and opened her arms, and he threw his arms around her. He'd dressed back in the clothes he'd been arrested in, but he looked rumpled and pale. "I can't believe I'm out. I thought I'd have to stay there." He pulled out of her arms and gave Kent a hug. "Kent, I saw you in the court-room. What are you doing here?"

"It's good to see you, kiddo. Your mother called me."

"They put me in stupid lockdown. I didn't even do anything."

"That was my fault," Kent said. "They were doing me a favor. It was my way of keeping you safe."

"To lock me up? It might as well have been a cage. I didn't even have a blanket. Just a piece of foam rubber and a metal bench. It was freezing in there and—"

"Honey, just say thank you."

Lance paused and studied Kent. "Thanks. I wish I'd known, though. I spent all weekend upset that I was being punished in the worst possible way." He turned back to his mother. "Did you talk to Jordan?"

"She's in the hospital, but she hasn't changed her story."

"Then let's go talk to her now."

"You can't," Kent said. "Stay away from her, Lance. That's important. Remember, you're not off the hook. You're still charged with kidnapping her child. You can't show up anywhere near the hospital."

"Then how can we talk her out of this?"

"I'll go back and see her after the graduation," Barbara said. "But right now, we've got to go home and get ready. It's Emily's big day."

Lance brooded as they drove home, but Barbara smudged her tears and thanked God that she had her child out of jail.

Chapter 32

The graduation was for Emily and another girl who'd checked herself in the same day as Emily, a year ago. Barbara, Kent, and Lance sat on the front row with the other family, wiping tears as Emily spoke about what the year had meant to her and how it had given her the tools to start a new life. Barbara laughed out of sheer joy as Emily accepted several certificates—for reading the entire Bible, for quitting smoking, for being a mentor to some of the younger girls.

The director spoke about all the changes she'd seen in Emily's life and gave her a reminder from Romans 12. "Therefore I urge you, my sweet sister, by the mercies of God, to present your body as a living and holy sacrifice, acceptable to God, which is your spiritual service of worship. And do not be conformed to this world, but be transformed by the renewing of your mind, so that you may prove what the will of God is, that which is good and acceptable and perfect."

As Emily said good-bye to all her friends and packed her things into the car, Barbara had a good cry. She hoped this era of Emily's life was completely behind her, and that they could move on to a brighter future for both of her children.

On the way home, Emily was in a good mood. "So how was the Big House?" she asked Lance, like he'd been on a field trip for school.

He didn't find that amusing. "A thrill a minute. What do you think?"

"And was lockdown all it's cracked up to be?"

"Lonely, cold, miserable?" he asked. "Yeah, everything I dreamed of."

She laughed. "And here I thought I was the only black sheep in the family. I never thought I'd see the day you'd end up in the slammer."

"Me either," Lance said. "Especially when I didn't do anything wrong."

"You did something wrong, all right. Driving my car without a license. They should have kept you there for car theft."

"Emily!" Barbara said.

Emily laughed. "I'm just kidding, Mom. But come on, you are gonna punish him, aren't you?"

"I think a weekend in jail was punishment enough."

"Seriously, Lance, if you do anything stupid like that again, you're gonna be in a lot more trouble, because you've already got this hanging over your head. You drive my car, and I'll turn you in myself."

"You're the one who told me to talk to her."

Barbara looked back over the seat. "Did you, Emily?"

"Yes, but I didn't expect him to get in my car and drive over there. I thought maybe he'd heard of the phone."

Kent laughed. "You guys are a hoot. I just realized I've never been around all of you together when you're not in a crisis."

"Hey, I'm in a crisis," Lance said.

"I'm just saying ... It's fun to see everybody happy."

Emily smiled, but Barbara sensed a wall between her and Kent. Emily hadn't expected him to be at the graduation. She'd acted happy to see him, but it would take time for them to feel comfortable with each other.

"Well, we're going to get happier," Emily said. "Don't worry, Mom. I'll take care of things today."

Barbara frowned. "What do you mean?"

"I mean I'll go to the hospital to talk to Jordan. We're good friends now. She'll listen to me."

"I don't know, Emily. That's probably not a good idea. You just got out."

"Mom, are you seriously gonna let her keep saying Lance tried to steal her baby?"

"No, not if we can prevent it. But I'll go myself."

"Her mother won't let you in. It has to be me. If Lance can't go, I'm the next best thing."

Lance leaned up against the back of Barbara's seat. "She's right, Mom. Let her go."

Barbara sighed. "All right, but I'm going with you. If her mother is still there, we're out of luck. She won't let either of us anywhere near Jordan."

"Her mother won't be there," Lance said. "No way she'd sit by Jordan's side like you would with us. She'll have to go out for a fix. And I almost forgot since lockdown kind of messed with my head, but when I was in the holding cell the other day, there were some dudes who told me that there's a guy in the hood who finds pregnant, addicted girls and offers to give them cash for their babies."

Kent turned around. "Did they say who it is?"

"No. But it sounds like there are other babies being sold. They pick addicts because they know they'll do anything for drug money."

Kent stared at him. "That's baby trafficking."

"What do they do with the babies?"

Kent shook his head. "It could be just black market adoptions—finding babies for a high fee. Or it could be something really evil."

"Like what?" Lance asked.

Kent swallowed and met Barbara's eyes. "I don't know. But I'll look into it."

Quiet settled over the car for a minute as that sank in. Finally, Emily broke the silence. "Don't worry, Mom. We'll get her to tell the truth."

Chapter 33

A whole year. Emily felt the lost days as she stepped back into her bedroom. Posters welcoming her home hung over the bed and across her wall.

Everything was organized and neat. Her mother had cleaned it up. Emily was sure that the last time she'd had an overnight pass, a month ago, she'd left her bed unmade and clothes over the chair. But that was a far cry from the way she'd kept it a year ago, when she'd been at the height of her drug use.

The furniture in her room hadn't been changed or moved, and the comforter and curtains were the same. But the absence of chaos and grime made it look unfamiliar and alien. She thought of how far she'd come. But was it far enough?

The phone sat beside her bed, plugged into the wall. She lowered to the bed and picked it up. But who could she call?

Not Paige, her former best friend. Paige was still deep into her addictions. Everyone else in her circle of friends was still ruining their lives. She had nothing in common with them now, and New Day had spent months drilling into her head how dangerous those old friends were to her sobriety.

But loneliness would consume her after a year surrounded constantly by other girls. She'd complained that she had no privacy, sharing her room with three other girls and standing in line for one bathroom. But the friendships had been good medicine.

Now the noise was gone, and Emily dreaded the silence.

"You okay in here?" Her mother leaned in the doorway.

"Yeah," she said. "It's good to be home."

"Karen Thompson just called and told me Maureen has left the hospital. Jordan's there alone."

Her spirits lifted as purpose returned. "Can we go now?"

Her mother studied her. "Are you sure you're up to this?"

"Yes, Mom. We've got to get Lance out of this. We can't let him go back to jail. And I have a few things to say to Jordan."

"All right," Barbara said. "Let's go."

As Emily stepped into Jordan's hospital room, she had the uncanny sense that she was standing outside her own body, looking at a potential version of herself. No, she and Jordan didn't look alike. But she could have ended up in the same place ... beaten and overdosed, with an innocent, homeless baby. Jordan's face was swollen and blackened with bruises. Bloody scabs had formed on her puffy lip.

Emily's anger at her friend vanished. No one wanted to be like this. Who would choose to go to sleep at night wondering where they'd get their next hit? No one wanted to wake up thinking about how to scrape together enough cash to score. And to be beaten and abused as a way of life ... What had Jordan's mother put her through to make her lie about Lance?

Emily sat down on the edge of the bed, like she had so many times at New Day when she and Jordan had talked into the night about what they might do with their lives when they truly kicked their addictions. She knew better than to wait for her to wake up. The girl was a sound sleeper even when she was sober, and she was withdrawing from her drugs, which meant she was utterly exhausted. She could sleep for days, except to eat and go to the bathroom. If Emily waited for her to wake up, it might be a long wait.

She shook Jordan's shoulder. "Jordan, wake up."

Jordan's eyes cracked open. "Leave me alone," she muttered.

"Jordan, it's me, Emily. I need to talk to you."

Jordan's eyes fluttered open again. Disoriented, she focused on Emily. "What are you doing here?"

"Thanks for missing my graduation," Emily quipped.

Jordan closed her eyes. "Yeah ... congratulations ... whatever. I was sorta busy ... having a baby and stuff."

"You know you never should have left in the first place."

"I still would have had the baby."

"Yeah, but none of this would have happened."

Jordan shifted and glanced back at her. "None of what?"

"You wouldn't have gotten beaten up. You were safe there. And my brother wouldn't have had to spend the weekend in jail. You're lucky I'm even speaking to you."

Tears rushed to Jordan's eyes, and she stared at the ceiling, as if remembering all that had happened in the last few days. When Barbara stepped into her sight, she sat up. "Have you seen Grace?"

Barbara came toward the bed. "Who's Grace?"

"The baby. I named her Grace."

Emily glanced up at her mother. Clearly, Jordan hadn't told anyone that.

"Are you keeping her?" Emily asked.

"That would be a disaster," Jordan whispered. "I didn't want Lance to go to jail. Is he okay?"

"He's out on bond. Jordan, tell the police the truth. You know Lance didn't kidnap your baby."

Tears rolled over her eyelashes, down her cheek. "My mother made me say it. She forced me. She's whacked out and I can't cross her."

Barbara came closer. "So what really happened?"

"She was arguing with Lance in the hall. I locked my door and went out my window and put the baby in his car. It was the only way I could save her. Mom was giving her to those people. I thought of going with him myself, but she would have known right away and chased us down. I thought if I went back in, I could buy them some time to get away."

"You have to tell the police that, Jordan."

Jordan wiped her eyes. "I know. And I have to make sure the baby's all right first. I can't let Mom give her to those people."

"She can't give the baby away without your approval," Barbara said. "If you don't want them to have Grace, then they won't."

"I want Loving Arms to handle the adoption. They're the ones I've been working with at New Day. I trust them."

"Then I'll call them for you," Barbara said. "We'll get them here. But, Jordan, I'm also going to get the police here, so you can tell the truth."

Jordan squeezed her eyes shut. "She'll kill me."

"She won't come near you if you don't want her to," Barbara said.

"Yes, she will. I'm a minor. She can do anything she wants. This adoption is important to her. She needs the money."

Emily's gaze snapped to her mother's.

"What money?" Barbara asked.

"The money those people were going to pay her."

Barbara caught her breath. "They were offering you money for your baby?"

"A lot of money," she said. "Forty thousand dollars."

Barbara's jaw dropped.

"Do you know how long that kind of money could keep my mom scoring? Once she saw those dollar signs, she couldn't think of anything else. She won't give it up. She'll kill me for telling you. I'm not exaggerating. She'll really kill me."

Barbara's voice grew thin. "Jordan, I need their names. The people trying to buy your baby."

"The Nelsons is all I know. I don't know their first names. I think my brother is the one who found them, which makes it even worse. All his friends are sleazy. I don't want anybody he knows having anything to do with my baby."

"I wouldn't either," Barbara muttered. "We'll make sure that doesn't happen."

Emily touched her hand. "Jordan, we need you to stay sober so you can do your part to make sure Grace is safe."

Jordan closed her eyes but didn't commit to anything.

Chapter 34

So do you think this will go on my permanent record?" Lance's question turned Kent from the grilled cheese sandwich he was making.

"Not if we get Jordan to drop the charges."

"But will I have to tell people I was arrested once, like on job applications and stuff?"

"No. They're usually only interested in felonies. You're innocent, Lance. We're going to get this cleared up."

Kent scooped the sandwich up with the spatula, turned it over, and watched smoke come up from the pan. Maybe he should have put more butter on the bread or sprayed more Pam.

"Are you sure you know how to cook?"

"I know how to cook bachelor food. Nothing anybody else would ever want to eat."

Lance came over to the stove and grabbed a glob of butter with his fingers. "Here, maybe this'll help." He dropped it in, and it sizzled and sent up more smoke. "I'm a whiz at grilled cheese. That, and macaroni and cheese."

"My two favorites," Kent said.

Lance wiped his fingers on his jeans. "So ... it's really cool that you came all this way to help me."

Kent smiled at the boy. "I'm glad your mom called."

"So ... are you two official?"

"Officially what?"

"You know ... a couple."

Grinning, Kent scooped the sandwich out and dropped it onto a plate. He shoved it across the counter to Lance. "I don't know. What do you think?"

Lance bit into it like he was famished. "I think you are."

"I'm not sure how your mom feels. There are a lot of miles between us."

"Yeah, I know. Makes it tough. Man, this is good. You know what you're doing."

Kent leaned over the counter. "Not burned?"

"Burned just enough." He chewed for a minute. "My dad used to burn them so bad they were stiff. I like them that way. He'd always scrape the burnt part off."

Kent decided to make another one. A weekend in jail had left the boy hungry. As he buttered the bread, Lance said, "You could visit us a lot more, you know. Especially with a friend who's a pilot."

"Yeah, but flying's not free, even that way. Fuel costs a lot, and he has a lot of costs for the plane."

"If you really want to, you'll work it out."

Kent dropped the sandwich into the pan and gazed at Lance. "I would if I knew your mother wanted me to."

"Are you kidding? Her face lights up when you're around."

"I think it was lit up today because of you and Emily."

He shook his head. "Different kind of light."

"And you don't have a problem with that?"

Lance shrugged. "Why would I? You make a mean grilled cheese."

As Kent laughed, his cell phone rang. Barbara's name filled the screen. He clicked it on. "Hey Barb. We were just talking about you."

"Kent, good news. Jordan has agreed to tell the police the truth."

Kent sucked in a breath. "Oh, man, that's great. Do you need me to contact the PD?"

"Yes, and get them here fast, before she changes her mind. Also, tell Lance for me, will you? I have to go."

Kent punched the air as he clicked the phone off. "Lance, Jordan told your mother the truth. She's ready to tell the police. If all goes according to plan, your charges will be dropped by the end of the day."

Lance's mouth fell open. "No way! Really?"

"Yes. I'm going to the hospital to be there when they take her statement. Then hopefully we'll get an arrest warrant for her mother."

Lance came around the counter and flipped the sandwich.

"You go on," Lance said. "I'll finish this."

"I hate to leave you here alone after you've been locked up all weekend."

"Hey, it's worth it." He scooped the sandwich onto his plate and turned off the burner.

"All right, but Lance, I want you to stay here until your mother comes back to get you. Don't do anything, got it? You're almost out of trouble. I don't want you to blow it."

"I won't. But will you call me when you know something?"

Kent promised he would.

Barbara waited in Jordan's room, pacing the floor. As she did, she prayed that Jordan wouldn't change her mind about confessing. What if her mother showed up and shut the whole thing down? What if Jordan feared repercussions for making a false statement to the police officer who'd taken her original statement?

When Kent arrived with two police detectives and a transcriptionist, they set up a tape recorder. Jordan looked ready to spill her guts as Detective Dathan sat down in a chair next to the bed.

"Jordan," Dathan said, "could you state your full name?"

Jordan cleared her throat. "Jordan Elise Rhodes."

A pretty name, Barbara thought. The name of someone whose mother might have given it some thought. Maybe Maureen had been sane at the time of Jordan's birth. Somewhere though, things had gone terribly wrong.

"Jordan, could you tell us what happened on Saturday, November 1?"

"I had my baby ... at home. The night before, I felt bad, cramping and back pain, and I didn't realize I was in labor. So I got high, and it helped with the pain."

"High on what?"

She sighed and looked down at her trembling hands. "Ice."

"Ice?" Dathan asked. "For the record, do you mean crystal meth?"

"Yes." She looked up at him. "Am I gonna get arrested for that? Because I don't have any with me right now."

"No. We're not here about drugs. Go on."

"So I was high and I didn't realize the baby was coming. But then I felt like pushing, and I told my mother that I needed to go to the hospital. But she said I was fine, that my water hadn't broken. She was a nurse's aide, years and years ago, when I was little. She thinks she knows everything. But then my water broke, and she still didn't take me. Even high, I felt worse and worse, so I shot some more, until I finally ran out. I didn't think about what it was doing to the baby."

"And what time did the baby come?"

"I went all night like that, and it finally came about ten in the morning."

"And what condition was the baby in?"

"She seemed okay, but every now and then she would get stiff and shake. I knew something was wrong. But my mom still wouldn't take me to the hospital."

"Did she tell you why?"

"It was because she wanted to give her to those people she found to adopt her, and she didn't want a record of the birth."

Kent glanced at Barbara. She pushed off from the wall and stood stiffly.

"Who were the people?" Dathan asked.

"She called them the Nelsons. They were paying her for the baby. They have some connection in town who looks for pregnant addicts. That guy hooked Mom and Zeke up with these people."

"How much?"

"Forty thousand dollars. My mother couldn't think about anything else." Jordan's face twisted, and she covered her eyes for a moment. "She was going to sell my baby. Just … sell her, like Grace was a car or something."

Dathan showed no emotion. "Were these people approved by an adoption agency? Were there papers?"

"I never signed anything."

"What happened when Lance came over?"

"He came to try to talk me into going back to New Day, and while he was there, the Nelsons showed up to take the baby. I couldn't let that happen. So I locked myself in my room while Lance was arguing with my mom and brother. And I went out the window and put the baby in Lance's car."

"So Lance didn't know the baby was in his car?"

"No. I figured his mom would know what to do. Mainly, I just wanted him to take her away from that place so they couldn't get her."

"Why didn't you go with Lance too?"

"Because I knew my mom would come after me if I did. I thought if he took off and I was still there, I'd buy them a little time. But I paid for it."

"How?"

"My mom picked my door lock and beat me bloody."

"So she's responsible for these bruises on your face?"

"Yes. And she forced me to call the police and report Lance. She wanted the baby back so she could sell her, but she also wanted to get revenge on Lance for getting in her way."

"Wasn't she worried about the birth record if she reported it?"

"I don't know what she was thinking. She was just raging." Her face twisted again, and a vein bulged on her forehead. "I didn't want to do it."

She looked at Barbara. "I'm sorry I lied. But she made me. I didn't want him to go to jail. He's the only one who cares what happens to me."

Barbara breathed a sigh of relief as Dathan wrapped up the interview. Jordan wept as she signed her statement. "I know what happens next. They'll arrest my mom and put me in foster care. But I don't want to go stay with some strange family. I want to give the baby up for adoption to a family who can love her and take care of her, and then I want to go back to New Day."

"We'll try to arrange that," Kent said. "For now, you've done the right thing. You've helped Lance, but more than that, you've helped your baby. Can we count on you to testify against your mother if it comes to that?"

"Yes. I have to," she said. "It's not just me now. It's Grace."

Barbara tried to comfort her as they finished up. But Jordan seemed to be waiting in dread for word about her mother's arrest. Until then, she wouldn't be safe. And neither would the baby.

When Kent was finished at the hospital, he followed Detective Dathan and his partner to the police station. Within minutes, one of them had gone to the DA for a warrant, based on Jordan's testimony. This was clearly a baby trafficking scheme. If they scared Maureen with jail, maybe she'd expose the others involved.

Kent went with the police to make the arrest. An old Dodge sat on the dirt driveway, and the front door appeared to be open. The crooked screen door had holes in it.

He waited on the lawn as the uniformed officers knocked.

Then Maureen emerged. She stepped out onto the rotting porch. Her graying roots looked as if they'd grown out four inches since she'd last colored it black. Even from where he stood, she smelled like she'd bathed in pig slop, and her eyes looked over-bright, as if she were high.

"Maureen Rhodes, we have a warrant for your arrest."

"What?" she spat out. "For what? I didn't do nothin'."

"For abusing your daughter and coercing her into giving a false statement to the police."

They left out the part about baby trafficking. They didn't yet have enough evidence to accuse her, but Kent hoped they'd be able to bring it up during questioning.

As they read Maureen her rights, Dathan put plastic cuffs on her. It satisfied Kent to see her rendered immobile after she'd called the police on Lance.

They took her to the precinct and sat her in the investigation room. Kent watched through the two-way mirror as the detectives questioned her, but she wouldn't talk. Clearly, her fear of repercussions from the traffickers and the risk of losing their money was more intimidating than her fear of the police. When they told her Jordan had changed her story, rage reddened her wrinkled face.

"Where is that little brat?" she demanded. "Is she still in the hospital?"

"Are you referring to your daughter?"

"She wants to keep that baby, so she's making up a bunch of stupid lies. The charges we filed were not false. Lance Covington forcibly took the baby. I didn't abuse her. He beat her up!"

Dathan glanced at the recorder. "Why did you keep her from giving the baby up for adoption through the Loving Arms agency, Ms. Rhodes?"

"I didn't. I don't care what she does with the baby. I just want it to go to a good home."

"Did anyone ever approach you about exchanging the baby for cash?"

Fear flashed across her face, and she stiffened. "No."

"Who were the two people who came to take the baby while Lance Covington was there?"

"They . . ." She paused, took in a deep breath, then looked down at her feet. "Those people weren't there for the baby. They were there looking at a couch I had for sale. That's all."

"A couch? That dirty couch in your living room?"

She didn't meet his eyes. "Yeah. They didn't buy it."

"So let me get this straight. On the day your daughter gave birth at home to a child who was obviously in distress, you took the time to show your couch to strangers?"

"That's right. I really needed some cash for the baby and all."

"Where did you list the couch for sale?"

She hesitated, clearly aware that they could check out her story. "It was word of mouth. I told some friends who told some friends."

"So no one ever offered you money for that baby?"

"Absolutely not."

Dathan leaned forward on the table. "Ms. Rhodes, are you aware that it's illegal to take cash for a baby?"

"Yes, I know that."

"Are you aware that baby traffickers don't always put the babies in homes of well-to-do people who want to adopt them? That sometimes there are much more sinister things going on?"

"Sinister things like what?" she asked grudgingly.

"Like taking the children out of the country, raising them in brothels. Or selling them to pedophiles."

She slammed her hand on the table. "I didn't sell nobody that baby."

"If you were to tell us who those people were and help us track them down, we might be able to keep the DA from charging you with conspiracy to commit child trafficking."

There was a long silence as she stared at the floor again. Watching through the window, Kent held his breath.

"I don't even know what you're talking about," she said.

When it was clear they weren't going to get any more out of Maureen, they took her to booking. Kent heard her shrill, raspy voice grow louder and louder, insisting that her own daughter was a lying tramp.

Kent couldn't blame Jordan for how she'd turned out. It was probably a miracle she'd made it to fifteen.

Chapter 35

Pride swelled in Barbara's chest at the way Emily attended to her friend. Today was supposed to be about Emily, but she'd unselfishly let Jordan become the center of their attention.

As Emily sat by Jordan's bed, updating her on all the drama at New Day, Karen came tentatively into the room. "Jordan, do you need some water?" she asked.

"No, I'm fine," Jordan said.

"If you need anything, just ring your call button."

Barbara knew it was time to introduce Karen to Jordan. She took her friend's hand and pulled her to the bed. "Jordan, Karen is a friend of ours. I asked her to look out for you when I realized she works on this floor."

Jordan seemed moved. "That's nice."

"Jordan, Karen has a special interest in you, because her

brother-in-law and his wife are on the Loving Arms adoption list."

For a moment, Jordan's face was blank, and Barbara braced herself for resentment. "Oh. You should have said something."

Karen swallowed. "I didn't want you to feel pressured. And if you're not ready to talk about it — "

"No, I am. I have to make some decisions."

"Jordan, Madeline and Ben have had four miscarriages. They want to be parents more than anything. I know you have a lot on your mind and a lot of options. But I'd love to introduce you to them. The baby's so beautiful."

Barbara couldn't tell how Jordan was taking this.

"Grace," Jordan said. "Her name's Grace."

Karen laughed. "Yes, Grace. That's perfect for her."

"Would they keep that name?" Jordan asked.

"I'm sure they would if you wanted them to. She looks like a Grace."

Jordan looked off into the distance. "She does, doesn't she?"

Emily nudged Jordan. "Why don't you meet them tonight, and see what you think?"

"Okay. We could do that."

Karen clapped her hands. "Then I'll go call them. I'm sure they'll come right away." She stood a moment, as if trying to decide whether to hug her. Jordan's expression remained closed, so finally, Karen backed away.

When she was gone, Jordan dabbed at her eyes. "She seems nice. Do you guys know the couple?"

"Yes," Barbara said. "You'll love them. Madeline would make a terrific mother. And Ben is amazing. He coaches his nephew's soccer team. They both teach first graders in Sunday school."

"Soccer and Sunday school," Jordan repeated on a whisper. "I like that. It's better than ... what I had."

"You couldn't go wrong with them," Emily said. "And Madeline wears the cutest clothes. You should see her. She has this really cool style, and she knows how to put things together. Grace would never look like a dork."

Barbara had to chuckle. She never would have used fashion to persuade Jordan, but maybe Emily was speaking her language.

"I want her to grow up like ... well, like you did, Emily."

Barbara's heart swelled. Was it possible that anyone really saw past Emily's mistakes and thought she'd been raised right?

Emily laughed. "I didn't turn out all that great."

"But not because of your mom," Jordan said.

Emily paused for a long moment. "No, not because of my mom."

Barbara backed up against the wall and looked up at some invisible spot on the ceiling. "Thank you, sweetie. I appreciate that." But I think you've turned out fine.

Later, when Madeline and Ben got to the hospital, nervous and teary-eyed, Karen brought them in to meet Jordan. As they talked, Barbara and Emily stepped out into the hall. "This could be a miracle," Barbara whispered.

"I know, right?"

"Let's go get a soda while they talk."

They were downstairs in the cafeteria when Madeline and Ben found them half an hour later. Madeline's nose was red from crying.

As she reached them, she raised her arms in the air. "Ben made her laugh. She's really sweet. She said we could have her!"

Barbara screamed and stood up, throwing her arms around her. "Did you call the agency?"

"Yes! We called our case manager together. They're getting the paperwork ready." She wilted into tears. "I don't know how to thank you."

Chapter 36

After Madeline and Ben left her hospital room, Jordan tried to sort through her feelings. There was some peace in knowing the decision was made, but unexpected sorrow crashed over her.

She felt the sudden need to see her baby. Getting out of bed, she tested her legs. She was weak, wobbly, but she made her way out into the wide corridor, rolling the IV pole behind her. She looked up and down the corridor and found the sign pointing to the nursery.

Keeping her hand on the wall to steady herself, she went to the display window. She looked across the sterile bassinets and didn't see a baby with brown curly hair. Where was Grace? What if her mother had already given her away?

She found the door and stepped inside. A nurse smiled at her.

"May I help you, hon?"

"My baby," she said. "I want to see my baby."

"The name?"

"Grace," she said. "Grace Rhodes."

The nurse looked surprised. "Oh, the Rhodes baby. Yes, she's right over here. Are you her mother?"

Jordan nodded, feeling like a fraud. She'd been called many things, but "mother" didn't seem to fit. She walked barefoot around the corner, pulling her pole behind her, and saw her little bundle lying in the bassinet, hooked up to a monitor. The baby lay sleeping on her back, her tiny hands on either side of her head. She was smaller than Jordan remembered, and her chest rose and fell rhythmically. Her skin was paler than it had been immediately after her birth. The purplish-pink had faded to white.

"Is she all right?"

"I think she'll be fine. Do you want to hold her?"

"Can I?"

"Of course. She's yours."

The nurse pulled a rocking chair beside the bassinet, and when Jordan was seated, she got the baby out of her bed, untangling the wires, and handed Grace to her.

Jordan was amazed at the warmth flushing through her the moment she touched her baby's skin. Grace had been cleaned up, and her hair had dried fluffy rather than curly.

The nurse stood over her for a moment. "Did you say you named her Grace? I'll put that on her chart."

"Yes, Grace," she said. As if in response, little Grace looked up at her, her gaze so clear and knowing that Jordan had the feeling she understood everything. Shame slammed her. Did Grace know she'd been born on her mother's dirty bedroom sheets? Did she know her mother was a tweaker? That she had chosen ice over prenatal care?

Maybe she'd be lucky and never find out. Never know darkness or pain ... or the truth about her family's betrayal.

As she rocked her baby, she realized it was the first time she'd felt a connection like this to any human being. The first time she'd had love for a blood relative, someone of her own. The first time she'd cared about anyone more than herself.

It was almost enough to make her want to keep Grace.

But then what would she do? She would have to get a job, and that meant she'd have to find someone to watch Grace while she worked. Even when her mother got out of jail, she would be no help—in fact, she'd be outraged that Jordan had destroyed her get-rich-quick scheme. She could go on welfare, Jordan supposed. That was a way to keep her.

But she was fifteen. What did she know about taking care of a baby? She had no safe place to live.

She pictured Grace growing up with Madeline and Ben. A swing set in the backyard. Frilly dresses. Photo albums full of firsts. All the things that had been absent from Jordan's life.

She wanted those things for Grace.

Giving her to Madeline and Ben was the best thing for her baby. If she didn't do this right, then nothing she did for the rest of her life would matter.

She wasn't sure it would matter anyway.

She started to cry, her tears wetting the little T-shirt that barely covered Grace's tiny belly. Her little navel was clamped off. She kissed the baby's round cheek, breathed in the scent of her baby skin, and let her lips linger there.

Suddenly, Grace let out a cry. Jordan felt the ache of her milk. Unprepared and flustered, she looked up for the nurse. "Can you take her?"

"Sure, honey."

Jordan stood and handed the baby back. As the nurse turned to put Grace back into her bassinet, Jordan fled from the sound of her child's hungry cry. Dragging her IV pole with her, she rushed back down the hallway toward her room.

She couldn't take this pain. She needed to get high, so she could forget she had a baby, one whose needs she couldn't meet.

She jerked the IV needle out of her hand, got dressed in her filthy clothes, and left her gown on the bed. Then she called a friend to come get her.

No one noticed her as she got onto the elevator. In mere moments she was out the door and waiting for her ride. Soon she could forget.

Chapter 37

Where had she gone? One minute Jordan had promised Madeline and Ben they could adopt the baby, and minutes later, while Barbara and Emily were downstairs getting her a milkshake, she walked out of the hospital and vanished.

"Mom, it's what she does," Emily said, standing in the doorway of Jordan's hospital room. "She runs away and uses when she's upset. It doesn't mean she's changed her mind."

Madeline and Ben had left the hospital after Jordan promised them the baby, but Karen had called them back to break the news. Madeline was grief-stricken, as if she'd just lost another baby. "But are we going to get the baby or not?" she asked through tears.

"I'm sure you are, Madeline," Barbara said. "Don't give up. Just pray. We're going to find her."

As Barbara and Emily went to the car, Emily said, "Let's

go back to the motel where you found her. That's the first place she would go."

"There's no 'let's.' You're not going. I'm taking you home."

"But, Mom, she's my friend."

"Emily, the last place I want you to go on the day you get out of treatment is a dope motel."

Emily threw her chin up. "I can handle it."

"You think you're strong, but you don't know that for sure. You're going to stay home."

Emily gave a long-suffering sigh. "All right, but when we find her, I'm gonna kill her. She shouldn't jerk people around this way."

After going by the police station to pick up Kent, Barbara dropped Emily off at her car, parked where Kent had left it. When Emily got home, she found Lance brooding in front of the television. She plopped down on the couch next to him. "So much for a warm homecoming."

"Hey, you didn't spend the whole weekend in jail. I at least expected them to throw us a parade or something." He poked at his game control and killed an alien on the screen. "Mom told me Jordan ran again. So where do you think she went this time?"

"I hope she's where she was last time so Mom and Kent can find her."

"If she really doesn't want to be found, she wouldn't go back there."

They stared numbly at the television. When the phone rang, Emily picked it up. "Hello?"

"Emily, it's Paige! How are you, girl? Why haven't you called me?"

Paige was her old best friend, who was still actively using. "I just got out of rehab today," she said. "How did you know I was out?"

"Jordan told me. She's here, and she's freaking me out a little. All beat up, can hardly walk. And now she's passed out."

Emily sprang up. "Jordan? Here *where*?"

Lance looked up. "She knows where Jordan is?" he whispered.

Paige's voice sounded sluggish, high. "Yeah. She's here at the house on Napa Street."

Emily closed her eyes. She knew the place—a dope house where people hung out for days at a time. Another one of Belker's places. "Paige, she should be in a hospital."

Lance stood up and put his ear next to the phone, trying to hear. "Paige, do you hear me?" Emily asked.

"Maybe she used too much. Took four bars ... you know, when you're weak like that ..."

"Four bars of Xanax could kill her! Paige, let me talk to her!"

"Can't. She's out cold."

Emily's throat grew tight. "Call an ambulance. I'm serious, Paige. She could die."

"Are you kidding?" Paige whispered. "Belker would kill me." The phone clicked off, and Emily stood staring at it.

Lance's face was only inches from hers. "What? What's four bars? What does that mean?"

"Four pills. It's way too much, that's what it means. It could seriously kill her, and nobody there is going to do anything." She grabbed her purse. "So I have to. I'm going to get her. Where are my keys?"

"You're not seriously going to a meth house, are you?"

Emily found her purse tossed on the counter, and dug out her keys. "I have to."

"No, you don't. Call Mom and Kent."

She turned back to him. "You don't understand. I can't just tell them who and where my suppliers were without serious payback. They'll know Paige called me and that I ratted them out. They'll burn our house down. They'll shoot through our windows. They'll kill all of us."

He stared at her. "And they won't get mad if you go there yourself?"

"No. They won't think I'm a threat. If I just go in and tell them I'm trying to help Jordan, they'll let me take her. They know I'm an addict, and they don't want to deal with a girl dying there."

"Emily, this is stupid. You think you can waltz in there and find Jordan and not be the least bit tempted to buy drugs?"

"I don't even have any money!"

"Jordan didn't have any money, either, but obviously somebody there got her some dope. And if you go there in your condition—"

"What condition?" she yelled.

"Fragile!" he yelled back. "Right out of treatment. You'll be making our worst fears come true. The last place Mom and I want you is in a dope house."

Emily threw up her hands. "Look, this is life or death. Jordan could die. She *wants* to die right now. We have to stop her. She's your friend too. Don't you care?"

"Then I'm going with you."

Why did he have to be so stubborn? "That's ridiculous. You just got out of jail. On bail. What would happen if you got caught near a place like that?"

"Emily, if you got caught there you'd go to jail too. We'd both wind up in jail."

"Shouldn't we put Jordan before ourselves? She's injured and sick. She just overdosed."

Lance wouldn't budge. "If you're going, I'm going. Period."

She stared at him. "All right, I don't have time for this. Jordan doesn't have time. Come on."

Lance got his jacket and followed her out to her car. "You sure you remember how to drive?"

"Yes."

"It's been a whole year."

"I drove home just now. I'm as good a driver as ever."

"And that's supposed to make me feel better?"

"Shut up." She started the car and pulled out of the driveway.

"If Mom gets home and finds us gone, she'll freak," he said. "This is wrong on so many levels."

"If we find Jordan and get her back to the hospital, Mom will be fine. She wants to help her."

Lance sulked as Emily drove. When she turned off the highway into a high-crime area, his mouth fell open. "Are you kidding? This is a bad part of town, Emily."

"I know. Just chill."

"Is this where you spent your time before treatment?"

"Some of it."

As she turned down a road next to a sleazy bar and drove through a neighborhood where men loitered on the corners, she realized just how right Lance was—this was a dangerous part of town. She'd never been clearheaded enough to worry about it before. Tension made her head ache as she slowed at the old rusted warehouse Belker had taken over after a factory closed down.

"What's this?"

"It's where she is," she said. "My old stomping ground."

"Jordan uses crystal meth. I thought you never used that."

"No, but I got crack here. You can get almost anything. It's a one-stop shop for junkies."

"That's not funny," he said.

"Do I look like I'm laughing?" She started to get out. "Wait here. I'm going in."

"No way! I'm not letting you go in there by yourself. Are you crazy?"

She groaned. "Lance, what kind of sister would I be if I dragged my little brother into a dope house?"

"And what kind of brother would I be if I let my drug-addict sister go into one the day she gets out of rehab, without some kind of accountability? We've been through too much with you, Emily."

"Where did you even learn that word? Accountability."

"Family counseling, hello-o! I'm not an idiot."

She sighed and got out. "All right, come on. We're in and we're out, just that fast. Don't talk to anybody. And don't argue with me. Let me do the talking. I know how to handle these people."

She closed her car door and went to the door, knocked, and waited as someone peered out through the window. She recognized the bouncer. His name was Charles, and he usually packed a pistol. The threat of anyone turning into an informant could turn him deadly. He recognized her and opened the door.

"Emily? Whassup, girl? Long time, no see."

"Yeah, I've been busy. Let me in," she said. He moved back as they stepped over the threshold. "This is my brother."

He gave Lance a once-over. "You sure he's cool?"

"He's fine. Would I bring anyone who's not?"

"New customer?" he asked Lance.

Lance shrugged. "Yeah. Whatever."

The bouncer seemed satisfied. As Emily moved farther into the building, she smelled the meth cooking. It smelled like chemicals burning and would get all of them decades in jail if the police were to raid the place now. The state didn't take meth labs lightly—not when they poisoned soil and drinking water and created fire hazards that put entire neighborhoods in danger.

Lance coughed and tried to get a clear breath. She hoped he didn't realize what was cooking. One unwise word from him could get them both killed.

"We ain't seen you since you murdered that chick," Charles said.

Emily's eyes flashed. "I didn't murder anybody."

"You were all over the news. What was it happened again?"

There was no one in the front room, so Emily looked toward the dark hallway. "I was rescued and cleared."

"So where you been all this time? I thought you was in jail."

Giving him a travelogue of her last twelve months wouldn't help. "Whatever. I'm out now. I'm just looking for somebody."

She glanced toward the makeshift kitchen. Through the doorway, she saw a table covered with syringes. A junkie sat there with a lighter's flame under a spoon, melting a rock of crack. The sight brought back a vengeful craving. All those months of sobriety hadn't taken away that door in her soul that opened and closed so easily. The dragon was still alive, and this was his lair.

Suddenly she was glad Lance was with her.

"Who you looking for, Emily?"

She glanced back at Charles. "Jordan Rhodes. She still here?"

"Maybe. Maybe not."

"I need to find her. She's sick and she could die. She had a baby and lost a lot of blood. They had to give her a transfusion, and she was dehydrated ... but she ran from the hospital."

Suspicion narrowed his eyes.

"Seriously," she said. "I need to find her. She might have it in her head to overdose on purpose. You don't want to deal with a dead body, do you? Please, if she's here, tell me where she is. I just want to help her."

"First you come with me." He put his arm around her and walked her away from Lance. She knew where this would lead. He would give her a freebie, get her started again. And as they'd taught her in treatment, every time she relapsed it would be worse.

Her mind groped for the Scripture she'd recited a thousand times in rehab. *God is faithful; He will not let you be tempted beyond what you can bear. But when you are tempted, He will also provide a way out so that you can stand up under it.*

She looked back over her shoulder at Lance. No surprise—he wasn't waiting quietly by the door. He was following her. She shook Charles off. Lance was right. This kind of place opened a craving in her soul. For her own sake, she had to leave now.

She felt a sheen of perspiration on her forehead. Her eyes burned, and her breathing was shallow. She grabbed Lance's arm for strength.

"Emily?" a girl's voice said.

She turned and saw Paige standing in a doorway. "Hey, girl!" Paige staggered over and hugged her. Paige smelled of body odor and oily hair. She looked awful. Her arms and legs were nothing more than thin skin stretched over bone, and the wrinkles in her dehydrated face made her seem thirty years older than she was. Her face was covered with what looked like acne, but it was probably sores from filling her bloodstream with toxic substances and then tweaking at her skin when hallucinations convinced her things were crawling on her. That was why they called meth addicts Tweakers.

It was the common look of a meth addict.

"You look great," Paige rasped. "I'm so glad to see you back. We need to hang out. You still have my number, right?"

"Maybe later," Emily said weakly. "Just ... show me where Jordan is."

"Back here," Paige said, turning back down the hall. "She looks really bad." Paige wobbled like a newborn colt, but in only a few steps they came to the room where Jordan was. Charles followed on their heels, his menacing presence reminding her that she was still in danger. Jordan lay passed out on a mattress on the floor, looking like death.

"Jordan!" Emily knelt beside her and took her pulse. She had trouble finding it, it was so weak. "Lance," she said quietly, "we've got to get her out of here. Her heartbeat is really faint. And her breathing's shallow."

"Let's call an ambulance."

"I don't have a phone," she whispered. "Where's yours?"

"Broken," he said.

"Nobody's calling nobody," Charles said. "You want to take her, go ahead. But we don't need no flashing lights here."

Emily wished they'd planned this better. She tried to lift Jordan up, but she was limp. Lance got on the other side of her and put her arm around his neck. They got Jordan to her feet, but her head lolled forward. This wasn't going to be easy.

God, help us!

"What are you doing?" Paige asked.

"She's going to die, Paige. Help us get her out of here."

Charles moved slowly aside, watching them suspiciously, and Paige led them back through the warehouse. But their commotion made too much noise. Just before they reached the door, Charles stepped back in front of them.

"Emily, what are you gonna tell the police?"

"Charles, let us out. I won't tell anyone where I found her, but she's really sick."

She heard the echoing clank of a metal door, and turned.

"Well, well. If it ain't the tragically beautiful Emily." The infamous Belker, who ran his dope houses like a CEO, stood smiling at her.

Emily shifted Jordan's weight. "Belker, we're taking her to the hospital, but we won't tell them where we found her. I know you don't want her to die here and have to deal with—"

"Leave her alone."

Charles took his cue from Belker's flat voice and drew his gun.

Lance gasped and held out a hand. "Whoa! Don't shoot. Please ..." Sweat dripped down his temples.

"Feel her pulse, Belker!" Emily said. "Listen, I could have told the police where to find her—they're looking for her. Instead, I came myself."

Belker moved in front of her, stroking the soul patch of hair under his bottom lip. "Maybe you didn't tell the police because you want to be able to come back," he said, bending down close to her. He pulled some rocks of crack out of his pocket. "This is what you like, isn't it? Or maybe some pills?"

Emily felt the sheen of perspiration dampening her face. "I really don't want it. Just let me out of here."

Belker kept his eyes on her, and for a moment she thought he could see into her soul, to the tangle of emotions smothering her. Finally, he dropped the rocks into Emily's jacket pocket. "On the house," he said. "Take her, but come back and see us. We've been missing you."

Lance's eyes snapped at Emily over Jordan's head. His cheeks blotched red, but he didn't speak.

"Lance, let's get Jordan to the car."

Paige opened the warehouse door, and they walked Jordan to the car and laid her in the backseat. Belker and Charles watched from the door, but they didn't stop them.

Lance got into the front passenger seat and held out his hand. "Emily, give me that stuff."

"Chill," she said, closing her door and starting the car. "I'll flush them when I get home."

"No, you won't. What are you doing?"

"I'm getting out of here before they change their minds. And we're in a hurry, in case you hadn't noticed."

As she turned the car around, he yelled, "Emily, you're scaring me. If you don't get rid of those rocks right now, I'm gonna go crazy."

She wiped the sweat from her eyes and drove as fast as she could out of Belker's sight.

"I can't believe this," Lance shouted. "Please tell me you're not gonna drag us through this again."

"I'm not dragging anybody through anything. I'm just trying to save Jordan."

"Then first save yourself. Give me the rocks."

"Shut up, Lance," she cried. "I haven't done anything wrong."

"This is a test, Emily. God is testing you. You're about to flunk!"

She drove, her hands trembling, intent on getting to the

hospital to help Jordan. But as she did, those nuggets of crack in her pocket called to her. She could so easily melt them down and shoot them into her veins or put them in a pipe . . .

She could even swallow them. It took longer for the high to kick in, but after a year of sobriety, that high would be amazing.

But as she reached the highway, she heard the echo of one of her twelve-step sayings. *Do the next right thing.*

The next right thing. What was that? Was it taking Jordan to the hospital or getting rid of the drugs?

She looked at Lance. There were tears on his face. He was so disappointed. It was bad enough that she'd led him into a crack house, but it would be even worse if she used. This was why she had to stay away from places and people like that. Why she had to cut herself off completely from anything having to do with drugs. Anything that smelled like them or dragged up memories. She had to make a clean break.

She pulled over to the curb. "Lance, get the rocks out of my pocket," she said, staring through the windshield. "Throw them out, and make sure they go down a storm drain."

He let out a huge sigh, tugged her jacket toward him until he could reach into the pocket where Belker had dropped them. His hands shook as he pulled them out. Opening his car door, he slipped out and found a gutter, threw them in. When he got back in and closed the door, he blew out a deep breath. "Thank you. You had me going there."

She started to cry and slammed the steering wheel. "I'm stupid," she said. "I'm weaker than I thought."

"No, you're not," he said. "You're stronger."

She stepped on the accelerator and pulled back into traffic.

"I wouldn't have been strong without you." The confession was hard to make, but there was no point in pretending.

"Well, I was here," he said.

"You were my way of escape. God does provide it." Her mouth was dry as cotton. "I'm sorry, Lance. I shouldn't have gone there, even for Jordan. I should have told Mom and Kent."

"As long as you don't do it again. It's good that you know this early on."

"I'll do better," she promised. "But don't worry Mom with this, okay?"

He just stared out the window.

Chapter 38

While the three of them waited in the ER examining room, Jordan drifted in and out of consciousness, giving Emily hope that they weren't too late. They had hooked her to an IV and done a tox screening, then started her on medications to fight the effects of the drugs. As soon as she could, Emily called her mother to tell her they'd found Jordan, careful to evade her questions about where they'd found her.

The hospital readmitted Jordan, and two nurses rolled her on a gurney to the same room she'd been in before. Emily followed them, but Lance waited in the lobby, afraid that his appearance on the same floor as the baby could cause trouble. When the nurses had transferred Jordan from the gurney to the hospital bed, Emily wet a washcloth and washed her friend's dirty, war-torn face. "We're not giving up on you, Jordan. You can make it. God can help you start over. You should see what He did for me today."

Emily sat quietly in a chair she'd pulled close to the side of Jordan's bed, wishing Lance had joined them to keep her company in the silence. She found the remote and flicked on the TV. She'd been unable to watch TV for the past year, except when she was home on passes or when she earned a half day off from her work at New Day. She had usually spent those half days off in the TV room watching a DVD or a favorite program that no one objected to. Freedom to choose when and what she watched now gave her a little thrill.

She channel surfed until she found her old favorite music channel, then sat back to see the latest videos. The first video that came up was blatantly sexual and hit her like a handful of sand in the eyes. No, that wasn't the image she wanted to trap in her brain. She switched to another channel. One of her old favorite singers, with black eyeliner caked around her eyes, sang a song that Emily knew was about cocaine. Even lingering there a moment caused those dreaded cravings to ache through her again.

Distraught, she changed the channel again, this time to a decorating channel her mother used to watch. Was this how it was going to be? Would she have to guard against every image that flashed before her eyes? Every smell? Every sound? Would the slightest slip send her barreling down the slope of addiction?

The words in Second Peter about a cleansed person relapsing into sin cracked like a whip through her brain. *For if, after they have escaped the defilements of the world by the knowledge of the Lord and Savior Jesus Christ, they are again entangled in them and are overcome, the last state has become worse for them than the first.*

They'd been over and over this in treatment. Relapses

always pulled you deeper, and the consequences were worse each time. Emily just couldn't go there. She had to stay clean.

A knock shook her out of her reverie, and her mother rushed through the door. "Emily, I saw Lance downstairs. Kent is taking him home." Barbara went to the bed and leaned over Jordan. In a low voice, she said, "She looks awful. Where did you find her?"

Emily hoped her mother couldn't see the guilt on her face. "Just ... in one of our old places."

Her mother's eyes flashed. "You went there?"

Emily swallowed and thought of telling her mom that it was no big deal, that she hadn't been exposed to anything, that she hadn't exposed Lance. She could deny the cravings that had almost done her in.

But secrets were her enemies. Things hidden in darkness had a way of attacking later.

Her mother wasn't going to like it. She drew in a deep breath. "Mom, I thought I could handle it. Paige called and told us she was there. Lance went with me."

"What?" Barbara whispered harshly. "Emily, do you know how irresponsible that was? I trusted you. The first day ..." Her voice broke, and her eyes filled with bitter tears. "The very first day you're out you go to a drug house and take your brother?"

"I know," Emily said. "Mom, you're right. I shouldn't have. It was stupid. But Paige said she'd taken too much, that she might have overdosed."

Barbara went to the vinyl couch under the window, sat slowly down. "What happened? Tell me every single thing."

"We found her, but I also found out that I'm weak." She glanced at Jordan, trying not to wake her. "I saw the drugs. They even gave me some. My old dealer put them in my pocket."

Her mother covered her face, as if it would protect her from this blow. "What were you thinking?"

"I thought I could do it." Her face twisted. "But it's okay. I gave the crack to Lance to—"

"You gave your brother crack?" Barbara said too loudly.

"No! Let me finish. I had him take it out of my pocket to throw away. That's so I didn't even have to touch it. He tossed it in a gutter."

Barbara sprang back up and walked across the room, clutching her head. Then she turned back, lowering her voice. "Emily, how could you do something so stupid and dangerous?"

"For Jordan! Yes, I could have sent the police, but if the people there found out I ratted them out, they might take revenge. I didn't know what else to do. Jordan could have died, so I had to move fast to get her to the hospital."

Barbara stood beside the bed, looking down at the fifteen-year-old lying limp under the blanket.

Emily looked at her mother across the bed. "Mom, she overdosed. I think it was intentional."

Barbara touched Jordan's forehead, then stroked her dirty hair back from her bruised eyes. Finally, she went around the bed and pulled Emily into a desperate hug.

Emily laid her forehead against her mother's shoulder, shame coursing through her.

"How are you ... after going there?" Barbara whispered.

"Confused," Emily said. "The triggers ... I didn't think they'd be that bad. Now I'm scared. What if I can't do this? What if I can't stay sober?"

"Of course you can."

"What if I fall again?"

Barbara pushed her back and stared into her face. "Honey, it makes me happy that you admitted all this. It tells me you're taking your sobriety seriously. We're going to help you. *God's* going to help you. But you have to make the choice to stay away from the people, places, and things that could make you fall."

"I don't know if I can. They're everywhere."

"It'll be hard until school starts. Then you'll have a whole new set of friends. New things to focus on. You can do this."

Emily wiped her face and turned back to the bed. Jordan's eyes were fluttering open. "Jordan?"

Jordan's eyes opened fully, and she stared at Emily for a moment, her eyes focusing. Then she covered her face with her blanket. "I hate you," she whispered in a weak, cracked voice.

Emily bent over her. "Why?"

"For bringing me here. Why can't you leave me alone?"

"We brought you back because you were about to die."

"I wanted to die. That was the point!"

Barbara let out a long sigh and shot a sorrowful look at Emily. Then she leaned down over Jordan, coaxing the blanket down so they could see her face. "Jordan, you don't have to die," Barbara said softly. "You just have to work hard for a few months to get this drug out of your head."

A vein on Jordan's forehead bulged. "It's not in my head. It's in my soul ... what's left of it."

Emily wanted to tell her that Jesus had died to redeem her soul, but Jordan was in no condition to hear it. It would only sound churchy. "Jordan, your soul can recover."

Jordan turned away from Emily onto her side and pulled her knees toward her chest.

Barbara stroked her back. "Honey, you've had a hard life, and it's no surprise that you're addicted. Blame whoever you want for that. But from this moment on, what you choose is in your hands, not your mother's, and not anybody else's. You can choose to have a healthy, happy life."

"Only way I can do that is with dope."

"No. It doesn't have to be a choice between drugs and death. Life is a choice you can make too, Jordan."

"Your baby is in there getting better," Emily said, "and somebody is gonna take her home from the hospital. If you don't sign the adoption papers, the wrong people are going to get her." Emily's voice had an impatient edge, though she did her best to constrain it.

"You think I don't know that?"

"If you've changed your mind about Madeline and Ben, that's one thing," Emily said. "If not, then sign the stupid papers and move on with your life. If you want to go down the toilet, then that's your choice. But at least your baby won't go with you."

Barbara speared Emily with a chastising look that told her to go easier on the girl.

But Emily didn't feel like pulling any punches. "Jordan, I know what you're going through. I understand. I almost relapsed myself when I found you. But both of us have to make the right choices, because if we don't, there won't be many chances left!"

"I didn't choose this!" Jordan yelled. "You grew up in your nice, cushy home, with a mother who loves you and puts you first. You don't know what it's like to have a mom who's been using since before you could talk, who puts everything before you, even her boyfriends. If anybody, *anybody*, offers to give her drug money, she doesn't care who or what she has to sell."

Emily was quiet for a moment. "Jordan, it's up to you to decide what you want to be. A corpse discovered in a gutter somewhere, or a tweaker like your mother, who goes from fix to fix, stepping on anyone in her way. Or, you could break the cycle and do better than your mother did. You could finish high school and go to college. Maybe meet a decent guy who doesn't use. You could have a family and be a good mother."

"You don't know what you're talking about. Those things don't happen to people like me. College ... like I'm going to get into Harvard or something. I'd be lucky to finish high school."

"I'm going to college. If I can do it, you can."

"You have a mom to pay for it."

"Don't even start, Jordan. I had to apply for grants and student loans, because my mom can't afford to pay my tuition. You could get the same financial aid I do—probably even more. But you're only fifteen. It's not too late to go back to high school."

"It's too hard."

"Give me a break!" Emily cried. "Rolling around in a dope house is hard! Scraping up money for a hit—that's hard."

Jordan grew quiet, staring through tears into the distance, as if trying to picture it.

Emily lowered her voice and sat on the edge of the bed. "Jordan, I want to help you, but I'm having enough trouble of my own. I want to stay your friend. But unless you go back to treatment, I can't. I'm drowning, myself. It's all I can do to keep my own head above water. Don't you want to get better?"

"I do," Jordan said. "I hate this! I don't want to always be fiending for drugs and doing stupid stuff to get them. I hate that I had a baby and couldn't even protect her. She could have died. I was high ..."

"Then change," Emily said. "I found out today that we

can't do it by ourselves. All the stuff they told us at New Day, it was true. We need God to help us do this, and He will."

"He won't listen to me!"

Emily's throat grew tight, and her heart slammed against her chest. "Yes, He will," she said through gritted teeth. "He promised to give us an escape if we ask for it. I tested it today, and it's true. But Jordan, if you don't choose to do the right thing, then you're one of those people I have to escape from." She slid off the bed and grabbed her purse.

"Go then. Everybody else abandons me."

"No, you don't. You're not gonna put a guilt trip on me." Emily looked wearily up at her mother. "Mom, I have to go."

As she headed for the door, her mother grabbed her arm. "Honey, where are you going?"

"I've had enough," she said. "I have to get out of here." She opened the door and saw Kent coming up the hall toward them.

"Everything all right?" he asked as he reached them.

Barbara put her arm around Emily. "I'll stay here for a while. But Emily needs to go home."

Kent gave her a weak smile. "I can take you home."

"No, that's okay," Emily said. "I have my car outside." She glanced back at Jordan. She'd turned back toward the window.

"Honey, I'll be home soon," Barbara whispered.

Emily headed toward the elevator, aware that Kent was on her heels. The doors opened, and she stepped in. He stepped in after her. They both looked straight ahead as the doors closed.

"You okay?" he asked.

She wiped her face and kept her gaze fixed on the buttons. "Yeah, fine."

"You sure?"

"Yes." What did he want from her? Yes, she owed him for saving her life. He was a good person, and her mother really liked him. But she didn't know him that well, and she wasn't in the mood to pour her heart out to him.

"Can I buy you a soda?" he asked. "Coffee?"

She sighed. He wasn't going to drop it. Besides, her mouth felt dry as gravel. "I guess."

The elevator stopped at the first floor, and he stepped off and headed for the cafeteria. Emily followed grudgingly.

She suddenly felt so tired. Just yesterday she'd had so much exuberant energy and had been excited about all the things she would do when she got out. Then Jordan had to go and mess everything up. Now Emily almost wished she was back within the safe walls of New Day.

In the cafeteria, Kent asked, "What do you want?"

"I'll get it." She got herself a Coke, something they didn't have at New Day. It was a rare treat. He paid for it, then nodded toward a table.

"So what's going on?" he asked, taking the seat across from her.

She sighed. "With what?"

"With Jordan. You seem really upset."

"I'm just mad at her, that's all. To see her being so stupid. Why would she choose what she has over New Day? It makes me sick."

He stared at her for a moment, and she knew she wasn't fooling him. "Emily, tell me about the place where you found her."

"I'm sure Lance told you plenty. Don't worry. I confessed everything to Mom." She sipped on the drink, felt the carbonation burning her tongue. "Look, I know you mean well, and you've been a big help to my mom."

"But stay out of your life?"

She looked away. "I didn't say that."

"You meant it. But that's okay."

She rubbed her temples. "No, I didn't. Really, I didn't. I don't want you out of it. I just ..."

"You just don't want me quite so involved?"

"I don't want you questioning me like I'm a criminal."

He blew out a breath. "Wow. I sure didn't intend to do that." He folded his arms on the table. "The fact is, I'm so proud of you I can't stand it. I know things are difficult for you right now. Your mom has tried real hard to keep things the same for you, so that when you got out you'd be able to pick back up on the good stuff and maybe find it easier to leave the bad stuff from your past alone."

"Yeah, well, it's not gonna be that easy."

"I know. But you've got a good start."

"Except for the dope house." She looked down at a spot on the table. "I didn't think that would be so hard for me. I didn't think they'd be so aggressive ... or that I'd react like that."

"When the dealer put the rocks in your pocket?"

Yes, Lance had told him everything. "If it weren't for my brother I don't know what I would have done."

"And it's still calling to you, isn't it?"

She thought of lying, but he'd never believe her. "Yeah ... only now it's not like a lover ... it's like an enemy luring me over the line. I don't see it as all beauty anymore. I know it's a monster, and I don't want to be won over. But there's still this part of me ..."

"You'll grow stronger."

She hoped it was true. She pressed the corners of her eyes. She didn't want to cry in front of him. "Mom's really been having a hard time. Financially, I mean."

"Yeah, she has."

"She lost her business because of me."

"Not because of you. Because of the economy."

"Yeah, but she could have saved her business if she'd gotten that governor's mansion job. But she couldn't get her proposal finished because she had to come looking for me."

"It wasn't like you chose to get kidnapped."

"I know ... but if I'd never started doing the stuff I was doing, then so many horrible things wouldn't have happened."

Kent rubbed his chin. "Well, God has a way of using everything. If it weren't for that, I wouldn't have met your mom, and I'd still be thinking that God didn't care anything about me. That He didn't even know my name."

She met his eyes directly for the first time. "Really?"

"Really. I was somewhere between an agnostic and an atheist. And then I met your mom, and realized that maybe God does care about me after all." He sipped his coffee, set the cup down. "For the past year, I've been going to church, doing Bible studies, meeting with a group of Christian men. And I've learned that Christ has funny ways of sweeping up the crumbs of our lives and making them into huge feasts."

She whispered a laugh. "I sure hope He can do that for me."

"He's already doing it." Kent smiled. "Listen, Emily. I don't expect you to be crazy about me from the get-go. But if we could just be friends because we have something in common, it would help us both."

"What do we have in common?"

"We're both big fans of your mom."

Her smile faded. "Guess Mom deserves a fan club, huh?"

"Yes, she does."

Okay. Maybe she'd give him a break. They were on the same team, after all.

Chapter 39

I don't blame her for being mad," Jordan said. "But she didn't have to come after me."

Upstairs, Barbara tried to comfort Jordan before leaving the hospital, but Emily's angry departure had only upset her more.

Barbara sat on the edge of her bed. "Jordan, for some reason, God tangled you up with my family," "We can't go after every addict we know every time they use and demand they get help. But Emily's right. There's a baby involved here."

"So if it weren't for the baby, you would have let me die?"

Her brooding, narcissistic question cut through Barbara's heart. "Jordan, we came after you because we care about you. It's not too late for you to start over. Ultimately, you'll make the decision whether to destroy yourself or not.

But first you have a responsibility to make sure Grace will go to the right home. Paperwork has to be signed."

"Okay," she said, reaching for a tissue. "Go get Ben and Madeline." When Barbara hesitated, Jordan said, "Don't worry, I'm not gonna run for it again." She blew her nose. "You're right. If I don't sign the papers, my brother will make sure those people get the baby."

"But, Jordan, this has to be final. I don't want to see Madeline and Ben jerked around."

"I know. Or Grace either. I'll sign."

Relief washed over Barbara. "I'll call them." She flicked through her cell phone's contact list to the number she'd plugged in earlier.

Madeline answered on the first ring. "Hello?"

"Madeline, Jordan is here at the hospital and she's all right."

"Oh, thank you, God."

Barbara's eyes stung with tears. "She wants you to come and bring the papers. Can you come?"

"I'll call Ben. He's ten minutes away. And even though it's late, I'll see if someone from Loving Arms can come with the papers."

It seemed like only a few minutes later when Madeline blew into the room. Jordan cringed as she faced her. "I'm sorry I ran," she said. "It wasn't about you. Really."

"I know." Madeline went to the bed and touched Jordan's hand. "Are you all right?"

Jordan ignored the question. "I want to sign the papers," she said. "I want Grace to be yours."

Madeline hugged her. "I just called Ben. He and the Loving Arms people are on their way."

"Good."

"But I want you to be all right."

Jordan squeezed her eyes shut. "Do you think … there will ever be a day when I'll have a real family, and children that I can keep and take care of?"

"I'm sure of it, honey," Madeline whispered.

"I want that," Jordan said. "But it can't be now."

Barbara watched as Madeline held Jordan, letting her cry against her shoulder. When Ben and the representative from Loving Arms arrived, she called Kent and he came back up and joined them. Jordan's sorrow slowly lifted. With nervous laughter and excitement, they presented her the papers to sign. Barbara and Kent acted as witnesses after Madeline and Ben had signed.

It was done. Grace had a home where she could go as soon as she was released, and when Jordan was strong enough, she could check back into New Day. For the next year of her life she would have a safe place of refuge. All she had to do was learn how to want it.

Chapter 40

By the next morning, Jordan supposed it was a blessing that they were treating her physical injuries rather
than her mental ones. If they'd called her incident a suicide
attempt, she'd be in the psych ward, and if they'd called it
an overdose, she'd be sent to detox. Instead, they attributed
her behavior to postpartum depression and let her stay on
the maternity floor. No one was monitoring her. She could
leave anytime. She could go back to the dope house if she
wanted to.

But this time no one would come for her.

Did she still want to die? What would life be like for
her if she didn't choose to get clean? The drugs would kill
her, one way or another. If they didn't kill her outright, she
would turn into her mother.

She remembered fifth grade, when they'd had the DARE

drug program at school, and she'd signed a pledge saying she would never take drugs. She'd learned a song about the stupidity of it, and they'd performed it for their parents. Her mother had stumbled in late and applauded wildly, high on her drug of the week.

It was a long way back to that innocence—too many years had to be erased. But she had made a good start at New Day. She had seen the glimmer of a future. She could get that vision back again.

She closed her eyes and tried to see it—the scars of her beatings healed ... a graduation gown ... a college dorm room.

"Get up, you little tramp."

The abrupt, hostile command opened her eyes. Her vision slowly focused, and she saw her brother standing over her. "Zeke?"

"Get up!" he snarled, his eyes wild. "Mama's in jail! And you're the one who did that to her, you maggot. Is that what you wanted? After all she was doing for you?"

She pulled her knees to her chest. "Zeke, leave me alone."

He yanked her IV cord, ripping the needle from her hand. Blood seeped out, so she pressed her other hand over it.

"How could you turn on your own mother?"

"The same way she could turn on me!"

Cursing, he grabbed her blankets and threw them across the room. "Keep your voice down, or I'll make sure you can't move your jaw. You're ruining everything. What were you gonna do? Raise a baby yourself? With no job? With no man to take care of you?"

She got out of the bed, her head spinning, and looked down at her bleeding hand. "Zeke, what do you want from me?"

"I want you to go get that baby and come with me."

"What? Why?"

"Because you can't keep it, that's why!"

"I know that. I've made all the arrangements. I signed adoption papers with Loving Arms."

"No!" With no warning, he hit her across her tender jaw. She stumbled back, almost falling. "You're coming with me! Do you hear me? If I get the money they're paying, I can get Mama out of jail and we can all score big." His voice dropped to a rippling whisper. "Don't you want that? To never have to worry where you'll get your next hit? To have it just sitting there waiting for you whenever you need it? We're talking forty grand! And they're good for it. They already paid ten."

She tried to focus, but her jaw was already beginning to swell. His voice softened, and he moved closer to her face. His breath smelled as if he hadn't brushed his teeth in months. His eyes didn't focus quite right. One eye seemed pulled to the right, as if some unseen force bent them out of sync with each other. "Don't you want that, Sis?" he asked, his voice trembling. "To have it right there, a whole stockpile of it? We can live in our own little world and nobody can bother us."

She did want it. At least the cells of her body, her neurons, her neurotransmitters — everything that had entangled itself with drugs wanted it. But then ... there was Grace.

"No. I don't want it. I want to go back to New Day. I want to give Grace to the people I've chosen."

"For free?" he asked, disgusted. "And nobody gets anything out of it?"

"I'll get something. I'll know she's safe. That she's got a shot at a better life than I've had. And she'll get good parents who love her."

He swung again, this time knocking her food tray off her rolling table. It clattered to the floor. She glanced at the door, hoping a nurse would hear the crash and come running. But he'd closed the door. They probably couldn't hear. She groped for the nurse's call button, but he jerked the control out of her hand.

"You and me and Mama will get nothing! She'll sit there in jail and you'll go into some perverted foster home with some fat guy salivating over you. You ignorant, empty skull—you're ruining everything!"

"I'm not ignorant," she said, throwing her chin up. "And I'm not empty. There's more to me than you've always said. There's more to me!"

Her rebellion only inflamed him more. He shoved the food table out of his way and grabbed her arm, twisting it. "Get dressed. Get the kid and let's go, or I'll smash every bone in your face, and nobody will ever want you for the rest of your life."

When she hesitated, he grabbed her by her throat. "Stop!" she choked out.

He released her neck and grabbed her chin, squeezing her face where it was already bruised. "Are you going to do what I tell you?"

"Yes," she said, trying to catch her breath. "Just let me go."

He released her and went to the closet, got her clothes, and threw them at her. "Get out of those pajamas. Get dressed and pull yourself together."

She got her clothes and went into the bathroom. She had to hold the rail on the wall as she steadied herself. What was she going to do? He would kill her if she didn't do what he said. He was half-crazed from meth and who knew what else.

She would try to wave someone down as she and Zeke

walked down the hallway—one of the nurses, or Karen if she saw her. She wouldn't even have to call attention to herself. If she made sure Karen saw her leaving, then she would surely call Barbara or the police.

She couldn't put on these clothes. Her jeans were bloody, and her T-shirt smelled of smoke. She looked down at what Barbara had brought her to wear from Emily's closet. Flannel pajama bottoms and a T-shirt that said Girl Power. She'd have to wear that out. Maybe someone would realize they were pajamas and it would raise a red flag.

She regarded herself in the mirror for the first time in days—her face disfigured and bruised black, her eyes swollen, her lip split. No one would notice a new bruise forming. What more would Zeke do to her?

She had no choice. She would have to go with him. But she wouldn't take the baby to the people who were paying for it. She wouldn't be able to live with herself afterward. There weren't enough highs to numb that pain. No, she would escape somehow.

The bathroom door crashed open and Zeke stood there. "Why aren't you getting dressed?"

"I can't," she said. "My jeans are bloody. I'll have to wear this."

"All right." He yanked her out. "Put your shoes on. Hurry up."

She was weak and light-headed as she bent down to pull her shoes on.

He slapped her chin, forcing her head up. "Hurry up, before somebody comes in here." He pulled a gun out of his pocket and cocked it. "I don't want to use this, but I will if I have to."

No, not a gun. "I don't even know if they'll let me have the baby. She's sick."

"You're her mother. You can get her if you want."

"But I signed the papers."

"You can change your mind. I know the law. There's a waiting period for you to renege."

She knew they would probably let her have the baby. The doctor had officially released Grace this morning — they were just waiting for the paperwork to be processed before Madeline and Ben could take her home. Jordan had been told more than once that she had every right to change her mind before then ... or even after, until the adoption was finalized.

She muttered a prayer for help under her breath as Zeke took her arm and hurried her out of the room, down the hallway to the nursery. Tears filled Jordan's eyes as she tried to make eye contact with the nurses hurrying past. But no one noticed.

She looked in the nursery window, hoping that Grace's bassinet would be empty, that Madeline and Ben had already taken her. But there she was, across the room, her little feet kicking in the air.

God, I don't expect You to answer my prayers, but Grace can't pray for herself. Please help her.

She knocked on the door and waited.

"Open it," Zeke said. "Go in."

She turned the knob and stepped inside. There were three nurses. The one in Grace's section looked across the room. "Hi."

Jordan swallowed. "I ... I came to get my baby. I'm leaving."

The nurse frowned. "The papers are still being processed. But ... I thought you were giving her up for adoption."

Jordan hesitated, and Zeke spoke. "She changed her mind."

The nurse studied Jordan. "Honey, are you sure?"

"Yeah," she said in a weak voice. "I need to take her now."

"But nothing's ready. We have stuff we'll send home with you. A package of formula and diapers, her picture, and some other things you might need."

"She doesn't need any of that," Zeke said. "We have everything waiting at home."

Jordan could tell the woman wasn't buying it, and she hoped she would pick up the phone and call someone ... anyone ... who would tell her this wasn't right.

"But what's the hurry? It'll just be another hour or so."

"We're just ready to get out of this place," Zeke said. "Jordan can't sleep nights with people coming in all during the night taking her blood pressure and stuff."

Jordan looked at him. He hadn't even visited her here. How would he know what was going on at night?

"But your injuries," the nurse said. "Honey, look at you. You aren't quite ready to go home yet, are you? Has the doctor released you?"

Jordan shook her head. "No, but I feel better."

"Do you? You really don't look better."

Zeke was losing patience. "Just get the kid, all right? It's her baby, and you can't keep it against her will."

The woman seemed to deflate. "All right. I guess I can speed up the paperwork. I'll have to get her prescriptions printed out, and instructions on her care, warnings about what to do in case of a seizure ..."

Zeke didn't press the issue, so Jordan kept quiet. But she knew he was on the razor edge of losing his temper and knocking every bassinet in this room over. And that loaded gun was still stuffed into the waistband of his jeans. Jordan sensed his insane rage next to her as he waited.

Finally, the nurse brought the paperwork. Jordan signed it quickly, knowing that any further delay could put all of these babies at risk.

"Do you have a car seat? We're not allowed to let you go home without one."

A glimmer of hope. "No, I don't have anything."

"Okay," the nurse said. "Let me call and get you one."

"That's okay," Zeke said. "She can hold her in the car."

The nurse dug in her heels. "I'm sorry, but we're not legally allowed to release her without a car seat."

Zeke began to pace between the bassinets, his hands trembling in fury. Babies began to cry.

"Please hurry," Jordan told the nurse.

The nurse was gone only a moment before coming back with a car seat on a rolling cart. A security guard followed her. "Ma'am, can I see some identification?" he asked.

Jordan had nothing. "I don't have any. I don't have a driver's license yet."

"Your bracelet," Zeke said, picking up her arm and showing the guard. "Her name is on her hospital bracelet."

The guard checked it, then gave Zeke a long look. "Jordan, you're fifteen?"

"Yes," she said.

"Where's your mother?"

"In jail," she blurted, her eyes pleading with him to stop this now.

"She signed adoption papers last night," the nurse said weakly. "But she still has the right to change her mind."

The guard said, "I'll go check on some things while you get everything ready."

Maybe, Jordan thought. Maybe he would realize how wrong this was and derail Zeke's plan. Maybe they'd arrest him and throw him in jail too.

The nurse looked troubled as she loaded a box of diapers and some formula on the lower shelf of the cart, then gently peeled the electrodes from Grace's skin. She removed the IV, then lifted the little ball of baby out of the bassinet and put her into the car seat.

"You slide the seat belt through the back of the seat, like this," she said. "You have to put her in the backseat. I'll walk you down and make sure you do it right."

"No," Jordan said. "That's okay."

"It's hospital policy," she said. "We have to do it."

"She didn't give birth here," Zeke said. "The policies don't apply to her."

"They apply to everyone. We're even supposed to wheel Jordan out to the car."

"Well, break the policy," he said. "Come on, Jordan, let's go." He lifted the car seat by its handle, holding it like a bucket. Jordan grabbed the diapers and bag of formula and followed him out, searching for the security guard.

The guard came out from behind the nurses' station and nodded to the nurse. What did that mean? That she had to let them go? Didn't he see she was being forced?

"Jordan?"

She turned back and looked hopefully at the nurse.

"What do you want me to tell the adoptive mother when she comes?"

Jordan's face twisted. "Tell her I couldn't help it."

Then she followed her brother down the hall and out to the rat-trap that they called the family car, and prayed for an escape.

Chapter 41

Morning came before Barbara was ready to wake up, its glaring light torturing her through her bedroom window. Fatigue ached in her bones. She would love to turn over and go back to sleep, but there was too much she had to do before she reported to work at ten. She'd hoped to take today off to spend with Emily, Lance, and Kent, but the store's owner was coming in today, and they needed all hands on deck. At least Emily wouldn't be home alone. Barbara had agreed to let Lance stay home from school today, to rest from his weekend in jail and keep his sister company.

But her heart was heavy. With Lance's case settled, Kent had no more reason to stay. She got up and showered, trying to prepare herself to say good-bye. But she didn't want him to go.

When he showed up at eight and knocked lightly on the door, she let him in, trying not to cry.

"I know you have to go to work in a couple of hours," he said. "But I wanted to see you before I fly back."

She took his hands. "Do you have to leave already?"

"I've booked a Delta flight for this afternoon. But I can stay longer if you want me to."

Yes, she wanted to cry out. *Stay. I need you.*

But that was selfish. "I know you have to get back to work. I really appreciate your coming. It was nice spending time with you."

He took her shoulders, pulled her close, and pressed a kiss on her forehead. "That wasn't really what I wanted you to say."

She met his eyes. "I want you to stay, Kent, but how can I ask you to do that after all you've done? I even borrowed money from you."

"Don't even think about that," he said with a grin. "I talked to the bond lady this morning. Showed her that the charges were dropped, and she gave me the money back."

"Oh, good. Kent, I don't want you to feel used. That's the last thing I'd want."

"I know that. And I don't feel used. I like helping you."

"But having you here just makes me hurt when you go." There they were, those tears she'd been fighting. She tried to blink them back. "You live so far away. I hate it."

He stroked the hair out of her eyes. "I hate it too. And there's something I want to tell you." He backed up and pulled out a bar stool.

"What is it?"

"The other day, when I met Chief Levin, he mentioned a position that's open in his department. He suggested that I apply for it. Pretty good position. I fit it to a T."

Her eyebrows shot up as her jaw dropped. "And you didn't mention it till now?"

"Wasn't a good time. And frankly, I didn't know whether I should consider it. I thought it might put too much pressure on you."

Her heart fluttered like the wings of a butterfly, almost taking flight. She stepped closer to him. "Are you considering it?"

He didn't take his eyes from hers. "I don't know. What do you think?"

She took his hand. "I think ... I'd really like to have you around more. But ... picking up and moving here, starting all over ... it seems like an awful lot to ask."

"You haven't asked."

"And I wouldn't." The look in his eyes told her that he wished she would.

"So ... then I shouldn't consider it."

"No, you should. If you want to. I mean ... if it's something you'd like."

She could see the frustration in his eyes. He stood up again, slid his hands into his pockets. "Barbara, there'd be only one reason I would consider this. It would be for you. It's not like I've always wanted to live in Missouri. Or always wanted to work in Jefferson City."

Something about his admission made her cheeks burn. "I know."

"So I need something from you. I need ... just some assurance that there's hope for us. That you wouldn't be against pursuing our relationship and seeing where it takes us. I know there would be pressure on you if I were here. Pressure to keep things going with me even if you didn't want to. I wouldn't want that. I need to want that job with or without you if I take it, enough to keep it if things don't work out for us."

"And do you?"

"Want it? I don't know. I need to pray about it."

She gazed at him. She knew she would mope around for days after he left. It had been so nice to have someone on her team, someone helping her carry the burden. Someone to lean on when she could hardly stand.

But promises? She couldn't promise that her life would be on steady ground a week from now. Her finances were a mess. Her children were fragile and unpredictable.

"Let's think about it, Kent. Let's pray about it. When do you have to tell him?"

"He didn't give me a time limit. He just said to call him if I decided I was interested."

"Then call him," she said. "At least find out if it's something you'd like."

A smile glistened in his eyes. "And you'd be okay with that? With my being around more? With my being a part of your life?"

Wiping tears, she laughed. "I'd be way more than okay with it. I don't want you to go home."

He pulled her into his arms then and kissed her. She loved the soft movement of his lips, the tender way he touched her face. She loved getting lost in his arms and touching his hair ...

"Mom?"

She jumped as if she'd been caught in a crime. Emily was standing in the doorway, wearing shorts and a sleep shirt. "Yeah, honey."

Emily just stared at her for a moment, resentment and surprise on her face. She shoved her tangled hair back. "Can you leave me the car keys so I can go see Jordan in the hospital?"

"Sure, honey. It's just ... Kent was thinking of going home today ... we were making some plans."

Emily padded in, her eyes groggy. "You don't have to go just because I'm out," she told Kent. "You can even keep driving my car."

"Thank you, Emily. But I don't want to intrude on your homecoming."

"You're not intruding."

That may have been all Emily could give him right now, but it was a lot, and Barbara appreciated it. She wanted to hug her and tell her how proud she was that she cared about her mother's happiness.

"Well, if I stay, I'll rent a car. You can have your car back."

She shrugged. "Then can I go see Jordan? I want to apologize for my meltdown yesterday."

"Yes," Barbara said. "There and back, okay?"

Emily nodded. "I'll go shower."

As Emily disappeared, Barbara looked up at Kent. "So ... are you going or staying?"

He grinned. "I think I'll stay another day or so. I'll go talk to the chief about that position."

Barbara smiled, then whispered, "I'm really glad."

They decided that he would take Barbara to work so that he could use her car until she got off.

Thrilled at the sudden turn of events and the fact that there were no impending good-byes—at least not today—she made him a quick breakfast.

Chapter 42

Emily had struggled with sleep all night, that bitter unease in the pit of her stomach. She'd gotten up around two and watched television for a while, wishing she had someone to call. There was no one.

Her friends from high school, the ones who'd ditched her when she went from being a partyer to an addict, had snubbed her so many times that she couldn't turn to them now. She couldn't forget the last time she'd gone to church with her mother, on a weekend pass from New Day. She had looked forward to showing everyone there that she was clean and sober, that her hair was healthy and her skin clear, that she had life in her eyes again. But the kids she'd been in youth group with, the ones she'd learned about Christ alongside, had refused to meet her eyes and had avoided her like they didn't know her.

So much for welcoming the Prodigal home.

She didn't blame them, though. If they'd welcomed her and spent time with her, and it turned out she'd still been using, their own reputations would have been damaged. But she missed them. As she showered, loneliness crept in. How was she going to do this? After a year of constantly being surrounded by other girls, the silence was deafening now. What did the graduates who didn't have family support do? Where did they go?

She wrapped a towel around her head and dressed, then went into the kitchen. Her mother was fixing her a plate of eggs and bacon. As Kent settled at the table with his own plate, her mother's phone rang.

Barbara looked down at the caller ID. "It's Madeline. They're probably heading to the hospital to get the baby." She clicked it on. "Hi, Madeline. What's up?"

Emily waited, listening for news. Her mother's face changed, and she closed her eyes and leaned back against the counter. "When?"

Emily said, "Mom, put it on speaker."

Her mother pressed the speakerphone button, and Emily heard Madeline's distraught voice. "She just took off. She told them in the nursery she'd changed her mind about the adoption. She left with some guy."

"What?" Emily asked. "Who was the guy?"

"They didn't know. They said she seemed nervous, but they processed the baby out. She's gone." Her voice broke, and they heard a quiet sob. "I guess it's over. I'll never get Grace now, and she could be in danger. What if something happens to that poor little baby?"

"Don't give up," Emily said. "Jordan's out of her head, fiending for drugs. It's not over."

"I can't keep hoping when she's so indecisive. I don't know what to tell Ben. He'll be devastated."

"We'll pray," Barbara said.

When her mother hung up the phone, Emily shook her head. "Mom, what should we do?"

Barbara slapped her hand on the counter. "Nothing. We can't do a thing. We've done everything we know to do for her, and we've offered her every opportunity. But we can't keep being jerked around, and neither should Madeline and Ben." She dropped her phone into her purse. "Just let it be. If she wants to get in touch with us, she knows where we are."

Kent came closer and rubbed Barbara's back. "I'm sorry this happened, you guys. But, Emily, your mom's right. I did this with my brother for years. I'd go to amazing lengths to get him help, to find a rehab facility that would take him, to get him there and pay the fee, and next thing I knew he was gone. Happened dozens of times before he wound up in prison."

"But the baby. Jordan can't take care of her. What if those people get her?"

Her mother looked so tired, and Emily saw the tears glistening in her eyes. "With Maureen in jail, they're probably out of the picture. The whole thing has called too much attention to them. Maybe Jordan just needed some time with the baby before she gives her up. Maybe good things can still happen."

But Emily didn't believe it.

After her mother and Kent left, Emily went back to her room and lay on her bed, looking up at the ceiling. Tears ran down her temples as she prayed for Jordan. But her mother was right. What could Emily do for her? Chasing her down and forcing her to get help wasn't working. Jordan had to figure this out on her own ... somehow. Emily closed her eyes and prayed, until she heard Lance moving around in the kitchen. When she went looking for him, he was lying on the couch playing a video game.

He glanced up at her. "Hey. Did you sleep?"

"Not much." She wondered if she should tell him about Jordan. He'd probably be more upset than she was.

He turned back to the television. "That guy, the one with the big nose? I have to help him get to the holy grail. But there's this little flock of vicious birds that keeps getting in my way. You ever played this before?"

She smiled and shook her head. "Nope. It's new, right?"

"Yeah. Just came out a couple of months ago." He worked the controller. "I can't quite win it."

She pulled her feet under her. "I feel behind on a lot of things. I'd hardly even heard of Twitter when I went into New Day. Now it's all I hear about."

"Yeah, well, I don't see the point in it."

"It's a way to stay in touch."

"With who?"

She didn't answer, but his question hung in the air. With who? was right. She glanced at the computer, thought of setting up a Facebook account and fishing for friends. But they wouldn't be like real, live friends. And that could become a whole new addiction.

"So how's Jordan? Have you talked to her today?"

Emily sighed but didn't answer. Lance knew her too well—he turned from the video game and watched her closely. "Emily? What's wrong?"

"Well ... she did what Jordan does. She took off again."

He dropped the controller. "No way. Not after we went into that horrible place and got her back. When did she leave?"

"This morning. And this time she took the baby."

His mouth fell open. "We did everything for her! I went to jail for two stinkin' days! Mom dragged her out of a crack motel. You and I went into a war zone to get her. You almost relapsed for her!"

"I know. But this isn't about us."

"Yes, it is. You don't turn on your friends like that. I forgave her, but now this! She's an idiot. Her brain is fried. Maybe there really is no hope for her."

"Don't say that. Of course there is."

He got up and kicked the ottoman. "Don't tell me she's gonna be okay, because you know she won't."

"No. You're right."

"And that baby ..." Lance looked as if he could put his fist through a wall. "She makes me sick." He stormed from the room. "I'm going to take a shower."

Chapter 43

Where are we going?" Jordan sat in Zeke's back seat next to the screaming baby, patting her chest to calm her. Zeke didn't answer. "Zeke, where are we going?"

"Shut up. I have to think."

She'd seen him like this before, his meth head full of schemes and stunts, and rage razor sharp in his eyes. "Let's just take her home. I think she needs to eat."

"Shut the kid up!" he shouted.

Jordan watched out the window, trying to figure out where they were going, but the baby cried harder. She found the bag with the formula in it—there were a couple of pre-mixed bottles in boxes. She tore into one.

"It's okay, sweetie," she whispered. The nipple was inverted, so she unscrewed the top and turned it right-side up. Was she doing this right? Her hands weren't even clean.

She shoved the bottle into Grace's mouth, and the baby hushed and began to suckle. The feeling of accomplishment—that she could do one thing right for her child—spread through her like an IV hit of meth. Motherhood.

She wanted to take Grace out and hold her, but Zeke was driving like a maniac, skidding around corners and running stop signs. He was on a mission.

"If you're taking her to those people, I'm going to fight you," she said. "I won't sign the papers."

"These people don't need papers."

What? "Why not? They can't adopt a baby without papers!"

He turned another corner, on two wheels.

"What kind of people are they?" Jordan asked, bracing herself. "What do they want with her?"

"They're people with money," he said. "That's all I care about. The kid'll be fine."

She leaned against the back of his seat and yelled into his ear. "I'm not giving her to them! Take me home now!"

"That's it." He swerved off the road onto the shoulder and stopped. "Get out."

She stared at him. "What?"

"Get out! Walk home, for all I care. I'm sick of your mouth."

Was this her escape? She could take the baby and walk to a phone, and he wouldn't be able to give Grace away. She opened the door next to the baby's seat, crawled out over her, then leaned back in to unhook the child's seat.

Zeke got out, shoved Jordan away, and kicked the back door shut. "Kid stays with me," he said. He got in and slammed his door. The car lurched back onto the road.

"No!" Jordan ran after him. "No, come back! She's mine! You can't take her!"

There was no traffic in either direction, no one to see her and help her. She ran until she couldn't see his car anymore, until she was about to collapse. Staggering to the shoulder of the road, she fell to her knees. *God, please help Grace! I don't know what to do!*

Chapter 44

Emily sat alone in the den, watching the video game figures move around the screen, waiting for someone to control them. She couldn't control herself, much less some alternative universe.

Thoughts of those crack rocks went through her mind, making her mouth dry. Her heart started pounding. If she went back to that gutter where Lance had thrown them—could she reach down the storm drain and find them?

The moment the thought crossed her mind, she snatched it back. No, she couldn't think like this. She had to do something. She had to talk to her counselor.

She grabbed the cordless and took it into her room. It was the first time she'd actually called Esther—she had to dig around in her purse for her business card. When she found it, she punched the number.

Esther answered quickly. "Esther's desk."

"Esther, it's Emily."

"Emily! Great to hear from you. How's it going out there?"

She wished she could tell Esther it was going great, that roses were blooming and friends were popping up, that she hadn't even had a thought of using drugs. But she had to be straight with her. "Not that great." She told Esther about their struggles with Jordan, the trip to Belker's warehouse, the problems she was having.

"Girl, get thee to an AA meeting."

She sighed. "I don't know where they're having any this time of day."

"That's no excuse," she said. "Do you have a computer?"

"Yes."

"Then get on it and go to AA.org. You can type in your zip code and see where all the meetings are. Some of them meet at noon."

"I thought you didn't like AA."

"I like the groups that are good. They aren't always good. Some of them are like sober nightclubs, all about hooking up with the opposite sex. But usually the ones meeting this time of day have people who are serious. You could also try the Christian version, Celebrate Recovery, but they usually only meet once a week."

"I just don't want my whole life to be about addiction. I don't want my days to revolve around those meetings, and I don't want all my friends to come from AA."

"Emily, just take it a day at a time. You need a little strength right now."

Emily sighed. "Okay, I'll go to the next meeting I can find in town."

After a pep talk, Emily hung up and went to the computer, pulled up the web site, and found a meeting that would start in thirty minutes at a church about ten miles away. She grabbed her purse.

Lance came out of his room, still looking sour. "Where are you going?" he asked.

"AA meeting."

He looked skeptical. "I'll go with you."

"Lance, I'll be fine. I don't need you to babysit me."

"That's what you said yesterday."

She hesitated. "I know. I just ... You can't spend your life carrying my problems. Play your video game. Do your homework. I have to work this out."

"But if you work it out the wrong way, the whole family blows up again."

"I won't do that. I promise."

"Are you sure? Because it would really stink if you did."

"I'm sure. That's why I'm going to AA. And, Lance, if I was going to use, I'd use. You couldn't stop me."

"I stopped you yesterday."

"That was because, deep down, I really wanted to be stopped. But now I'm nervous and depressed and lonely. And Esther thinks the meeting will help."

He sighed and leaned against the counter. "I could go and pretend to be an alcoholic."

She laughed. "That would be fun. But no. I have to do this alone. And just in case there's anyone who knows us, I don't want your reputation ruined."

"It's Alcoholics *Anonymous*. I thought it was confidential."

"Yeah, well. Trust me, Lance. I'm doing what I need to do to stay healthy. But I can't take you with me."

When he finally let her go, she drove to the small Episcopal church. Several people stood outside, smoking before going in. There were only a few cars here. She hated the small groups, where she couldn't blend into the crowd. But, swallowing back her trepidation, she went in.

She took a seat at the back of the room and tried not to make eye contact with anyone. But she couldn't miss the ragged guy sitting across the room, reeking of smoke, his face unshaven for days. He looked like he'd just crawled out of some alley. What was she doing here?

A guy sat down next to her and mumbled a quick hello. She answered without looking directly at him. He slid down in his seat, crossed his legs, and began doing a rapid drumbeat on his legs.

Not sober. She looked around the room as others came in. Sober. Not sober. Sober.

There were people here who could lure her back in. If someone stuffed one more rock into her pocket, she didn't know if she could resist.

Her mouth went dry. Her heart pounded. Heat prickled her skin, and she began to sweat.

No, she couldn't do it. She sprang to her feet and headed for the door. Rushing through the doorway, she bumped into a woman, stopping them both. "I'm sorry," Emily said.

The woman had a frizzy halo of red hair. "Where are you going?"

"Out. Away. I don't think this is the right meeting for me."

"How do you know? We haven't even started yet."

"I just ... I'm a year sober, okay?" She kept her voice low. "I'm trying to stay that way."

"Just come back in and sit down."

Emily shook her head. "I can't. The smell of smoke, the look in some of their eyes ... It's just not what I need."

The woman touched her arm and gave her a sympathetic smile. "Just got out of treatment, huh?"

How did she know? "Yeah. Just yesterday."

"Good for you."

"What?"

She lowered her voice. "Good for you for having some discernment. Truth is, this probably isn't the right group for you. I come because I lead it. I work the night shift, and it's not far from my house. A lot of these people come from the shelter down the street. They're forced to come. They have to get a form signed saying they were here, or they can't sleep there at night."

Emily swallowed and glanced back in.

"I keep doing this one because these people need hope. And some of them get it. I was like them about ten years ago."

Emily found that hard to believe. The woman, who looked about forty, was clean and nicely dressed. "Really?"

"Yeah." She took Emily's shoulder and walked her outside, away from the door. "Listen, I have a really great AA home group that meets at seven o'clock once a week. It meets tonight. Why don't you come to that? I think it's a healthier group."

Emily shrugged. "I don't know."

"Seriously, most of us in that group have been sober for a long time. And there are also some who are just days or weeks sober. We take them under our wings and help them. But it's a safe group. You'd like it. You could find a good sponsor there."

"Where is it?"

The woman gave her the address—even closer to Emily's house than this one. "Okay, maybe."

"What's your name?"

"Emily."

"I'm Jan. Nice to meet you. Hang in there, okay? It gets better."

Emily felt better as she crossed the tall grass and got back into her car. Maybe that was the kind of meeting she needed. As she started her car, she noticed Drew, one of Belker's dealers, approaching one of the smokers. What better place to find new customers?

Disgusted, she drove home, praying that God would help her. The last thing she wanted was to go back to drugs. Her addictions had almost gotten her killed. She didn't want to repeat those mistakes.

Would it be this hard if all this with Jordan hadn't happened? If Emily could have come home to a celebration and not had to think about drugs for a while?

The Jordan factor had definitely complicated things. If the girl wanted to throw her life away, Emily had to let her. She couldn't fool herself into thinking she could save Jordan or her baby. That was codependence, an enemy to recovery.

No, all she could do was pray for her friend and ask God to protect baby Grace. But for now, Emily's first priority had to be keeping herself on track.

Chapter 45

Before going back to the police station, Kent went to the hospital to talk to the nurse who'd released the baby to Jordan. This wasn't just a case of an indecisive birth mother. She could be planning to sell the baby after all.

The nurse described the man who'd been with Jordan. After a call to Detective Dathan, Kent managed to get a copy of the security tape in the nursery and hallway when Jordan checked out of the hospital. He'd sent the picture of the man to Barbara's cell phone, and she'd identified Jordan's half-brother. There was a bulge in the waistband of his jeans, under his shirt. A gun, probably. That explained why Jordan had gone along.

So if Zeke had Jordan and the baby, that probably meant he was going ahead with selling the child. With every moment that passed by, the baby was in greater danger.

He asked Detective Dathan to put out an AMBER Alert for Jordan and the baby, and an APB on Zeke Rhodes. Then he called Lance and drilled him about the man and woman he'd seen in the Rhodes's home that day, trying to take the baby.

"The man looked a little like Sean Penn," Lance said, "but his hair was kind of light brown and cut short, like a buzz cut that had had a couple of weeks to grow out. The woman's hair was black, shoulder-length, with straight black bangs. I didn't think of it then, but it might have been a wig. It didn't go with her skin, you know? She was really pale, and her eyebrows were light."

"How old would you say they were?"

"Old. Probably the same age as you and Mom."

Kent breathed a chuckle. "How were they dressed?"

"The man had on a black bomber jacket, and the lady had a trench coat."

"Do you think you remember them enough to help an artist draw a composite sketch?"

"Sure," Lance said. "That'd be cool."

Since Dathan was tied up getting information on Zeke Rhodes's vehicle, Kent took a moment to call the police chief.

"Detective Harlan, good to hear from you."

"Chief Levin, I hope I haven't disturbed you again."

"Not at all. Detective Dathan is keeping me informed on this case. It sounds like a case of child trafficking, doesn't it?"

"No question. And it's bigger than this one case. Listen, I got a description of the man and woman who were trying to take Jordan Rhodes's baby. Do you think we could get a composite artist to work with Lance to get a sketch of them?"

"We don't have our own here, but I could get one from another city. It would take a while to get her here."

"Might be worth it. He thinks the woman was in a wig, so maybe we could put some different hair on her. I'd like to put this out to the press. See if we can catch them and track down this baby."

"I don't know about that," Levin said. "Dathan already put out an AMBER Alert, even though it's a little iffy. Since the baby's mother's involved, it's not really a kidnapping. I can't go to the press with accusations against this man and woman, because we have absolutely no evidence that they've done anything wrong."

"We have Jordan's statement. And if we tell the press, maybe somebody else who's been approached about selling their baby would come forward."

"Let's wait until we have a little more evidence. Giving that information to the press could open a real can of worms, and give the perps time to get out of town. Jordan never saw any money change hands. I agree with your conclusions, but we can't pull the press in until we've got a little more on them."

Kent wasn't surprised. "I understand, but I thought it was worth a shot. Could you brief your patrol officers and fill them in on what we're looking for?"

"Yes, I'll do that right away. Track down the baby, and my guess is you'll find the traffickers too."

"I sure hope so."

"Listen — keep me updated. We're trying to make a good impression so you'll come work for us. Given that any more thought?"

"Actually, I have. I'd like to talk more about that when all this is over, if you have some time."

"I'll look forward to it."

Kent hung up, disappointed that there wouldn't be a press conference. He refocused on the description of the traffickers, hoping he could find them before they skipped the country. "Hey, Dathan," he said.

Dathan looked back at him. "Yeah?"

"Could you come with me to Juvie and interview the guys who were arrested Saturday night? Lance says they knew about these traffickers. Might be they could give us a little more information."

"Good idea," Dathan said. "Let's go now."

Chapter 46

Jordan sat for several moments, trying to make her head stop spinning and her breath settle. She heard a car coming, half a mile up the flat road. She forced herself to her feet, stumbled toward the road, and tried to flag it down. But it kept going.

She tried to get her bearings. They were on a lonely road outside of town. What roads had they taken to get here? Which direction? She had seen some buildings, a store and gas station, people. She heard a plane overhead and looked up. The plane banked and then came in low, descending, apparently about to land. But they were still too far above her to notice her.

She could walk home. She took in a few deep breaths, then started back in the direction they'd come. She couldn't be that far from home. They were still on her side of town, she thought. She'd see something she recognized soon. She just had to keep walking.

She was about to collapse when a minivan turned onto the street and came her way. She waved her arms. This time it slowed, then pulled over beyond her. Jordan stumbled to it and got in.

The driver looked like a soccer mom on her way to carpool, and she gasped when she saw Jordan. "Honey, are you all right?"

"Yeah, my brother just dumped me out of his car. I need a ride somewhere."

"Your face! What happened? Did he hit you?"

"It's a long story."

The woman looked stricken. "Should we call the police?"

Jordan's mind raced. Would the police even listen to another kidnap accusation from her when she'd already admitted to lying about Lance? No, they'd blow her off as some messed-up meth addict. They wouldn't even look for Grace.

Besides, they might think she'd hurt Grace herself when they heard how she'd taken her from the hospital.

"Honey?"

Jordan shook her head. "No ... not the police." She made up her mind. She would go to Lance's house. He would think of something.

"But, sweetie, they need to know."

"I'll call them from my friend's house. His mother's friend is a cop. He'll help me."

"Okay, where is it?"

She told the woman the street. She didn't know the number, but she'd seen it before—joyriding in the family Dodge, just cruising the good side of town to see how the other half lived.

On Lance's street, she pointed out the house. "That one." There wasn't a car in the driveway. She hoped Lance was home.

"Do you want me to go in with you?"

"No, that's okay."

The woman couldn't let go. "Honey, you might need medical attention. You look pretty bad."

"I'll get help. Thank you for the ride." She got out, feeling suddenly dizzy and drained of all energy. She took a moment to steady herself, hand on the car door.

"Honey, how old are you?"

She shook the fog out of her head. "Eighteen." She hoped the lie would keep her from slowing Jordan down with Child Protection Services. They had already been notified when her mother was arrested.

Jordan knew the woman wouldn't leave until she got into the house. She walked unsteadily to the door and banged on it, praying Lance was there. The minivan idled out front, the woman watching her with a troubled look. Finally, she heard movement inside, and Lance's voice.

"Who is it?"

"Lance, it's Jordan," she called through the door. "Let me in! It's an emergency!"

The door flew open. "Where have you been?"

Jordan stumbled inside. "I need your help!"

Chapter 47

The baby's guttural cries were driving Zeke nuts. He wiped the sweat from his forehead on the sleeve of his army-green T-shirt and considered taking a quick detour to his supplier. It had been six hours since his last hit, and he was beginning to come down. Fatigue weighed on him like a lead jacket, and his eyelids were heavy. But he didn't have any cash. If he could get to the ten grand his mother had deposited, he'd be fine. But the cops had put a freeze on her account, and now he couldn't even scrape together twenty bucks for a quarter gram.

He glanced in his rearview mirror, certain the cars behind him were tailing him. What had he been thinking, kicking his sister out of the car? The little tramp would call the police for sure. What if they were on his tail now, letting him lead them to the buyers?

The baby's screams made his head hurt. He wiped his nose on his sleeve and turned the radio loud, trying to drown her out. The heavy thrum of the bass guitar hit the off-beat as voices rapped about the upside of death.

He tapped his hand on the steering wheel and glanced in the mirror again. The car he'd been watching had turned off, and now a new one followed. A yellow VW Bug, with some blonde-haired chick whose window was open, her hair flapping in the wind. She didn't look like a cop.

He amped the music up, feeling the vibration with every beat. It almost drowned out the sound of the kid. Swinging his head to the beat, he turned off the main road, taking the back way. The girl didn't follow. He was good. Nobody was tailing him.

But there were those cameras. They were on the tops of buildings, on stoplights, in street lanterns, though you couldn't always see them. They were watching all the time ... mocking him in his hunger ... in his highs ...

Right in front of him, a plane descended as if coming in for a landing. It might be them—the buyers. They'd told him to look for a private jet sitting on a landing strip beside a hangar.

These people were made of money. He wondered where the plane had come from, where it would be going next. He hoped they'd brought the other thirty grand in cash.

The industrial buildings grew farther apart. He drove past a company with piles of lumber, then a lot with hundreds of old trailers lined up bumper to bumper. Then for a few minutes, only weeds and dirt ... then, finally, what looked like a small airfield.

Adrenaline jolted him like a hit of crank, lifting his fatigue, delaying his pangs. This was going to be good. Thirty grand in his hands ... would it be small or large bills? How would they pack it?

He would head right over to Belker's after he got the money and buy a couple of eight-balls. Then he'd stash the money somewhere safe. He could postpone bailing his mother out for a while. He'd ride high, with no one to stop him. Maybe he could gamble with a couple thousand, and win even more.

He found the hangar, and just beyond it, the landing strip. A small jet was slowly making its way up the runway toward the building. As he put the car in Park, the door to the hangar opened.

Zeke cut off the radio, and once again, the baby's high-pitched crying scratched through the air. "Calm down, kid," he said. "You're about to go on a airplane ride."

He got out and walked toward the man who appeared in the doorway. "Hey, man," he said. "I got the kid. You got the cash?"

The man went to the car, looked in at the baby. His face didn't change. "Good job. Get it out and bring it in for me."

Zeke wasn't crazy about that. First, he didn't want to touch the baby. He'd seen it when it was first born, all slimy and sticky, as his mother yelled at Jordan to tie off the cord. Second, he didn't like the idea of going into the building without somebody backing him up.

But he supposed he'd have to if he wanted the cash. They weren't going to count it out here in the open.

He unhooked the seat belt and, lifting the baby seat out by its handle, he followed the man into the building. The swinging motion of the seat seemed to quiet the baby. He stepped into the hangar. There were a couple of cars parked there, and the woman he'd seen at his house and another man across the room.

They crossed the building and peered into the car seat.

"What about the seizures?" the man who called himself Nelson said.

"She stopped having them," Zeke said, not knowing whether that was the truth, and not really caring. "They sent some medicine. It's in my car. You can have all the stuff they sent from the hospital."

The woman took the baby out of the seat and inspected it like it was an antique vase. The kid kicked and squirmed, mouth open wide, letting out a scream.

"What about the girl?" the woman asked, setting the baby back in the seat. "Where is she?"

"I don't know," he said. "She got out of the car and I left her."

The woman's eyes flashed to Nelson.

"We told you to bring her with you," he said.

Zeke shook his head. "Nah, then she would have known where you were. She would have told the police. And she never would have let you take the kid."

"That was the deal," Nelson said. "We told you to bring them both."

Zeke was getting sick of this. Were they trying to renege? "No, man, you didn't. You told me to get her out of the hospital and make her get the baby, but you didn't say nothing about bringing her here too."

The woman rolled her eyes as if she couldn't believe how stupid he was. Her gaze shot to the other man. He had dark greasy hair and dark eyes and spoke with a heavy accent. "No, we have girl too. She worth more than *bambino*."

Zeke frowned. "Wait ... you want Jordan to go *with* you?"

The woman stiffened. He noticed her eyes for the first time. They were blue, but too blue, like she wore contact lenses. Her face was stretched in a bad face-lift, but her neck was wrinkled and droopy. "We need her to take care of the baby until we get it to the adoptive parents," she said.

He shook his head. "No, she's no help. She's a raving lunatic right now. She screams louder than the kid. You'll have to take care of it yourself."

"Zeke," Nelson said, "this is not negotiable. Your sister is part of the deal."

"You never said that!" he bit out. "Not to me or to my mother. Now where's my money?"

Nelson let out a long-suffering sigh, then he motioned for the others to follow him across the hangar.

Zeke should have brought his gun in, but he'd been so excited to make the exchange that he'd left it on his seat. He looked toward the door.

The three came back, and this time the stranger spoke. "You get girl to us, we give you twenty more."

He frowned. "Twenty thousand *cash*?"

"Yes. Total fifty thousand."

This was a trick. They thought he was an idiot. "No way. I'm not leaving here without the thirty thousand you promised me. I have an appointment." He wiped the sweat dripping into his eyes. "An important appointment, and I need the cash."

"We'll give you a thousand now, and the rest when you bring her back," Nelson said in a cold, flat voice.

Zeke shook his head. "I'm not stupid, man! You said forty thousand. You gave my mother ten, and you owe me thirty. I want it now."

Nelson gave the woman another look, then he nodded. The woman disappeared into one of the rooms inside the hangar and came out with a backpack. She tossed it to Zeke.

He caught it at his gut, then dropped to his knees, his hands shaking as he unzipped it and looked inside. There were six stacks of hundred dollar bills. He pulled one out and fanned through it.

"Fifty to a stack, six stacks," Nelson said.

Zeke's mouth grew dry and his skin prickled as he counted out each stack. Thirty thousand. He zipped the backpack and got to his feet, unable to restrain his grin. "And if I come back with Jordan, twenty more, right?"

"That's right," the woman said. "But we need her now."

"And you're flying them out of the country? The feds aren't gonna show up at my door?"

"We will be far from here," the foreigner said.

How would he find Jordan? By now, she'd probably had time to get back home, and she might have called the police. But he doubted it. More likely, she'd gone to one of Belker's spots.

In fact, since he had the cash, he would head over there himself and get high before he looked for Jordan. Everything would be easier if he did that first.

"All right," he said. "I'll bring her back as soon as I find her."

"You have two hours," Nelson said. "If you aren't back by then, we leave. But we'll come back for you later."

Zeke knew the man didn't mean they were coming back to pal around. "Don't worry, guys," he said. "I want that other twenty. I'll be back in time."

They followed him back out to his car and he handed them the baby supplies. Then he screeched out of the concrete lot and headed out to score.

Chapter 48

The interview with Turk and the guys who were arrested with him didn't turn up much. They swore they'd never told Lance anything about people wanting to buy babies. It was a clear case of kids not wanting to bring more trouble on themselves from someone who might not appreciate their loose tongues.

As he and Dathan drove back to the precinct, Kent tried to work it all out in his mind. "Who would have access to pregnant girls in these neighborhoods?"

"I'd say doctors, but poverty-stricken teens, especially the ones on drugs, aren't big into prenatal care."

"But is there any kind of free clinic in that area? Or an abortion clinic? Some place these girls might go?"

"No abortion clinic. But there is a church-run clinic there, where doctors volunteer their time. Could be that somebody who works there gives the names to the traffickers."

Kent's phone rang, and he saw that it was Lance. He clicked it on. "Lance?"

"Kent, you've got to come!"

He frowned and looked at Dathan. "Come where? What's wrong?"

"Jordan's here. Zeke took the baby, and he's selling her to those people."

Dathan turned his siren and lights on, turned the car around, and headed to Barbara's house to take Jordan's statement.

She spilled out the story of Zeke's appearance at the hospital, his insistence on her getting the baby and leaving in the family's blue Dodge, his admission that he was selling the baby, and his dumping her in the street to get her out of the way. Unless they acted fast, they wouldn't find the perpetrators before they got the baby out of the country. But they had no idea where Zeke had taken the baby.

The girl still looked sick and in pain, but she refused to go back to the hospital until her baby was found.

"Jordan, we need to get into your house," Kent said. "Maybe Zeke or your mother wrote something down—an address or phone number or anything—that would tell us where they could be."

"Okay," she said. "Let's go now."

Lance followed them to the door. "What about me? Want me to stay here?"

Kent thought about that for a moment. With Lance on the traffickers' radar and Zeke on the loose, it didn't seem wise to leave him here alone. "Why don't you come with me and keep Jordan company while we search the house?"

"Okay," Lance said as he grabbed his shoes.

Jordan and Lance rode with Kent, with Detective Dathan following in his car. Kent watched for Zeke's car as they drove slowly past the decrepit houses on her street, then the woods that set the Rhodes house apart.

There was no car on the dirt driveway.

"Jordan, do you have a key?"

"No, not with me," she said. "But I know how to get in."

Kent pulled into the driveway, and Dathan pulled in behind him. Two cruisers parked on the street, and uniformed cops got out. One looked to be about forty. The other looked so young he couldn't have been out of the Academy for more than a couple of months. The whole group followed Jordan to her open bedroom window. She shoved it further open. "I can climb in."

Kent shook his head. "I'll do it." He drew his weapon, just in case, and climbed in through the window.

The house smelled rank and rotten. Dust motes floated on the sunlight beaming in. He stumbled over clothes and towels on the floor, saw blood-stained sheets wadded in a corner.

He went through the house to the front door and let Dathan and one of the uniforms in. Pointing to the rookie, he said, "What's your name?"

"Agora," the man said.

"Agora, you stand guard at the door. Log us as we come in and out, and don't let anybody in. Jordan and Lance, you guys just wait out here."

They sat on the porch steps, Lance stroking Jordan's back as she cried into her hands.

Kent turned back to the mess inside the house. It reeked of spoiled food, cigarette smoke, and other odors he couldn't name. The kitchen sink was full of dishes. Flies clustered over them.

There were lots of places to look for evidence—stacks of papers and garbage bags full of trash. The kitchen table was cluttered with notes and junk mail. He flipped through some of the handwritten notes. "Here ... phone numbers. And a deposit slip." He picked up the slip. "Perfect. A bank account number showing a deposit of $10,000, dated last week."

Detective Dathan examined it. "Just what we need." He put it into a paper sack, then looked at the phone numbers. "I'll call these in and see whose they are."

Kent flipped through another stack. Mostly junk mail, nothing helpful, until he came to a writing pad with several notations.

$40,000

$10,000 deposit

Newborn—no paperwork

555–1348—Call the minute she's born—Need imme-diate delivery

Beneath that was an ad printed out from the Internet, about the "adoption agency" willing to pay "ample expenses" to aid in adoptions. There was another phone number.

"Here's what we're looking for," Kent said, handing the two papers to Dathan, who still had the phone to his ear. Dathan grinned and gave the number to the detective looking the numbers up. Putting his hand over the phone, he said, "The phones were wireless and without GPS, but we're trying to find out what cell tower they last pinged from."

Kent nodded and kept looking. That info would only give them a general area where the baby could be. They needed an address, directions, anything that Zeke might have written down.

He hoped he'd find it soon. Once they took Grace out of the area, the odds of ever finding her were negligible.

Chapter 49

Barbara got a coworker, Lily, to drop her off at home, since Kent had her car. As they pulled into her driveway, Emily pulled in beside them. She was alone. Where had she been?

Barbara thanked Lily and got out. She waited on the driveway as Emily got out of her car. "Emily, where were you?"

Emily looked like she'd been crying. "I went to a meeting."

Barbara frowned. "An AA meeting?"

Emily nodded.

They'd been all through this in the last weeks of Emily's treatment—whether to encourage her to go to AA meetings or not. Since New Day's program was a Christian one, their policy was to offer information about AA if needed, but not to insist their graduates commit to going. At its inception, AA had been a God-centered program created by Christian men who recognized they couldn't kick addiction without God's help. But after years of political correctness had rubbed the polish off the program, Alcoholics Anonymous now recognized God as only a "higher power." Members were encouraged to plug into the Power of their choice.

Though it couldn't be denied that AA did help many people turn their lives around, she wasn't sure it was what Emily needed right now. But she had left the decision up to her. The last she'd heard, Emily had planned not to attend.

"Why didn't you tell me you wanted to go to a meeting?"

"I didn't want to bother you at work. I didn't think it was a big deal."

Barbara set her purse on the kitchen table and turned to her. Emily was clearly distraught. "What's wrong? Did something happen?"

"No, nothing."

"Really? Nothing?"

Emily's face twisted as tears overflowed. "Okay, everything."

Barbara pulled out a chair and patted the seat. "Honey, sit down."

Emily sat and pressed her face into her hands.

"I know being out isn't like you expected. We never had your welcome home dinner, and we haven't been home much for you to relax and enjoy your freedom. I know it's been a letdown, but the stuff with Lance and Jordan was a distraction. I'm really sorry about it all."

"It's okay. Jordan's my friend too. I feel like she's a little sister. We had to do what we did." She wiped her face. "Has anybody heard from her?"

"Yes. She came here. She's with Lance and Kent now. Zeke kidnapped the baby, and they're trying to find it."

"Oh, no. Mom!" Tears assaulted her again. "That poor baby."

"Kent will find her." Barbara tipped Emily's chin up. "Honey, what else is wrong? You were crying when you got home. What is it?"

"I'm just really disappointed in myself."

Fear tightened Barbara's chest. "Why? Did you do something?"

"No, don't get all freaked out." Emily stood up and went to the sink. "I didn't. I just ... can't stop wanting to."

Barbara didn't want to hear that, but Esther's warnings from Saturday came back to her. "But I thought you said you hardly thought about it anymore. That you didn't feel the cravings after a year of sobriety."

"I didn't—when I was at New Day. I was protected in there. Now there are reminders and triggers everywhere. I know where to get it. And it's on my mind all the time."

"Is it from being around Jordan?"

"Not really. It's from being in the world. In real life. I thought I was farther down the road than that. I called Esther and talked to her for a little while, and she told me to go to an AA meeting."

Barbara stroked Emily's hair. "Honey, I think that was a good sign. That you called her when you were craving. You held yourself accountable. You fought the temptation. You didn't just let it overtake you. I'm proud of you."

"Yeah, well, the meeting was disastrous. I saw right away that it was the wrong meeting for me. I just left."

Barbara's heart ached. "Is there anything I can do for you?"

"No, Mom. I have to do this myself. I'm just telling you because secrets don't help anything. I have to keep everything out in the light. I don't want to pretend I'm doing well and have it all pile up in me until I break down and use again." She wiped her face. "I really don't want to use, and I don't want to smoke. But there are triggers everywhere, because I used to get high everywhere." She sighed. "Maybe I'm making a mistake applying to a college so close to home. Maybe I just need to get out of this town."

Barbara hadn't expected that. After losing the last year with her daughter, she didn't want to have her out of reach again. "We can talk about that." She kissed Emily's cheek. "When all this is over with the baby and Jordan, we're going to have a real celebration."

"Whatever. Anyway, I'm trying another meeting at seven tonight. I met a girl who told me about a better group where people have been sober longer. She invited me."

Barbara stiffened. "Are you sure you want to do that?"

Emily wilted. "No, I'm not. But I need some reinforcement. I know how you feel about AA, but I realize now that I need a sponsor to keep me from getting off-track, and daily reminders that I'm not who I used to be. There are bad groups, like the one I tried today, but if I keep looking until I find a good, solid one, it might be just what I need."

"Then you should do it. No further explanation needed. The first few months you're out are going to be tough. But once you get a job and start working, you'll make friends whose biggest dramas are their boyfriend woes. That's what most girls your age think about."

"I know. If only ..." Her voice trailed off.

"If only what?"

"If only I hadn't taken that first hit. I'd be in my third semester of college, and I'd be dating and studying and hanging out with friends. I'd be moving ahead, instead of figuring out where to go from here."

"You're still young, honey. You can start over without
a blip."

"I feel old," she said. "Like I missed years of my life, and
I keep thinking about the people I'm leaving behind. Jordan
and Paige ..."

"Pray for them when you think of them. As for you,
remember what they said at New Day. God is good at repay-
ing the years that the locusts ate."

"I remember. Joel 2:25. But is that true even when we
invited the locusts ourselves?"

"You bet. God's going to show you what that really
means."

She sighed. "I hope He shows Jordan too."

"That's up to her," Barbara said.

Chapter 50

The detectives were taking too long. Jordan wanted to scream for them to hurry up, that every minute that ticked by put her baby in greater danger. Finally, she got up and looked through the screen door. Kent was still going through the stack of papers on the kitchen table.

"There's another place she has stuff," Jordan called through. "Can I come in and show you?"

Kent straightened. "Yeah, come in."

She stepped into the filthy house, assaulted by the smells she had grown up with. After being away for a few days, the stale, rotten air made her want to gag.

She led him to her mother's closet, where more stacks of bills, notes, and journals covered the floor. She had read some of the journals when her mother wasn't home. They'd been irrational rants about various men in her life and her fantasies of revenge.

She watched Kent and the other detective go through the papers for a few minutes, then went back into the living room.

Her baby ... where was she? Had Zeke already turned her over to them? Would they take care of her? Surely they wouldn't pay that much money for a baby they intended to hurt. Maybe the police would find her, and she'd still be okay.

But Zeke said they wanted to take her out of the country. What if they already had?

She looked out the front window, across the dismal yard. Lance and the other cop were still on the rickety front porch, talking quietly. What had she gotten her child into? Jordan was no better than her own mother—they had both chosen this vicious cycle of drugs and abuse and neglect. How had she let this happen? How had she allowed her sick brother to kidnap her baby and sell her?

He was driving high, screeching around corners like a maniac. What if he had a wreck and hurt Grace?

Nausea roiled in her stomach, and her head began to hurt. She was weak ... trembling ... sweating even in the damp cold. She needed a fix.

No. That wouldn't help. They needed her here, and her baby deserved a mother with a clear head.

But if she just had one hit, her head would clear, and she would feel normal.

She could walk out that door, slip past Lance and the cop somehow, and up the street to one of her suppliers. She could get a hit before anyone even knew she was gone. Besides, if she never came back, little Grace would probably be better off. Jordan had only brought horrors into her daughter's life.

The moment she let her thoughts head in that direction, the battle inside her ceased. The decision was made. No fighting required. She looked back up the hall to make sure the police were still focused on her mother's closet. She stepped out the back door onto the creaking steps. Dizziness assaulted her again, but it was only temporary. A little ice and she'd be fine. Back to normal.

She crossed the backyard, kicking through the tall grass, and went quietly around the house, out to the street, the same route she'd taken so many other times, when her mother withheld her own stash from Jordan. It was only a few blocks.

She plodded up the street, her eyes set on the road lined by forest and the houses just beyond it. She couldn't help her daughter now. She could only help herself.

Chapter 51

Sitting on the porch, Lance caught movement out of the corner of his eye. He turned and saw Jordan slipping through the trees toward the road.

"Hey—where's she going?" he asked the cop guarding the door.

"Got me."

Lance got up. "Hey! Jordan! What are you doing?"

She didn't answer, just kept walking.

"No way!" Rage shot through him. Crossing the yard, he ran and caught up to her and grabbed her arm. "So what are you gonna do? Just walk away? Right now, when you have a chance to do the right thing?"

"I did the right thing!" she shouted. "I called the police. If anybody can stop Zeke, they can. I can't do anything for her. So I might as well do it for myself."

Lance couldn't believe his ears. "You're going to get high? Now?"

"You don't understand," she said through her teeth, shaking him off and starting down the road again. "Just leave me alone. I told them everything I know. Just let me go." Her steps were fast and slightly unbalanced. She was breathing hard.

"What about your baby? And your future?"

She swung around, her face a red, wet mass of rage. "I don't have a future. Why don't you get that? Why can't you let go? I'm not gonna change. I can't even protect my baby. I'm gonna be just like my mother, whether I like it or not."

"That's not true, Jordan. You have a choice. You can walk up that road to a meth house, or you can choose freedom."

She gave a bitter laugh. "Freedom? There's no chance of freedom for me! I'm in prison. I didn't want to be here, but I am, and I can't get out."

"How is getting high gonna help?"

"It helps with the pain! It helps me hate myself less!" she screamed. Her voice echoed through the trees on either side of the road, silencing the crickets and birds calling overhead. Even the wind seemed to still.

She wilted into sobs, and Lance tried to put his arms around her, but she twisted away and lowered herself to the curb, bracing her elbows on her knees. "It hurts, Lance. I lost my baby. I was all she had, and I let him take her. I need to feel better. I'm not like you."

"It's not a matter of being 'like' anybody. It's about the choices you make. I've had the same opportunities you've had to do drugs. I just decided that I wasn't gonna do that. I wasn't gonna be that."

"It's not the same when you grew up in a house where your mother was perfect. It's just not."

He couldn't argue with her that they'd ever stood on level ground. "I know. Everybody would agree that you can look back and say you got a bum deal. You were born into a messed up family. But that doesn't help you now."

She looked up at him, wiping her face, and in her eyes, he saw a longing to change. He glanced back toward the house, but the trees hid it now. "Jordan, this is your moment. Why don't you make up your mind to be the kind of person you want to be?"

"Oh yeah. It's that easy. Just make up my mind."

Wind whispered through the trees. "You're making up your mind to surrender and drown yourself in dope. Why can't you make up your mind to do the opposite? I know you'll need help. But you have New Day. It probably sounds cheesy to you, that God will help you and everything. But it's true. He helped Emily. It's not just a bunch of bull that they came up with. It's real."

She wadded her hair with fisted hands. "What if they don't find Grace, Lance? What if she's gone forever? Do you know what it would be like to live with that?"

"Jordan, if that's true, then you'll have to deal with it somehow. The right way or the wrong way. Deal with it the right way. Come back to your house with me now. If anybody can find her, Kent can. They've already found some phone numbers. They're getting close. God already knows where she is, and He'll help you if you just make up your mind to let Him."

She covered her face again, and Lance waited, knowing he couldn't force her to choose the right thing. She could walk away right now, and no one would be able to stop her. Somewhere down the line, she'd wind up back in the hospital, or in jail, or dead somewhere. And he would go to her funeral and mourn the fact that drugs had taken another life.

She wiped her hands on her pajama bottoms, and he half expected her to get up and keep walking up that long road to her destruction. Instead, she let out a long, ragged breath. "Let's go back."

Relief flooded through him. They got to their feet, and he hugged her. He heard a car coming, its heavy engine sounding like it was in dire need of a new muffler. As he let her go, there was the squeal of brakes, and there it was beside them ... the blue Dodge.

Zeke leaned toward them and held a .38 through the open passenger window. Lance froze. "I was hoping you made it home, little sister," he said. "And looks like you brought company."

Jordan flew to the car. "Where is she? Where's my baby?"

"With people who really, really want her," he said with a grin. "And you know what, Jordan? They really, really want you too. The idea of a pretty blue-eyed brunette who's controllable with a little meth ... it upped the ante. They're paying me another twenty grand for you." He let out a bitter laugh. "Who knew you were worth that? Get in."

Lance felt the blood draining from his face. He glanced in the direction of the house, but couldn't see it through the trees. Where was the cop who was standing guard? Couldn't he hear the car? "Zeke, come on. She's your sister."

"Half-sister," he said, "which is practically nothing at all. And you. I should have killed you the other day. They wanted me to after you saw them, but you were in jail."

So jail had kept him from getting murdered. But Zeke had the capacity to kill. There was no question about that. "Hey," Lance said, holding his palms out, as if it would calm him. "Just put the gun down. You won't get away with it, and why have a murder and a kidnapping on your record?

The police are right over there, at your house. They're probably moving this way already."

Zeke peered uneasily toward the house, but then relaxed. They were hidden. "If they do, I'll have hostages. Both of you, in the car. Jordan, backseat. Lance, my friend, you come sit up here by me. I'll hand Jordan over, and then I'll take care of you." He cocked the hammer. His hand was shaking. "Or I could drop you right here. Don't really matter to me, but it might call attention to us."

Jordan didn't wait to be forced. She got into the backseat. "I want my baby."

"You'll be with her soon. Come on, Lance."

Lance moved slowly toward the car. Where was Kent? Why hadn't Agora heard the rumbling car? As he closed the car door, he looked in the direction of the house, but no one came. Zeke made a U-turn in the street and headed back the way he'd come.

Chapter 52

ere it is!" Dathan's voice echoed over the house. "I've got it!"

Kent crossed the hall, saw Dathan in what must be Zeke's room. He stood by a dirty bare mattress, brandishing a notepad with childish print. "It's directions, with the same phone number. And it has the money amounts again."

Kent examined the notepad. It gave cryptic directions to what sounded like an airstrip behind an industrial area. "All right, let's go."

He called out as he headed up the hall. "Lieutenant, let's go!" The patrol officer in the living room held the door open for them.

The other uniform who stood outside was focused on his BlackBerry. He turned. "We done here?"

Kent stepped outside. "Yeah. Where are the kids?"

The rookie pointed up the street to the trees. "Went for a walk. The girl was upset."

Kent's jaw dropped. "A walk?"

"Just up the street."

Kent's heart thudded as he went to the street. There was no one in sight. He broke into a run. "Lance! Jordan!" He ran toward the area where trees cloaked the sides of the road. No one there.

He shouted out their names as he jogged the half mile to the aged neighborhood. A man was outside working on a rusty car on cement blocks. Kent was sweating now. "Did you ... did you see a teenaged boy and a girl? Boy's about five-seven, brown hair, girl's the neighbor that lives past those trees?"

"No, I didn't see nobody."

How could that be? "How long have you been out here?"

"Coupla hours. You a cop?"

Kent turned back, looked up the street. "Did anybody come past here toward the Rhodes house down the street?"

"Yeah, that scuzzball Zeke come by in that clunker of his. Didn't stay long. Came right back out."

In that moment, Kent's world spun out of control, and he stood in disbelief. Zeke would have seen the kids on the road. If they told him the cops were waiting, he might have taken Jordan as a hostage. Apparently Lance too.

Barbara would never forgive him.

His legs felt like iron as he went back to the road. By now, the stupid cop who'd been posted at the front door was behind him. He looked shaken.

"Sir, I'm so sorry. I didn't think—"

Kent grabbed his collar. "You let them walk away, and now they've vanished!"

The cop swallowed. "I wasn't told to babysit. I was just guarding the search area."

"You weren't doing anything except playing on your stupid phone!" Kent spat out.

Dathan's car rolled up beside them, and Kent let Agora go and jumped in. "Zeke was here," he told Dathan, breathless. "He has them."

"Not for long," Dathan said, and as the cruisers' sirens came on to escort them, they headed toward the side of town where Zeke's directions led them.

Chapter 53

Zeke had a manic look in his eyes, and from the sores on his skin, Lance guessed he was deep into his meth abuse. The gun shook in Zeke's left hand as he steered with his right, and Lance knew it could go off at any moment, even if Zeke wasn't trying to pull the trigger.

"Put the gun down, Zeke," Lance said. "Please."

"Shut up!" he shouted, keeping the gun on Lance. "You helped get my mother locked up, so I owe you. And you, kid sis, you and your mouth brought the cops on our family. I'll show you. You're a brainless teenaged meth head, and you think you're gonna do anything right for the kid? Fighting us when we're trying to help you?"

"You sold her for money!" she screamed.

"So what? You think you're smarter giving her away for nothing?"

"The police are looking for her," Jordan said. "They're gonna find everybody involved, and if you're involved, they'll arrest you too."

The gun went off, its blast shattering the glass on Lance's window. He jumped and Jordan screamed. Glass sprayed the street.

Sweat broke out on Lance's face.

"Zeke!" Jordan screamed. "Stop it! Put the gun down. We don't want any trouble. Just let Lance out."

"No. I'm gonna kill him when we get there. And then I'm handing you over."

Lance's heart raced. "Zeke, you only have two family members left. Why would you put Jordan in this kind of danger?"

"She's always been nothing but trouble to us, ever since she was born."

"I hate you," she cried. "I've always hated you!"

Lance tried to think of something to say … something that would change Zeke's mind. But every time words came to his mind, he saw that gun barrel, and that trembling finger, right over the trigger.

Lance tried to think ahead. If Zeke was taking them to the people who stole the baby, then maybe he could gather some evidence, escape somehow, and call Kent. Maybe he could help the police blow this case up. But what if he couldn't? He had nothing to defend himself with. Once he was there, those people had no reason to keep him alive.

Maybe they weren't as evil as Zeke. Maybe they were just a high-powered underground adoption firm. It could be that they cared about babies and valued human life, but just had an illegal way of doing business.

No, that made no sense. They wouldn't have asked for Jordan too if they were really trying to help. And Lance was a witness, so they'd have to get rid of him. They had no choice.

It was completely out of his hands.

Chapter 54

Kent turned on the siren in Dathan's unmarked car as they raced to the site Zeke had written down. Barbara needed to know her son was missing, but dread of that phone call strangled him. She would never forgive him if anything happened to Lance. He would never forgive himself.

But he couldn't leave her in the dark, not after Dathan had expanded the AMBER Alert to include Jordan and Lance. Media outlets across the town were probably already getting word, and announcements would be made on TV and radio within the half hour. It was unfair to let Barbara hear about it that way.

Gripping the door handle to brace himself for the race through town, Kent called Barbara. When she answered, he closed his eyes. "Barbara, I have to tell you something."

She paused. "Is that a siren?"

He pressed a finger to his ear. "Yes. We're on our way to where we think Zeke took the baby. We found directions."

"That's great! Where's Lance?"

He sighed. "That's why I called. Barbara, he's missing. Jordan walked away from the house, Lance went after her to bring her back, and they vanished."

"*What?* No!" Her lungs seemed to empty with the word. "Did you look for them?"

"Yes, and I found out Zeke had been there minutes before. I think they're with him."

There was silence for a moment, and then he heard her hard breathing.

"Barbara, are you okay?"

"He could die." Her voice rippled with panic that rose to near hysteria. "He could be dead already. Kent, you have to find him! You have to get to him before they kill him!"

"Barbara, I'm headed there now. We've put out an AMBER Alert, and everyone will be looking for them. Just pray."

He couldn't bear the sound of her shocked grief. He hated himself for having no words to calm her down. There was no way to sugarcoat the fact that Lance was with a meth-crazed madman.

Why hadn't he watched him more closely? Why hadn't he told that rookie not to let them out of his sight?

God, please don't let anything happen to him!

But as they flew to their destination, he had a sinking feeling that he might be getting there too late.

Lance's gaze slid from one window to the other, looking for some source of help, as Zeke drove them up a long road, where factories and industrial buildings stood without a soul in sight. Zeke still held the gun in his left hand, aimed across his stomach at Lance.

Bezel, a local carpet manufacturer, had a parking lot full of cars, but no one walked outside. Not even a security guard. Zeke sped past it, crossed a railroad track, then drove in front of a shipping warehouse for a local department store. Lance saw men at an open bay unloading an eighteen-wheeler, but before it even registered, they had passed it and were speeding by abandoned factories with For Sale signs out front, and warehouses with boarded windows.

The farther they drove, the less likely it was that anyone would notice the insane man in the blue Dodge, holding two people hostage.

There was no one to signal, no one who would hear if Jordan screamed or Lance cried for help.

But Jordan wouldn't scream, because she didn't want anyone to stop them. Lance could tell from the determined look on her face that she saw this as a way to rescue her baby. For the first time in her life, she was putting someone else first. But her zeal to save her baby could keep Lance from finding an escape.

Zeke was going to kill him unless Lance could find a way out. His mind raced through options.

He could open the door and hurl himself out, but Zeke's finger was still on the trigger. He would fire for sure, and if Lance wasn't hit by the bullet, hitting the ground at eighty miles an hour would kill him anyway.

He could wait until they stopped and make a wild run for it. But Jordan wouldn't come with him—not until she had her baby. And he couldn't leave her.

Bottom line ... he was toast.

He looked back at Jordan, willing her to take what-ever chance they had for escape, but she wouldn't meet his eyes. She stared over Zeke's shoulder, out the windshield, as though trying to anticipate their destination.

They slowed and turned off the road as they approached another building. Beside it, Lance saw a long airstrip with a fuel tank beside it. As Zeke pulled up to the closed doors of the airplane hangar, he honked his horn.

"What is this place?" Jordan asked, her voice hoarse.

"You'll know soon enough," Zeke said. "And when I hand you over, I'll get another twenty grand." He slapped his hands on the steering wheel and laughed. "You know how much ice I can do with that much dough?"

Lance's hand closed over the door latch, but Zeke raised his gun. "Zeke, who are you turning her over to?"

"Somebody who can make good use of her," Zeke said. "Nobody else ever has."

Lance heard a noise; the hangar's bay door was opening slowly. Inside, just beyond it, he could see the man who'd been at Jordan's house with the woman that day.

God, please help us.

Carrying an automatic rifle, the man walked over to Lance's side of the car, opened the door, and told him to get out. Lance slid out, holding his hands above his head. His knees threatened to buckle. "Don't shoot," he said. "I haven't done anything wrong."

Jordan bolted out, seemingly without fear. "Do you have my baby?" she demanded.

"Hold it." The woman emerged, her gun aimed at Jordan. "What's the boy doing here?" she yelled.

"He was with her, so I had to bring him," Zeke said. "Don't worry about him. I'll take care of him myself."

The man stared at Zeke as if he wasn't pleased. Lance raised his hands innocently. "Let me go, man. I swear I won't tell anybody."

"Inside," the man bit out, looking up the road. "Pull the car in."

The man went back to the door and yelled something, and the door to the second bay rolled open. Zeke pulled his car in.

As they walked Lance in, a gun against his back, he saw that there were two cars, a sleek plane that looked like something a corporation would own, and at least one other guy in the dimly lit building. As the door closed behind them, Lance's lungs locked—he couldn't breathe. This was it.

"Give me the gun, Zeke," the man barked.

Still behind the wheel, Zeke handed his gun out the car window—then gasped as Nelson lifted it to Zeke's head. "Out of the car, Zeke."

"What? Put the gun down, man. We're on the same side."

"Where is my baby?" Jordan screamed, her voice echoing through the metal building.

"We'll bring her to you," the woman said in a calm voice. "Come back here with me, and we'll get her for you. Hands over your head. All of you."

Lance did as he was told. He followed Jordan into a small room that looked like a manager's office. It had a metal desk in the center of the room and some folding chairs.

Lance took the seat by the wall, as far from the man's gun as he could get. Jordan sat down, watching the man hopefully, as if he'd produce Grace at any moment. As Zeke stepped over the threshold, the man lifted Zeke's gun ...

... and shot him in the back.

Jordan screamed as her brother hit the concrete. Lance grabbed her and pulled her against him, pressing both of them against the wall.

God please help us. God please help us ... He was going

to die. Jordan too. They would find them here in a pile on the floor.

The other man and woman looked undaunted as they dragged Zeke's body from the doorway. Jordan's screams bounced off the walls, echoing through the building—but Lance doubted anyone was close enough to hear. "Shut up!" the man yelled, his voice booming her into silence. She sobbed, sucking in breaths, trying not to make noise.

"Take your jackets off," he said. "Darlene, get two syringes."

Sweat dripped from Lance's chin as he pulled off his jacket. His eyes searched for an escape. The walls were some kind of heavy corrugated metal, but there were no doors except for the ones they'd come in. No windows either.

The woman came back, syringes in hand, and came to Lance first. He drew back. "What is that?"

"Something to help you relax." She slid up his sleeve.

Lance jerked his arm away, but the gun barrel pressed against his temple. He squeezed his eyes shut, bracing himself for death.

Darlene put a tourniquet on his arm and shoved a needle in. He heard Jordan's anguished scream just as liquid fire burst through him. His vision went blurry ... his ears muffled Jordan's cries.

As he prayed for God's intervention, Jordan's screams grew more distant. Unconsciousness hit like a sledgehammer, blacking through his brain. As he sank into it, he heard voices over him.

"Put the girl in the plane with the baby. We'll set up Zeke and the kid to look like they killed each other. Put the pistol in Zeke's hand, and shoot the boy with it. Then get in the plane and we're outta here."

Chapter 55

Across town, Barbara sat by the phone with Emily, watching the news for some mention of Lance. Part of her still expected him to come ambling up the driveway with some perfectly logical explanation for where he'd been. After all, they didn't know for sure he'd been kidnapped.

But if Zeke hadn't taken him, where was he?

"Mom, it's a press conference!" Emily's voice pulled her out of her thoughts, and Barbara turned up the TV. The spokesman from the police department—the same one who talked to the press on every major case—stood in front of a podium with four or five microphones from the local channels.

She listened, astonished, as they focused on the baby trafficking scheme and the missing baby and her mother, failing to mention anything about Lance. The public relations officer for the police department showed a poster with Zeke's face.

"If you have any information about the whereabouts of this individual, or information about someone you know who's been approached to exchange her baby for cash, you're asked to call the Jefferson City Police Department at 555–3214."

"Nobody will recognize that," Emily said. "He doesn't look like that anymore."

It was true. Zeke was at least thirty pounds lighter now. His meth use had left him a skeleton.

Finally, the officer said that an AMBER Alert had been put out on Jordan, Lance, and the baby, and their pictures flashed up. The picture was one they'd taken from Lance's Facebook page; it was last year's school photo. His hair was shorter and he'd grown a lot since then. She hoped his image imprinted itself on viewers' memories.

"At least we don't have to wait thirty-six hours or whatever for them to call him a missing person," Emily said.

Barbara sat down on the couch, put her arms between her knees, and tried to imagine what Zeke might do with them. If he was still trying to get the money the traffickers were paying for the baby, maybe that was all he wanted. As horrible as it would be for the baby to be handed over, at least Lance might be unharmed.

But a lump rose in her throat as she realized that no one involved would let Lance go if he were a witness. In fact, there was only one reason Zeke would have taken him in the first place. To kill him.

If Lance were dead, would she know, somewhere deep in her gut? Would there be some jolt of pain the moment he stopped breathing?

"Mom, are you all right?"

Barbara looked at Emily and thought of telling her that, yes, she was fine ... that everything would be all right.

But she couldn't force any words out of her throat. Slowly, she shook her head.

Chapter 56

Jordan didn't sink as quickly as Lance had, because she'd developed a tolerance to the effects of all kinds of drugs. She kept fighting, trying to keep them from giving her another dose. But they held her down and injected her again.

Then she heard a baby crying. Wrestling away from them, she tried to get to the door. The cry was coming from the other side of the hangar, in one of the cars ... or in the plane. She struggled to get to it, but it was like swimming through mud.

They tackled her again, all three people holding her down. As the needle found another vein, her screams fell into a whimpered prayer.

"When the swelling on her face goes down, she'll be pretty," someone said.

"Yeah, we can put her into service right away. Keep her high and she'll do whatever we want."

No, she thought, but the words wouldn't come out. I won't ... never ... But even as she tried to protest, she knew she'd done worse things for drugs.

The baby's panicked cry rose hoarse and tinny through the building.

I tried to save you, she wanted to say.

But her mouth was dry, and a bittersweet numbness warmed her. She felt her arms and legs going limp, her eyes falling closed.

Don't hurt her ... Grace didn't do anything ... suffering for my mistakes.

But wasn't that always the way it went? She'd known dozens of mothers who'd sacrificed their children to the altar of drugs.

She was one of those children.

As the drug pulled her under, she hated her mother ... her brother ... her captors ... herself.

God was the only One who could save her now. But she didn't even know if she was still on His radar.

Chapter 57

Kent was surprised when Dathan told him the Chief was alerting the SWAT team. He hadn't expected the Jefferson City police department to have one. Even then, he expected a ragged crew of patrol officers who doubled as sharp-shooters on the rare occasions that required the big guns. He was impressed with how quickly they gathered, though, and hoped they were well trained.

He and Dathan met the squad a couple of miles from their destination. The men were assembled in a van, with assault rifles and bulletproof vests. Kent pulled one on, then hurried back into Dathan's car.

They drove to the scene with lights and sirens off to keep from alerting the perps. He tried to switch his brain into detective mode, focusing only on the choreography of getting inside the headquarters, disarming and restraining the bad guys, and rescuing the victims. He forced his affection for Lance out of his mind. Letting emotion get tangled with crime scene strategy could cause lethal mistakes.

They paused a few hundred yards from a building that looked like an old airport hangar, maybe for a corporate charter service that had shut down long ago. Kent used binoculars to scope out the hangar. The doors were all closed and there were no cars in sight. On the side of the building were a fuel tank and a long runway.

"If that tank is full, it could be a problem if we start firing," he said to Dathan. "Tell the SWAT team to shoot clear of it."

As Dathan radioed the men in the van and the other cruisers serving as back-up, Kent got out of the car and walked a few feet to get a better look at the other side of the building. If these men could afford a jet and forty thousand dollars to pay Jordan's family, they could afford a team of hotshot lawyers. That meant they'd probably come without a fight, knowing they could bond out and fight any charges against them.

A Piper Jet sat on the airstrip, poised to take off. Exhaust heat rippled in the air. Through the plane's windows, Kent saw a pilot and the silhouettes of passengers. The plane looked ready for take-off. Then he saw the beacon light on the tail flash on.

He ran back to the car. "Plane about to take off!" he said. "Let's go now!"

Dathan relayed the message into the radio, then yelled, "Let's go! Let's go! Move in around the plane!"

Blue lights flashing, the cars sped to the airstrip as the plane began to taxi down the runway. Kent drew his weapon and steadied it on the dashboard as Dathan pulled onto the grass beside the plane. The pilot saw them, but kept taxiing, picking up speed. The sirens came on, warning them to stop, but the plane went faster, faster ... ready to take off. Dathan kept up with them, going forty, fifty, sixty miles an hour ...

"Shoot out the wheels!" Dathan yelled as he drove. "I can't get in front of them."

Kent took aim, getting the wheels in his sights, and he squeezed off a round. One of the small tires blew, tipping the plane slightly, pulling it to the right. He fired again, targeting the other tire. The plane skidded and slowed. Its take-off was aborted, but the plane kept its trajectory down the runway.

"Hang on!" Dathan tore around the plane and screeched to a stop in front of it as the other cars moved in, blocking the plane in every direction. The piper rolled to a halt. The pilot's door flew open, and he saw the barrel of a rifle as the pilot fired. Kent fired back, aiming low to knock the shooter out, but a bullet shattered Dathan's windshield. Kent got out of the car and ducked behind it.

Someone on the passenger side of the plane began shooting now, bullets flying from both sides. Kent fired back, praying he wouldn't hit Lance or Jordan or the baby if they were in the plane.

The pilot fell back inside the plane, pulling the door shut.

Kent turned his fire to the other shooter, hoping to take at least one of them alive. He fired toward the leg of what appeared to be a woman.

But other cops surrounded the place, SWAT team snipers positioning themselves around the plane.

"Stand down!" Kent cried into the radio. "Victims may be in the plane! Hold your fire!"

Before Dathan's firing stopped, the woman was hit. She tumbled back, hit the wing, and slid off onto the tarmac.

The firing stopped. Kent braced his gun in both hands and made a run for the plane, hoping to get underneath it before the pilot rallied. If there were only the two of them, maybe he could climb in, take the pilot, and find Lance and Jordan. But where was Zeke? And what if there were others?

A shot from the cockpit burst through the plane's windshield, the bullet ricocheting off the concrete next to Kent just before he reached the plane. Fire ripped through his shoulder. He fell back, lightning flashing in his brain as his head hit the ground.

Chapter 58

Gunfire shook Jordan out of her stupor. She forced her eyes open. She was in the plane, lying on the backseat.

The world swirled, a tornado of confusion spinning around her head. What had they given her?

Bits of glass showered her as the guns kept firing. Were they shooting at her? She tried to get up, but her head was as heavy as lead and felt as big as a watermelon. She pushed her knees under her, tried to push up with her hands.

"What you shoot for? You crazy, man? They kill us!" a man's voice said in the cockpit.

"We can't let them take us." Nelson's voice was raspy, and he was breathing hard, as if in pain. "There are two bodies inside. They catch us, we're going down for murder. We've got to get this plane off the ground."

Jordan lifted her head and squinted toward the front

of the plane. The man with the accent squatted behind the front seats, firing out between the seat and the door. Nelson crouched on the floor, blood soaking his shirt.

She looked around for an escape. Behind the backseat was a cargo area. If she got back there, maybe she would be safe.

Then her baby started to cry, its tinny, angry voice rising. Jordan followed the sound and found Grace strapped in a car seat on the seat in front of her.

Bullets shattered the glass beside Jordan, and she screamed. Grace would get caught in the crossfire. She started toward Grace just as a bullet whizzed past her head.

She hit the floor, keeping her head low. She could slide back under the seat to the cargo bin, but she couldn't leave Grace here, vulnerable to the spray of bullets.

Jesus, I need You ...

She crawled to the baby's seat, aware that the foreign man was just two feet away. But he ignored her and kept firing through the shattered window. Her hands trembled as she fumbled with the straps. Finally they came free and she grabbed her baby up.

The child kicked and squirmed and yelled, her little mouth open in a desperate O.

Holding the baby tight against her chest, Jordan got down on the floor and, lying sideways to shield Grace with her body, pushed herself along until she was in the cargo space. She slid to the back of it, shielding her baby as bullets flew through the fuselage.

Chapter 59

Kent regained consciousness, unsure whether he'd been out for seconds ... or much longer. He made himself roll under the plane, out of the line of fire. His right shoulder was numb, and he couldn't use his right arm. He grasped his gun with his left hand and tried to get to his feet.

"The fuel tank!" he heard someone say above him, inside the plane. "By the hangar! Hit the fuel tank!"

There was more gunfire, more yelling—and then the fuel tank a hundred yards away went up in a blast that knocked him back to the ground. Black smoke mushroomed over him ... he heard the sound of a crash ... felt himself rolling as metal smashed and tumbled around him.

Jordan felt the blast, and the plane bounced upward,

flipping over. Metal ground and broke as she felt the wing breaking, the plane rolling.

She clutched the baby to her chest, pulled her knees up, and rolled like a lottery ball in the cargo bin. When the plane settled on its side, she examined Grace.

The baby was still screaming, but Jordan could see no injuries.

Jordan managed to catch her breath, her heart thudding against her chest. "Shhh," she said. "It's all right. Mommy's here."

Smoke was filling the cabin. She had to get out of here. She put the baby under her shirt to protect her lungs from the smoke and found the small door to the cargo area. It was over her head now, and she tried to kick it open.

She heard two more gunshots, a grunt and a thud ... then men's voices. "Two dead inside! Is there anybody in here?"

She looked through the smoke and saw a man at the door to the plane. "Help me!" she cried. "Please help me!"

In minutes they had gotten her out and away from the flames and smoke, to fresh air. "Lance," she cried. "He's in the building. I think they killed him."

She sat on the grass, comforting her child, as the police turned their attention to the hangar.

Chapter 60

Lance ...

Kent stared at the flames engulfing a collapsed wall of the hangar, a hundred yards away. It looked like a war zone here—flames and smoke and broken pieces of cars ... and the plane everywhere, its wing broken into three pieces.

He had to find Lance.

Dathan pounded toward him. "Kent, you all right?"

He got to his knees, accepting Dathan's offered hand, and staggered to his feet. "The plane ... the victims ..."

"We pulled the pilot and his partner out dead and found the girl and the baby. They're alive."

He sucked in a breath. "Lance ... where is he?"

"She said he's in the hangar. She thinks he's dead."

His heart balled into a fist, squeezing blood from its chambers. He squinted toward the hangar. The fuel tank blast had knocked down a wall, and flames had spread across the ceiling. Through the fire, he saw Zeke's blue Dodge.

Lance must be in that building with Zeke, about to be burned. If Jordan was right, he was already dead.

He ran toward the hangar, his left hand still clutching his firearm. On the side of the building not yet engulfed, he kicked in a door and went in.

He stumbled over a body. In the smoky light, he saw that it was Zeke. He lay dead on the floor in a pool of blood, a gun in his hand ... aimed at another body.

Lance!

Kent stumbled toward the boy lying on the ground, a bloody gunshot wound in his left side. He knelt and turned him over. He felt for a pulse, but couldn't find one. Awkwardly throwing Lance over his left shoulder, he ran back the way he'd come in, through the flames and smoke.

Chapter 61

As Kent cleared the flames, he ran to a score of sirens ... fire trucks and ambulances racing toward the scene. He kept running until he was clear of the building, in case the fuel tanks of the cars inside the hangar went up next.

When he couldn't run another step, he collapsed on the dirt and lay Lance down. Blood from Kent's own wound had soaked Lance's clothes, but Lance was still unconscious. Kent ripped Lance's shirt open. The wound was low, through his lower ribs, and there was an exit wound. Blood still seeped from both front and back. He pressed his hand over the exit wound to stop the bleeding. If blood was still flowing, there must be a pulse. He put his ear to Lance's chest. Yes—there was a faint heartbeat, a whistle of breath. "Lance!" he said. "Hang on, buddy!"

An ambulance crossed the field to them. Paramedics

jumped out and took over. Only then did Kent collapse beside Lance.

Don't take him, Lord. Take me. Please let him be all right.

Chapter 62

Barbara sat in the surgical waiting room, Emily's head on her shoulder, as they waited for word. They had taken Kent to Radiology to evaluate the shoulder that had been shattered by a bullet. She thanked God that he'd been wearing a bulletproof vest. But Lance ...

They had brought him in an ambulance. She'd gotten a glimpse before they rolled him into surgery, and he was limp, his face drained of color. Pasty, like he was already dead.

The bullet had shattered ribs and punctured a lung, filling it with blood. The doctors weren't sure if they could save him.

Suddenly, the doctor she'd spoken to earlier came into the waiting room, his mask around his neck. "Mrs. Covington?"

Emily lifted her head and got to her feet. Barbara

wanted to stand up, but she found she couldn't move. She didn't want to know if he'd died. To plan another funeral, buy another casket—she'd thought she'd never recover from burying her husband, but burying a son would be worse.

"Is he ... alive?" Emily asked.

The doctor looked tired, but he managed a smile. "Yes. We removed the torn lobe of his lung, and his vital signs are good now. I think he's going to be okay."

Relief burst like fireworks through her heart. Had she heard him right, or had she merely wished it? Was Lance really going to live? Slowly, she got to her feet.

"Mom, it's a miracle!" Emily threw her arms around her.

Yes, it was true. She was going to get her son back.

Lance woke hours later to bright, blinding lights. His vision was blurred, and his head felt like it had gotten between a sledgehammer and its stake. His side burned like he'd been blasted with a welding torch.

"Lance, can you hear me?"

A face hovered above him, blurred at the edges. "Mom?"

His mother burst into tears and whispered, "Oh, thank You, God." Her face became clearer. "Lance, how do you feel?"

He tried to answer, but the words just rotated through his head like numbers on a slot machine. He couldn't settle on any.

How had he gotten out of there?

"You were shot." Emily's face came into view. "You're a hero. Half the school is in the waiting room. It's all over the news."

Shot? He tried to remember, but he could only think of the syringe shooting something into his veins.

"They gave you a very high dose of horse tranquilizer, honey. Then they tried to make it look like Zeke shot you."

He shook his head. "No, he was dead before ..."

"We know."

He frowned and tried to lift himself, but pain stopped him. "My side hurts."

"You were shot through your ribs and your lungs. Kent saved your life. You've had surgery, and the doctors say you'll be okay."

"Throat hurts," he whispered. "Water."

His mother held up his glass, and he sipped through the straw, the liquid cooling the burning in his throat. Horse tranquilizer? A gunshot? Who would believe that?

"Jordan?" he whispered.

"She's fine too," Emily said. "So is the baby."

He dropped his head back down with relief. Then fear gripped him again. "Kent?"

Barbara stepped away from the bed, and he followed her with his eyes. Kent lay on a hospital bed beyond the open curtain next to him, his shoulder braced and bandaged.

"How ya doin', buddy?" Kent asked.

Lance managed a smile. "Not so good," he slurred.

"Tell him about it," Emily said. "He was shot trying to save your hide."

Lance peered at him. "You too?"

"The bullet cut through bone," Barbara said. "Shattered his rotator cuff. He had surgery too."

It seemed like a miracle. Someday Lance would share it all with his grandchildren, and he wouldn't even have to embellish the story to get gasps. "Thanks, man," he said. "I was hoping you'd come."

Kent gave him a grin that belied the pain he must be feeling. "No problem, kiddo. Glad to do it."

Chapter 63

The next day, Emily pushed Lance in his wheelchair to Jordan's room, so they could support Jordan when she gave Grace to Madeline and Ben. Jordan put Grace into Madeline's arms, and Madeline melted into tears. Ben's face was awestruck as he cupped her little head.

Jordan couldn't stop weeping after they left. She rebuffed their efforts to comfort her, and covering her face, she walked out into the hall.

"Come on," Emily said, turning his chair around. "Let's go after her."

"No, let me," Lance said. "I've got this."

Emily stayed in the room and Lance rolled himself after Jordan, following her to the window at the far end of the corridor, where she stood looking out into the night.

He rolled up beside her, facing his reflection in the window. "You okay?" he asked her finally.

She wiped her face with the sleeve of her gown. "Yeah, I'll be all right. I just … wish my mom wasn't in jail. That none of this happened."

"She's not there because of you."

"If I hadn't got pregnant, if I hadn't had a baby …"

"Then your mother and Zeke wouldn't have been able to use you that way. But they would have found other illegal ways to get money. Neither of them wanted to hold a job, but they both wanted to do a lot of drugs. How can you miss her?"

Jordan expelled a life-weary sigh. "It's not that I miss her. I just miss the idea of having a mother who cares what happens to me. Like, maybe if she got sober and her head cleared … she might be more like your mom."

Lance understood. "When they shot me up with that horse tranquilizer, I felt my life slipping away, like I would just fall asleep and wake up in heaven. I saw my mom standing beside my casket, grieving again. I was sick that I hadn't saved you. I'm glad it was a dream."

Jordan nodded. "God listened. He sent Kent and the police to save us."

"He did," Lance said. "Kind of makes me want to be a better person now, you know?"

"I know." She wiped her face and drew in a deep breath. "Sorry about the tears in there. It was just so hard."

"We knew it would be."

"But watching Madeline and Ben with her, I couldn't help thinking, some day I'm gonna be a parent like that." She lifted her chin. "I'm not just a junkie."

"Nope, you're not. You risked your life to save your baby. You put her first. You're not like your mother at all."

"She'll be happy, won't she? She'll have a good home with Madeline and Ben. She'll get to be a happy little kid. I hope she never has to hear about those traffickers—people trying to sell girls into a life of horrible things …"

"By the time she's old enough to understand, they'll have rounded up everybody involved. They've got a real good start already. Kent told me they've had two girls come forward with information. They've made several arrests."

She smiled. "That's good."

Lance looked at her reflection in the glass. "So have you decided what you're gonna do next?"

"I'm going back to New Day," she said. "You were right that day on the street, before Zeke got us. I can choose. And I choose to get better and have a better life."

"See? You've already broken the cycle. You made the right choice … did the right thing."

She breathed out a laugh. "Who woulda thought?"

She turned back and looked up the hall. A nurse was coming out of a room wearing scrubs, a stethoscope around her neck. "I was thinking maybe I'd be a good nurse. I don't know if they'd take me with my background, since I'd be around drugs and stuff. Maybe I could be an X-ray tech or something. Do something important that helps people." She breathed a laugh. "I like the idea of wearing scrubs to work."

"If you put your mind to it and get clean, you can do anything you want to do."

"That stuff New Day told me about the damage meth does to your brain. You think I have too many holes in mine to make anything of myself?"

"Nope," he said. "I think if there wasn't a God, maybe that would be true. But He has a way of filling in holes, healing hurts, setting things right."

She smiled through fresh tears. "At New Day, I learned what Jesus said. 'He has sent me to proclaim freedom for the prisoners and recovery of sight for the blind, to release the oppressed, to proclaim the year of the Lord's favor.' I think that was written for me."

Lance smiled. "At church they used to sing this hokey song about beauty coming from ashes, and I never understood what it meant. But now I do. You may never be a rocket scientist or a brain surgeon, and neither will I. But you can have a good life and be smart and raise healthy kids. You can have a husband someday who loves you."

She met his eyes. "Somebody like you?"

"Somebody a little less stupid, hopefully."

"You're not stupid. You're brave."

He wanted to believe that. But he'd gotten into so much trouble lately. He'd been to jail, and now he could no longer say he'd never used drugs. Even though he hadn't chosen to use, he still felt tainted, damaged. But if he believed what he'd just told Jordan, God would overcome that. Still, he didn't like what he'd seen. Gunfire … dead bodies … his own veins being shot full of a lethal dose of drugs.

Salvation had new meaning. Jordan had risked her life to save Grace. Kent had risked his life to save Lance … just as Christ had done for all of them.

It didn't make sense.

Yet it was true.

Chapter 64

The night Lance was released from the hospital, Barbara made a special dinner. Kent's arm was outstretched in a brace to keep his shoulder immobile, but he tried not to complain. He wanted Lance to be the celebrated hero, the center of attention. He and Barbara laughed through the meal as they told stories of their childhood, and the kids talked about what they wanted to study in college. Lance was more certain than ever that he wanted to go into Criminal Justice and be a detective. He'd already taken a bullet, after all.

Afterward, Kent took Barbara outside, and they sat on her backyard swing under a jasmine-covered arbor. She laid her head against his good shoulder as they swung, clearly allowing herself this moment of unhindered joy.

And then he ruined it. "I guess I have to go home tomorrow."

She met his eyes. "I don't want you to go. Why don't you stay here and let me take care of you?"

He smiled. "That's nice to hear. But I have bills to pay." He kissed her, then gazed down at her. "There's still that job opening, though."

Barbara was silent, and his heart sank. Didn't she want him to stay? He didn't know how to respond to her silence, so he pulled his arm from around her shoulder.

She touched his back. "I don't want you to give up your job and come here," she said. "I don't want to take you away from everything you've built. You have a life in Atlanta."

"Not much of one, Barbara."

She slipped her arm through his, laced her fingers through his fingers. "The thing is, I've been thinking that maybe it's not such a good idea for us to stay here."

He squinted, not sure where this was going. "What do you mean?"

"I mean, there are a lot of bad memories here, and a lot of triggers for Emily. Lance ... I don't know. He's been exposed to some bad stuff. I feel like I need to get him out of here and start over clean."

His heart locked. "Where would you go?"

A soft smile changed everything. "Emily talked about applying for school in Atlanta. So maybe we should think about going there. I have a lot of reasons."

He looked into her smiling face and realized he was one of them. Suddenly, his throat was tight. Swallowing came hard. "I hope you can tell how crazy I am about you."

"Really, I can't," she teased. "Why don't you tell me in words?"

Tears stung his eyes. "I'm absolutely in love with you."

"I know," she said. "I love you too."

"Then we can move forward with this relationship and not just try to do the long-distance thing?"

"I hope so," she said. "If I were to move to Atlanta, get a house there, get Lance into school and Emily into college, maybe I'd have more opportunity to get back into the interior design business. It's a bigger city with more opportunity. You and I could date ... see how it goes."

"We know how it'll go," he said.

"Then let's let it go that way. We'll take a little time to see if you can stand having me around more often."

"And you can see if you can tolerate me. Especially as I heal. I can be pretty grumpy."

She shook her head. "I know how I'll feel about that. Having you around is always a joy. I've never felt so safe or so loved."

"Yet every time I'm around, you or your kids are in mortal danger."

She laughed. "Does seem that way. But it's not because of you."

He sat back, pulled her against him, and kissed the top of her head. "Lance isn't gonna like it," he said.

She shook her head. "No, he won't be happy about moving away from his friends. But he'll be happy about being around you more. He needs a man in his life, and you're his hero."

"Then you'll call the realtor tomorrow?"

She laughed. "I called her today."

A Note from the Author

If you've read many of my books, you know some of the life issues I struggle with on a regular basis. There are times when I feel life coming at me in unwarranted and inexplicable ways, offering crises where my best-laid plans had promised only peace. As a Christian, I often try to make sense of those times, searching for God's purpose among the fallout of my shattered plans, struggling to understand how God will use this one day.

As part of my never-ending quest to find those answers, I take Bible courses to help me better understand the nature of my Creator, and His interest in my life. But sometimes the more I learn about Him, the farther away He seems, and the smaller and less significant I feel. However, in a recent lesson about the dimensions in which God lives, as opposed to the dimensions I live in (width, height, depth), I began to understand that God isn't bound by those dimensions or by time or by gravity. He lives in many more dimensions — some which my mind can't even comprehend. He can go through walls and fly across the universe; he can hear everyone's thoughts at once; He can know us before we're even knit inside our mother's womb. He is the One who builds and breaks down nations across the world, rescues desperate and war-torn refugees, makes the sun come up each day, and keeps our feet on earth's ground by maintaining the perfect gravitational force to keep us from hurling into outer space ... and still He cares about the prayers of a child in his bed.

God is not bound by time or space, as I am, so my thinking about God's dimensions is limited by my own experience. He can be everywhere at once and attend to billions of problems at once. He can be touching me and also touching you. He can be so close that His breath is sweeping my skin, yet He can be that close to you as well, even if you're across the world from me. He can hear all my prayers and not just give me what I ask for, but thankfully, He can assess what's best for me given His purpose for my life and the desires of my heart.

I find this comforting, especially when I pray for things and can't see immediate answers. If I think of my life in human terms, as a parade, for instance, and God hovering over it in a helicopter, able to touch down at the beginning and the end and any point in between—seeing the end *from the beginning,* and the beginning from the end, and the end from the middle, then I can trust that all my prayers have been answered at some point in that timeline. My frustration at what I see as unanswered prayer is unwarranted, because He has already sent those answers even though I may not have caught up to them yet. Daniel prayed for Israel and his prayer was answered immediately, but it took three weeks before the angel came to tell him.

No one living in America can deny that our culture has changed. The drug culture alone is killing our kids. In times like these, it's easy to throw up our hands and declare that there must not be a God, that if there were, why would He allow people to suffer this way? Why would He allow children to be born into dysfunctional and dangerous homes? Why would He allow substances on earth that destroy us? Why would He allow such evil to hold us in bondage?

But if you see this life as a training ground for a greater purpose that has everything to do with eternity, and if you see that Jesus came to offer us an escape from the hell that was calling to us and threatening to swallow us whole, by taking the consequences of our dysfunctional, dangerous choices (which he calls sin), and enduring our punishment so that we could emerge whole and flawless, then you'll see how everything has meaning. Everything has a purpose. You are an important part of God's plan, and you have a purpose in His eternity. If you understand and accept that Jesus Christ took away your sin by taking it on Himself, then you too will someday live in a sinless heaven of miraculous, immeasurable dimensions—where human limitations are taken away, and nothing inhibits us from living up to our eternal purpose.

Just imagine ...

Thinking that way makes my parade a lot more joyful, even when I'm at a place on the timeline where things aren't going like I'd hoped. This place in time is not all there is to my life ... or to yours.

There's so much more.

Terri Blackstock

For more information about this concept of God's dimensionality, read "The Extra Dimensional Nature of God" at http://www.godandscience .org/apologetics/xdimgod.html. (I haven't read everything at this site so I can't vouch for it, but I agree with this article.)

Predator

A Novel

Terri Blackstock,
New York Times Bestselling Author

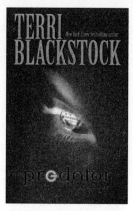

Bestselling author Terri Blackstock presents another stand-alone novel, *Predator*.

The murder of Krista Carmichael's fourteen-year-old sister by an online predator has shaken her faith and made her question God's justice and protection. Desperate to find the killer, she creates an online persona to bait the predator. But when the stalker turns his sights on her, will Krista be able to control the outcome?

Ryan Adkins started the social network GrapeVyne in his college dorm and has grown it into a billion-dollar corporation. But he never expected it to become a stalking ground for online Predators. One of them lives in his town and has killed two girls and attacked a third. When Ryan meets Krista, the murders become more than a news story to him, and everything is on the line.

Joining forces, he and Krista set out to stop the killer. But when hunters pursue a hunter, the tables can easily turn. Only God can protect them now.

Intervention

A Novel

Terri Blackstock,
New York Times Bestselling Author

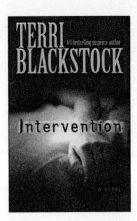

It was her last hope — and the beginning of a new nightmare.

Barbara Covington has one more chance to save her daughter from a devastating addiction, by staging an intervention. But when eighteen-year-old Emily disappears on the way to drug treatment — and her interventionist is found dead at the airport — Barbara enters her darkest nightmare of all.

Barbara and her son set out to find Emily before Detective Kent Harlan arrests her for a crime he is sure she committed. Fearing for Emily's life, Barbara maintains her daughter's innocence. But does she really know her anymore? Meanwhile, Kent has questions of his own. His gut tells him that this is a case of an addict killing for drugs, but as he gets to know Barbara, he begins to hope he's wrong about Emily.

The mysteries intensify as everyone's panic grows: Did Emily's obsession with drugs lead her to commit murder — or is she another victim of a cold-blooded killer?

In this gripping novel of intrigue and suspense, bestselling author Terri Blackstock delivers the up-all-night drama that readers around the world have come to expect from her.

Available in stores and online!

Double Minds

Terri Blackstock,
New York Times Bestselling Author

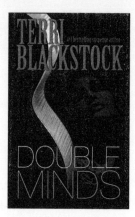

As talented singer/songwriter Parker James struggles to make her mark on the Nashville music scene, she finds the competition can be fierce — even deadly.

When a young woman is murdered at the recording studio where Parker works, Parker is drawn into a mystery where nothing is as it seems. Unraveling the truth puts her own life at risk when she uncovers high-level industry corruption and is terrorized by a menacing stalker. As the danger escalates, Parker begins to question her dreams, her future, and even her faith. Does stardom even matter anymore?

Double Minds is a compelling suspense novel that unfolds in the middle of the Christian music industry in Nashville. Terri Blackstock grabs readers at page one and keeps them riveted until the final plot twist is untangled. This well-turned mystery is Blackstock's first stand-alone title in several years, and it was worth waiting for.

Available in stores and online!

Last Light

Terri Blackstock,
New York Times Bestselling Author

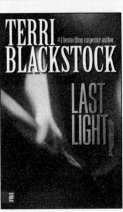

Today, the world as you know it will end. No need to turn off the lights.

Your car suddenly stalls and won't restart. You can't call for help because your cell phone is dead.

Everyone around you is having the same problem ... and it's just the tip of the iceberg.

Your city is in a blackout. Communication is cut off. Hospital equipment won't operate. And airplanes are falling from the sky.

Is it a terrorist attack ... or something far worse?

In the face of a crisis that sweeps an entire high-tech planet back to the age before electricity, your family faces a choice. Will you hoard your possessions to survive — or trust God to provide as you offer your resources and your hearts to others?

Yesterday's world is gone. Now all you've got is your family and community. You stand or fall together. Like never before, you must rely on each other.

But one of you is a killer.

Number-one bestselling suspense author Terri Blackstock weaves a masterful what-if novel in which global catastrophe reveals the darkness in human hearts — and lights the way to restoration for a self-centered world. *Last Light* is the first book in an exciting new series.

Night Light

Terri Blackstock,
New York Times Bestselling Author

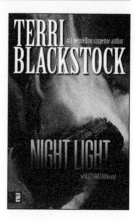

In the face of a crisis that sweeps an entire high-tech planet back to the age before electricity, the Brannings face a choice. Will they hoard their possessions to survive—or trust God to provide as they offer their resources to others?

Number one bestselling suspense author Terri Blackstock weaves a masterful what-if series in which global catastrophe reveals the darkness in human hearts—and lights the way to restoration for a self-centered world.

An era unlike any in modern civilization is descending—one without lights, electronics, running water, or automobiles. As a global blackout lengthens into months, the neighbors of Oak Hollow grapple with a chilling realization: the power may never return.

Survival has become a lifestyle. When two young thieves break into the Brannings' home and clean out the food in their pantry, Jeff Branning tracks them to a filthy apartment and discovers a family of children living alone, stealing to stay alive. Where is their mother? The search for answers uncovers a trail of desperation and murder ... and for the Brannings, a powerful new purpose that can transform their entire community—and above all, themselves.

Available in stores and online!

True Light

Terri Blackstock,
New York Times Bestselling Author

The darkness deepens in a world without power.

But, daring to defend a young outcast, one family strikes a light.

In the face of a crisis that sweeps an entire high-tech planet back to the age before electricity, the Brannings face a choice. Will they hoard their possessions to survive — or trust God to provide as they offer their resources to others?

Number one bestselling suspense author Terri Blackstock weaves a masterful what-if series in which global catastrophe reveals the darkness in human hearts — and lights the way to restoration for a self-centered world.

Now eight months into a global blackout, the residents of Oak Hollow are coping with the deep winter nights. But the struggle to survive can bring out the worst in a person — or a community.

A teenager has been shot and the suspect sits in jail. As the son of a convicted murderer, Mark Green already has one strike against him. Now he faces the wrath of all Oak Hollow — except for one person. Deni Branning has known Mark since high school and is convinced he is no killer.

When Mark finds himself at large with a host of other prisoners released upon the unsuspecting community, Deni and her family attempt to help him find the person who really pulled the trigger. But clearing Mark's reputation is only part of his battle. Protecting the neighbors who ostracized him is just as difficult.

And forgiving them may be the hardest part of all.

Dawn's Light

Terri Blackstock,
New York Times Bestselling Author

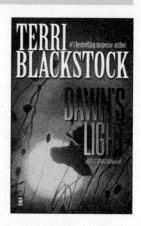

In the face of a crisis that sweeps an entire high-tech planet back to the age before electricity, the Brannings face a choice. Will they hoard their possessions to survive — or trust God to provide as they offer their resources to others?

Number one bestselling suspense author Terri Blackstock weaves a masterful what-if series in which global catastrophe reveals the darkness in human hearts — and lights the way to restoration for a self-centered world.

As the Pulses that caused the outage are finally coming to an end, thirteen-year-old Beth Branning witnesses a murder. Threatened by the killer, she keeps the matter to herself. But her silence could cost her life.

Meanwhile, as Deni's ex-fiancé returns to Crockett with a newfound faith and the influence to get things done, Deni is torn between the man who can fulfill all her dreams and Mark Green, the man who inhabits them.

As the world slowly emerges from the crisis, the Brannings face their toughest crisis yet. Will God require more of them than they've already given? How will they keep their faith if he doesn't answer their prayers?

Available in stores and online!

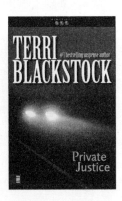
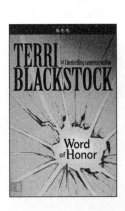
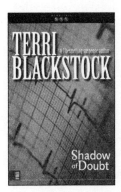
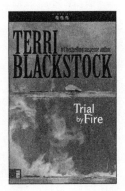
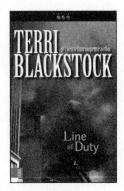

CAPE REFUGE SERIES

This bestselling series follows the lives of the people of the small seaside community of Cape Refuge, as two sisters struggle to continue the ministry their parents began helping the troubled souls who come to Hanover House for solace.

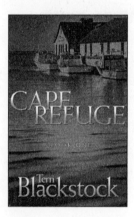

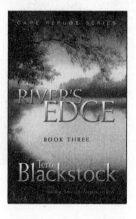

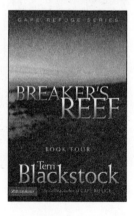

Available in stores and online!